Enigmatic Thoughts
Paradoxical Existence

Written by
Mehran M. Rezaei

Imagination Paradox
P.O. BOX 1086
Wildomar, CA 92595

ISBN-10: 0996073833
ISBN-13: 978-0-9960738-3-7

http://www.imaginationparadox.com/

To my parents, for always enduring life's challenging moments with an unparalleled stance for hope, and to keep an unbreakable bond through love and determination within the family. And for all their self-sacrifices in providing a better future for their children, and to remain the best role models as they possibly could by staying the course through morality, belief and forgiveness.

To my two beautiful sisters for always being there for each other, for our family, and for their own families to unselfishly provide wise moral support and unmatched loving care.

And for their endless love, to let strangers and those in need into their hearts and into their lives with open arms and with no strings attached.

To my beautiful wife for enduring my thoughts and always keeping me on my toes, and for being a great mother that she is. And also for her beautiful heart and the wonderful person that she is.

To my beautiful daughter who will always remain the most precious blessing and dream that I could have ever asked for. She is, and will forever remain the center of my universe.

And lastly to everyone in my bigger family and all my friends, and to you as well, as we all share the same faith at the end…

Disclaimer

The contents in this book should not be used for any educational purposes, as they are mostly based on my own personal thoughts, studies and beliefs.

The stories, events, characters and environments in this book are fictional, and any similarities of such are coincidental and not intended by the author.

Contents

Preface

This book is a subset of "Scattered Thoughts: The Eternal Search for Answers", and only offers the science fiction short stories. Whereas in the first version, all "what if" ideas and philosophical thoughts are wrapped around every story.

The stories in this book mostly reflect upon an artificial existence, and that our reality might just be another prefabricated paradox...

The infinite thirst for control

The year is 2089, and on an early April morning day in Stockholm Sweden, a long waited annual science seminar is about to start as the program announcer walks up to the podium.

"Good morning everyone, my name is Anna Lindgren and I am your program host during today's events." She says with a smile and continues after a short pause.

"I hope that you are all excited and ready to start our schedule... I know that many of you are here to hear about the recent breakthroughs in space travel technologies, and the discovery of several habitable planets that are top candidates for in-person explorations. -- But first, we have a surprise guest that announced his participation late last night with yet another breakthrough in brain science."

The crowd is instantly very displeased and unhappy with this announcement, and someone through the crowd says

"Not another two hours of brain junk please..." with an unpleasant tone, and then another person with an angry and demanding expression says

"What else could we possibly learn from the brain?"

Anna then smiles and continues to say

"Even though he's been gone for almost a decade working under the radar, he is no stranger to anyone in this room... so without further ado, please welcome Doctor Norman Walker!"

The crowd is still displeased, and no one is really happy to see him as he walks up to the stage with a big smile on his face.

"Obviously I am much happier to see you all in one room, than you are to see me in the same very room... but, I promise not to disappoint anyone." He says as he signals his team members to bring his equipment up to the stage.

He then faces the audience again and continues to say

"As you all know, or at least I hope you do... you were all handpicked to be personally present for this event, and my presentations are 'only' shared with you... all our remote viewers are currently watching some introductory high-tech media about how to explore other worlds, and will tune-in as soon as we're done here."

"We're done!" Someone says quickly from the audience and everyone laughs. And at the same time some people are getting up to leave the auditorium.

Doctor Walker puts his head down and starts walking slowly to the left of the stage and continues to say

"And leaving this place won't be an option, I am afraid... until you have seen what I have to show you, of course."

He then lifts his head up and looks directly at the few standing by the door trying to leave, and gives them a sarcastic smile and continues to say

"The doors are closed and locked, so please indulge my presence for just ten to fifteen more minutes, and I will be forever in debt to all of you... thank you!"

He then walks over to his equipment, which is a tilted back black lazy-chair that looks more like an over-sized comfortable car seat with built in racing straps, and with a black rectangular box attached underneath. And there are two other large boxes next to it separated by a couple of feet from each other.

With the help of a staff member, he then starts removing the covers of the first box closer to the chair.

And then he continues to say

"In order to travel in space and to explore new worlds, we need reusable bodies that can operate independent from the host…"

The first box is now uncovered and there is a human like robot sitting in a chair. And while he moves over to the second box another person in the crowd says

"So what now, you are here to show us surrogates and avatars? You've only been gone for a decade but this technology is probably as old as most of us here."

And there are follow up taunting language and laughter from the crowd.

Doctor Walker turns around to face the direction of the voice, and then he says

"Assumption is one of our costliest weaknesses. And no, this demonstration is not what you think it is."

And then he uncovers the second box, which is a human wearing an oxygen mask.

He then goes on to say

"The first subject to the left is a robot that can operate on its own, or to be controlled remotely as a surrogate. And the person, who is sitting comfortably on the chair, is a clone of one of my staff members."

Suddenly people in the room are protesting and shouting out unpleasant phrases such as

"This is outrageous!"

"This madman has no rights to be on this stage!"

"It's not even legal to clone a human!"

But Doctor Walker peacefully looks at his watch and stands relaxed while smiling. And he patiently waits for everyone to settle down.

On the lower left side of the auditorium closer to the stage, a security guard is looking through the crowd watching every person who is making a comment. And through his right eye, he is receiving a live feed of information about every person that he is focusing his eyes on, like an internal built-in screen.

And in his mind in form of a thought he says

"I think he is about to reveal the technology..."

And a voice though his earpiece replies

"Move in when you see a window."

"Copy!" He then says in his head.

"Please don't focus on the legalities of these procedures as I assure you, the laws will change much sooner than you think... and may I also remind you, that this is a science exhibition and not a courtroom." Doctor Walker says with a low and calm tone, and continues to say

"I have always been a man of science, and truly believe that science must be shared with everyone. But this vision is not always shared as a common goal of humanity, or by the higher powers at play, which also explains my absence as I was 'forced' to lay low."

He looks at his watch again and continues to say

"Since we are now running out of time, I must skip the demonstration... which was really an attempt to show you all, that the content of a brain can be successfully copied over to another brain regardless of the supporting media... to prevent aging or to correct many brain illnesses,"

The crowd is now dead silent as they continue to listen to Doctor Walker

"But since you wouldn't remember any of this anyways, let's just move on to the next demonstration, which is why you're all here." He says under his breath, and the last sentence is barely heard by anyone as he says it while signaling his staff by nodding his head.

He then continues with a commanding voice to say

"The human mind has always been obsessed to control its environment. But our lack of unity 'begs' to be controlled and to find a common ground with our brains, which hasn't yet reached acceptable levels of maturity to understand the desire." He says as he walks towards the door at the back right corner of the stage.

At the same time the security guard seems to be trying to analyze Walker's speech, but then he says in his head
"Something is not right, I'm moving in!"
And then he walks toward the back door on the opposite side of the stage where Doctor Walker is headed.

"And that is why we have to bypass our natural evolutionary path, and to avoid yet another dead-end leading to more questions that our minds are not capable of seeing the answers to... now please, enjoy the show!"
Walker says and then he walks out through the door.
Behind the door, he then turns to Anna and says
"Release the Nano-bots and proceed as planned!"

The security guard works his way around the backstage people and manages to catches up with Doctor Walker as he is walking out through the back door.
And before Doctor Walker has reached the street, the guard then quickly says
"Doctor Walker, I need you to come with me please..."
And after a short pause, he then continues to say
"And I would appreciate it if you didn't make a scene."

Walker looks to his left where his vehicle is parked with one of his personal guards waiting for him outside.
The man has sensed that something might be wrong and is ready to take action. But Walker signals him by nodding his

head to let him know that he can relax, and that everything is fine.

Walker then puts his hands in his pockets and breaths in the fresh air with his eyes closed. And a few seconds later he then starts walking to his right towards where the security guard is trying to lead him to.

"Where are you taking me agent Miller?" He says with a pleasant conversational tone.

"How do you know my name?" Miller replies.

"I designed you... along with several other clones of course. But you were the most polite one as I recall." He says and peeks at Miller with a smile as they walk towards the line of driverless robotic taxis.

These vehicles are oval shaped with sliding doors opening towards the side walk.

There are four seats in the vehicle facing the sliding doors.

And when the doors close, they would rotate to create two rows with costumer's settings of either facing each other or all facing one direction.

The seats could also stretch out to allow clients to rest during their travel.

The wheels would rotate to slide the vehicle in and out of any spot. And they would retract while raising the cabin to an upright position when parked without any costumers, which would allow the vehicle to occupy minimum space required at designated locations.

These vehicles are fully electric. And their batteries are charged through magnetic fields generated by the underlying roads, dedicated exclusively to them and other transportation vehicles alike.

Every vehicle would essentially become a part of various networks as they moved through different physical locations as zones. And as individual swarm-bots, they would become members of each zone, and would obey the traffic rules of the zone while traveling through.

Miller walks up to a vehicle in the middle of the line and reads the taxi's identification in his head

"Sierra, Echo, Zero, Two, Zero, Six, Seven, Zulu, please upload destination."

Within seconds the taxi pulls out to the street, expands its wheel base and lowers the cabin while opening the sliding doors.

The seats line up facing agent Miller and Doctor Walker.

And as they take their seats Miller says

"English please!"

And the taxi replies

"Language confirmed!" And continues to say

"Good morning! -- Your destination coordinates are confirmed. Please place your luggage beneath your seat and select your seat position when ready."

Agent Miller selects his seat to face the opposite direction of the ride, where he could face Walker while going backwards.

The taxi repositions the seats, closes the doors and starts the fair.

"Would you like to have any entertainment while traveling?" Says the taxi.

"Privacy please and no entertainment..." Miller replies.

"Request confirmed!" The taxi responses and dims the windows.

"You have an agreement with the agency Doctor Walker, to not disclose any information around the clone technology. -- But today you broke that promise... would you care to explain why?" Says Miller while looking directly into Walker's eyes.

"How can you or whoever else is listening to this conversation, ever think that I've dishonored our agreement... when you didn't even stay long enough to see what the main show was about?" Walker replies with composure while raising his eyebrows to mark the question.

"The agreement was not to disclose any information about your work." Miller replies with an expression clearly showing that he is disappointed.

"But that project was finalized many years ago, and there were no agreements on any further research… the question that you need to ask agent Miller, is how could the agency know anything about my participations in today's events, when I announced my appearance only hours before? --

Unless of course, I had already brought it to their attention ahead of time… wouldn't that explain the lead-time for your preparations as well?" Walker says as he is looking at Miller with a concerning expression, hinting that the agency might have kept him out of the loop.

Miller gives Walker a quick sarcastic smile as he sinks into his seat. And while he is still looking directly at Walker, he then says

"So, what was today's event or show really about?"

"Agent Miller, your suspicions are irrelevant since you are clearly still missing the bigger picture…"

"Please enlighten me."

"I could, but that's not something I would choose to freely share with the agency… if you know what I mean."

"I don't understand. You just said, that you had already informed the agency about your new projects!?"

"No… I said… that I had informed them about my attempts to show up at the event, to share my new research of course. But that, still wouldn't say much about the bigger picture."

"And you would willingly share it with me knowing that I work for the agency…?"

"Yes, on a personal level, and for the old times' sake… even though you obviously don't remember much about. -- I always liked you because you were very cooperative and always very polite."

"So you're telling me, that my memories have been erased...?"

"I'm not saying anything... I was just simply assuming that it might have been in the best interest of the agency, to protect the information from falling into the wrong hands. -- And thought that you might agree with me knowing the policies better than anyone else... but I realize now that if you never knew anything was missing, then your suspicions would also make perfect sense... so I apologize if I have foolishly implied an idea, that could potentially implicate your relationships with your employer."

"I need to go offline for a while to find out where this is going." Miller says in his head after being quiet for a few seconds.

"No, you cannot disconnect, that's a direct order! He is just trying to manipulate you..." The voice from the other end replies.

"We need to know what he is up to." Miller says calmly in his head.

"He does have a point." Says an analyst to the lead on the other end.

"Going dark was never an option for this operation." Says the lead. But Miller doesn't say anything back, and then he switches off his communication link by touching the face screen of his wristwatch.

On the other end in the agency's control room, the analyst says

"Okay, he just switched off... that's just beautiful..."

"Keep tracking the cab and see if you can enable the built-in microphones." The lead replies.

Back in the taxi, Walker smiles at Miller when he switches off his communication's link. And then he says

"Have you ever had a dream where you consciously try desperately to wake up from? Your consciousness is awake, but your brain is not responding to your commands... you feel somehow trapped in a prison and fight to wake up, and every second feels like an eternity." He then pauses for a second and then continues to say

"What if I told you that only in that moment, you are who 'you' really are... and only in that moment, you are one with yourself as a conscious mind...?"

"I'm not sure I follow..." Miller says.

"Your memories are not lost, they are just locked away."

"How...?"

"Aren't you controlling this body right now, even though you are probably hundreds or even thousands of miles away? Is it really that hard to believe in mind control?"

"Are you saying that someone is controlling me?"

"I'm just simply implying another possibility... but if I was right, then what could 'you' do about it?"

"So, I'm a puppet controlling a puppet." Miller says with another sarcastic smile.

"Or, you are not a puppet, not yet at least... but you might be taking instructions from a puppet, as of course yet another possibility..."

Miller stares at Walker with a serious look on his face and doesn't say anything. Walker then turns his face away and looks at the outside scenery and continues to say

"My ambitions go far beyond what you might think right now. And please don't get me wrong, I would love to share more with you. But I also know if I do, it might mean the end of my research or another decade of sleeping in the shadows..."

He then pauses for a couple of seconds before continuing to say

"Unless, you give me your word that my research could continue regardless of its usage and this conversation... I mean, sooner or later someone might decide to use it with wrong intentions, and I'm sure that you must be curious enough to know what it is."

"You know that I can't make that promise... but I'll do my best." Miller says and Walker extends his arm out for a handshake.

While Miller is looking at him unsure of what to do, Walker then says

"I would like you to confirm it with a handshake as well .. what can I say, I am an old fashion guy."

Miller then leans forward and shakes Walker's hand and says

"I'll do my best."

And while Walker is holding Miller's hand with a tight grip, he says with a smile

"I know you will."

But right then he stops smiling and says

"John Miller, zero one six subcommand, Pause!"

And then he releases Miller's hand.

Miller is sitting still with his arm in the handshake position, and while looking directly at Walker.

"Relax your arm and sit back." Walker says and takes out a button like device and puts it in his own ear. And then he continues to say

"Pull up the decoy cab and begin the synchronization... and don't forget to switch their core IDs."

In less than a minute, another taxi pulls up and locks in its speed and position with the one Miller and Walker are traveling in. And after a few seconds a voice in Walker's ear says

"Tracking matched and synchronization is complete!"

"Excellent, break the link and upload new coordinates to this vehicle." Walker says and takes out a small flashlight like device from the inner pocket of his jacket.

He then puts the lower wider side of the device on Miller's head and presses a button located on the top end.

The device flattens over Miller's head in a circular shape and a blue hologram shows Miller's brain.

"I know how terrible it must feel right now, being in a prison... which is why I'm trying to complete this process as fast as I can." Walker says while Miller is sitting frozen in his seat and looking straight ahead.

"Initiate full copy. -- Main functions." Walker says and a process indicator starts showing the copy process over the brain image in the hologram.

There are now two images, and the destination brain image is getting new dots very rapidly and randomly across different areas.

"Hang in there son, it'll be over soon... your complete personality profile and basic brain functions are needed first to revive and access your memories, which is what I'm trying to get to. -- You see, as one of the agency's top agents, your brain carries vital information to assure complete success for the final steps of my ambitious plan... and soon, a prosper future is guaranteed for humanity, and that, I promise." He says as the copy process reaches eighty-five percent.

At the agency, the analyst working with the lead says
"Something is wrong, something is very wrong!"
"What?" The lead asks.
"His brain functions are being accessed!"
"What do you mean accessed?"
"I mean exactly what I said!"

"Can you interrupt it? And should I be concerned?"

"Not without killing the link between Miller and the clone… and yes, because this is not good!" He replies with a shaking voice.

"Is he doing this?" The lead asks.

"Who…? Walker? I'm not sure… Wait, it stopped " The analyst says while holding his hands, and then he just gets quiet and unsure of what had just happened.

In the taxi, Walker rotates the image around while checking for flaws as soon as the copy process has completed successfully. And then he says

"Commence full memory extraction and purge sequence." And as the hologram displays additional required actions, he removes the verification of data integrity option and chooses to copy and purge data in a single step mode.

He then confirms the execution and the process starts.

Over at the agency, the analyst notices additional activities initiated from the other end and reacts explosively to what he is seeing. And then he suddenly jumps out of his chair and shouts

"Oh no, his memories are being copied!"

"Kill it! Kill the link now!" The lead shouts back.

The analyst tries to break the link and after a few seconds he says

"I can't, the link is locked!"

The lead drops her dimmed translucent control pad on the analyst's desk and starts running towards the door.

She then pushes the glass door out and shouts

"Get out of the way!" While running through it. She then continues to run through the office and down the hallway with the same urgency.

Midway through the hallway she then stops at a double door and puts her hand on the bio-scanner next to the door.

The door's scanner then scans her face and checks the patterns in her eyes, and the door opens within less than a second thereafter.

She runs inside the room towards a transparent coffin like control unit where Miller is laying inside of.

She then quickly pulls up the hologram by the unit and enters in a combination code, and after a second the bio-scanner lights up where she then puts her hand on.

The scanner then starts the verification process and she says

"Come on... come on!"

The scanner turns blue and as she removes her hand, the top of the scanner simultaneously lifts up with it, exposing a keypad with various emergency commands.

She then pushes the key in the lower right corner with the label that says 'SHUT DOWN' on it. And right then the unit immediately shuts down.

She then manually lifts up the lid of the capsule by unsnapping the lock in the middle and says

"Miller, are you alright? Miller... John, wake up!"

But agent Miller is unconscious and completely unresponsive.

The analyst then enters the room and stops when he sees Miller's condition.

The lead then looks at him with a worried expression, and then she says

"Go get the medical staff now!"

The analyst is clueless and takes a step back in confusion.

But then he quickly turns around and runs back out to get help.

In the taxi, Walker sees that the process has suddenly stopped at forty-nine percent, and now the hologram is showing the phrase 'CONNECTION LOST'.

"Well, I was hoping for better results... but hopefully that'll do it..." He says calmly and continues to say

"John Miller, zero one seven subcommand, Standby!" And Miller's clone shuts his eyes and drops his head.

"We are done here... ready the transport." He says while removing the device from the clone's head.

A week later, Miller is waking up from a deep coma in the agency's medical facility. And the first thing he sees is a woman sleeping in a chair next to him.

He then starts looking around the room but comes back to the woman again.

She is a brunet in her early to mid-thirties and has a fitness looking shape. Her hair is black and straight and drops right below her shoulders, and it's also covering her face as she is curled up in the chair.

He then looks at the monitor on his right wrist and slowly brings his left hand over to the monitor, and then he pushes the display to feel its connections against his skin.

The display then turns on and a hologram pops up showing his heartbeat, blood pressure and temperature.

He touches the heartbeat display and it changes to a graph showing his conditions over the past twenty-four hours.

He then grabs the monitor and slowly pulls it off of his wrist without turning off the hologram, and then tries to sit up on the bed.

His back feels stiff but he manages to sit up, and then he slowly tries to stand up on his feet.

His balance is slightly off and he quickly reaches for the side rails of the bed. And right then a nurse comes rushing in since the monitor was disconnected from his arm. And right behind the nurse a female doctor then walks in as well.

The nurse quickly grabs him and says

"It's okay, you're okay... you just need to take it easy right now."

The woman in the chair wakes up and it is the same lead operator who turned off the link between him and his clone.

"Hi there, I'm Doctor Holden, and this is my nurse Mrs. Turner."

"You can call me Elisabeth." Mrs. Turner says, and then Doctor Holden continues with a pleasant smile to say

"Can you sit back on the edge for me? I need to make sure your levels are normal before you can walk around on your own."

Miller sits on the edge and the nurse attaches the monitor back on his arm again and pops up the monitor.

Doctor Holden then checks Miller's eyes and ears and starts going through different screens of the hologram.

"Is he alright?" The lead operator asks.

"He seems fine." Holden replies and turns off the hologram.

She then looks into Miller's eyes again and snaps her fingers next to Miller's left and right ears. And then she asks Miller

"Do you feel okay?"

"Where am I?" Miller asks.

"Do you remember anything of what happened?"

"Where is my wife? Where is Kate?"

"Don't worry… your memories will come back to you slowly. And I'm sure that Agent Smith here, will make sure that you will be taken care of and back on your feet in no time… she's been here by your side almost every day since the incident, and friends like that are hard to come by." Doctor Holden says as she fills out her report on a translucent pad.

Smith looks at Miller and smiles, and Miller looks back and tries to smile back. But he doesn't know her and his smile comes off very generic and somewhat fake.

"Well, everything looks good to me and you're good to leave anytime you want." Says Doctor Holden.

"He just woke up from a coma lasting a week... wouldn't it be better to keep him here for another day or so, just to make sure?" Smith says while confused by the Doctor's decision.

"He can stay for comfort and peace of mind if you want him to, I have no problem with that. -- His coma wasn't caused by any trauma, and I think he'll probably have difficulty sleeping over the next forty-eight to seventy-two hours if anything. And being a little more active would also help him recover much faster." The doctor replies.

She then turns to Miller and continues to say

"If that is still the case in three days, then let me know and I'll see what we can do... but up to seventy-two hours is normal."

Miller looks at the doctor and nods his head in confusion, and the doctor then gives them both her pleasant smile and walks out of the room.

Miller peeks at Smith and sees her worried expression.

He then lifts his head up and looks at her and says

"Where do you know me from?"

"I'm Angela... I'm another agent, agent Smith... we've worked together for quite some time now..." She replies while trying to stay collected and optimistic.

"What happened? Is Kate ok?"

"What do you remember last?" Smith asks.

Miller closes his eyes for a couple of seconds, and then he says

"We were coming back home from Mike's wedding, Kate's brother... did we have an accident? Please tell me she is fine."

Smith walks over and holds Miller's hand and says

"Don't worry right now... the answers will come to you... I'm sure." She then turns around and grabs her bag and continues to say

"I need to report your status to the board and we'll catch up as soon as you're done here... we have a lot to talk about so give yourself some time." She then gives him a warm smile and a kind rub on his hand and says

"It's good to have you back John!" And then she walks out while trying to hide her painful but happy tears.

"What day is it?" Miller asks the nurse who is still in the room recalibrating the equipment.

"It's Thursday, May second... and still 2089." She replies with a smile.

"2089? How can it be? The doctor said that I've only been gone -- for only a week."

"I'm sorry, but I really don't know what happened... you're probably still in shock so, just go easy on yourself." She says and turns off the equipment next to the bed. And then she continues to say

"You're ready to leave if you want, or you can stay... just let me know if you still need to talk to the doctor. But I personally think you should wait and give yourself a little more time. Either way, I'll have the release forms ready at the front-desk. -- Your clothes are in the closet, and let me know if there's anything else Agent Miller."

"Agent...?" Miller says with a terrible confusion.

"Goodbye now." The nurse says as she walks out just as confused.

Miller is really bothered by not being able to connect the dots. He looks outside the windows and doesn't recognize the environment.

His sense of displacement makes him wonder if he is just having a dream. But since he is able to intentionally process his actions and thoughts, his wary mind suggests otherwise and his keen logic is giving him explanations that he is not attentive to process.

A car grabs his attention, and he gets a memory of his time with Kate driving back home while laughing over his stupid corny dance at the wedding.

He remembers that cars looked different back then, and then he slowly walks over to the bathroom and sees his own face in the mirror.

He realizes that years have gone by leaving him with no memories of his life beyond that night with his wife Kate.

He remembers that he had surprised Kate with a weekend trip to one of the first publically affordable space hotels around earth's orbit, for her twenty-fourth birthday right before the wedding.

It was 2067 and he was twenty-five years old, and Kate was filled with joy around him as if she was walking on clouds.

He then opens the closet and sees several different suits with matching shoes and shirts to the left, and a pair of jeans and several t-shirts to the right. He looks down at his left hand while touching his ring finger with his right hand, remembering the silver ring that he used to wear. But he can't even see a mark on his finger anymore.

He then changes his clothes into a light-blue dress shirt, the pair of jeans and a pair of dress shoes. And then he walks out of the room and over to the front-desk.

A security agent is already waiting for him by the front-desk. And when Miller walks up to the desk, the agent says

"Agent Miller, Agent Smith is waiting for you in the board room, if you are ready to leave…"

Miller nods his head and turns to the nurse behind the desk. But before he can say anything the security agent continues to say

"Your release forms are also confirmed sir, and there's nothing else you need to do here."

"I just need the wrist monitor." The nurse says with a smile.

Miller then takes off the monitor and hands it to the nurse and looks back at the agent.

"This way please…" Says the agent and leads the way.

As they walk through the corridors and office areas, people greet him in different ways. But Miller is unable to recognize anyone, and he just looks back at them with a confused expression on his face and a general quick smile and a "hello" here and there.

In the board room, Smith is talking with two other men when Miller walks in.

"Ah, there he is." Says the man behind the desk with a smile.

"I'm sorry, but I seem to have a problem remembering who is who, or any of this for that matter." Miller says.

"This is Agent Carter, our chief of operations and the head of our agency... and this is Agent Ortega, one of our top field operators." Smith says as she points at each person with her left hand.

"It's good to have you back sir." Says Ortega with a smile.

Miller studies the two guys but unable to remember anything. Carter is a black male in his mid-forties. He is six feet and a couple of inches tall, and about two-hundred and fifteen to twenty pounds with a solid frame and an athletic body. And Ortega is a Latin-American male in his mid-thirties who is about the same height, but has a smaller frame and weighs somewhere around one-hundred and eighty-five to one-hundred and ninety-five pounds lean.

"Yes it is, we're all glad that you are okay, and sorry to put you through all this without any breathing room... but the fact is, that the circumstances are forcing us all to be prompt from this point on, until we can figure out what went wrong during your last assignment." Says Carter.

"The last memories that I can recollect are with my wife. And evidently from a very long time ago. So please, before we go any further, can someone explain where my wife is and why she isn't aware of my situation." Miller says with a collected but pleading tone while he grabs a chair and sits down next to agent Ortega.

"Do you have any other memories besides what you can remember about your wife?" Carter asks.

"I do have fragments here and there but nothing that I can put together."

"Okay here it is and I hope you're ready for it." Smith says with a very fast paced tone, and continues with the same tone to say

"Agent Miller and her team were led in to a trap while doing an undercover co-op involving other agencies to bring down a terrorist group who were trying to take control over all nations using nanotechnology as viruses."

Miller suddenly interrupts Smith and says

"Nanotechnology...?"

"Yes, mechanical viruses designed to target specific DNA information, which could be narrowed down to wipeout families or even an entire race..." She replies and waits for a second to see if Miller has any more questions. And then she continues to say

"At first, they were only going after powerful individuals and families to gain momentum. But, when they realized that their actions were not being taken seriously, they decided to cause one of the largest mass genocides in the recorded history of our species... killing one point six billion people globally."

As Miller was listening to the story, he didn't seem to be bothered by it as someone who had heard this for the first time. He was getting images of the events in his head, as if segmented memories were trying to resurface.

He could remember short news clips, and glimpses of busy streets and sidewalks replaced by bone chilling fear and barren emptiness.

"How did we fight them back?" Miller asks as he interrupts Smith again.

"We didn't have to…" Smith replies.

"What do you mean?"

"During the preplanning of one of their organized attacks, they all fell victim to their own technology, which was seen as a mistake at first. But when their leader was recovered pierced to the fuselage of a weather drone flying around the globe. Only then, we realized that it was most likely an inside job to avenge the brutality of the program."

Miller was recollecting memories of reprograming devices containing the Nanites. And attaching a stitched up body covered in blood to a metallic surface with a high-power nail gun, as Smith was explaining the events.

"Why do you think it was personal and an inside job?" He then asks.

"Because every single bone in his body had been surgically removed except his skull and his spine, while kept alive… and no one could have had access to their bio-bank to retrieve the DNA information of every single member of the group, other than someone with direct access and proper knowledge to use it… and to reprogram the Nanites."

Miller was again remembering images and sounds of breaking into the lab facilities, taking out security guards, cutting the throats of some of the key members of the group, and cutting out the bones of a screaming man…

And as he was absorbing the information and injecting his own leftover memories, he was mostly looking down at the floor. The room became quiet for almost half a minute past Smith's last sentence, and Carter finally breaks the silence and says

"Alright, now that you know the past, let's focus on 'now' and what happens next… after all, and as harsh as it might sound, you wouldn't have enrolled to become an agent if it wasn't for Kate."

"What do you mean?"

"In your profile, it says that you had mentioned to honor her spirit. And to follow through with what she believed in during her funeral ceremonies."

Miller can't even process the thought of Kate not being around anymore. And instead, he sinks right back into his treasured segmented memories of her.

He remembers some of their intimate moments together and how he was interrogating Kate in the best way possible to figure out things about her work.

It was before they were married, and he was talking her in to skip work and spend the day with him while they were taking a morning shower together. And he remembers saying

"Why don't you stay home today and we could take the boat out." while kissing her around her neck.

"That sounds very tempting but I have to work today, and so do you!" Kate had replied with a smile while gently pushing his head back to look into his eyes.

"Just sign in and inactivate your status for today... and if anyone asks, just tell them that you're not feeling good and need some time to clear your head... I mean, I took the day off to spend it with you..."

"What? That I've caught the worst kind of 'mad-love' disease and need to be quarantined?"

"That would work for me... I already have a bunker where we could lock ourselves in, and survive for years if needed..."

"Okay, I can see that it's better for everyone if 'YOU' stayed home, since you're talking like a complete madman." Kate said as she was walking out of the shower.

"What...? I'm just giving suggestions here..." He had replied back as he was running out of ideas, and feeling somewhat defeated.

Miller then remembers looking out of his kitchen window that morning. It was a foggy morning and the lake in-front of his small mansion, which was built in twenty-twenty-five, was free of ripples. And he could see Kate's reflection in the window as she poured the protein-shake that he had prepared for breakfast, into a tall glass.

She was wearing a white shirt and a dark blue skirt down to her knees, a dark blue coat, and a pair of black low-heel shoes. She wasn't wearing any jewelry or any makeup, and he was thinking that her flawless look wasn't in need of any either.

"So, what's your typical day like at work?" He had asked Kate.

"Well, you know, the usual office work... going through memos, scheduling meetings, reviewing forms and documents before they are signed." She had replied as she walked over to give him a kiss on her way out.

"And there's no one else that could step into your shoes for a day..."

"Working for the boss of a large private company has its pros and cons, what can I say... enjoy your day and stay out of trouble. And make me something good for dinner, Captain."

"Miller, Miller... Are you okay...? We could stop if this is becoming too much... I can imagine how overwhelming all this must be right now." Carter says when he notices Millers watery eyes.

"Oh no, please continue... I was just trying to remember what my profession was before all this, since you mentioned that I had enrolled after what happened to Kate." Miller says as he tries to snap out of his thoughts.

"You got your master's degree in 'electronics' when you were sixteen, and became the first teenager having two master's at the age of eighteen when you added 'deep space science and theoretical physics' to your achievements as well. -- Then, you were awarded to further your educations and were offered high level positions with many prestigious companies worldwide. But instead, you enrolled in the Navy and became a 'SEAL' before your twenty second birthday... also, while you were in the Navy, you had picked up your educations through remote classes when you were twenty-one, and finished your third master's in biology right after your twenty-third birthday. -- After that, you started working as a contractor on the side for one of the largest privately owned space agencies, as an inventor. -- And while you were making your fortune on the side, your main focus remained on the SEAL's program, and you were promoted to the captain of your team at twenty-four. -- You became the leader of a highly specialized infantry team designed to carry out most sensitive operations at twenty-five, right before you met Kate." Smith says and stops by looking at Miller with raised eyebrows, as to see if he needed to hear any more about himself.

"Your application to become an agent didn't even last an hour in the system, before the agency was urged by the department of defense to pretty much hire you on the spot... and since your team was involved in most of our cases anyway, you seemed to be the perfect match when considered from all angles." Carter follows up, and then he continues to say

"We also believe that you were targeted, and set up to be at the annual science meeting in Europe."

"Targeted?" Miller asks suspiciously.

"Yes, targeted... there are very few men who know about highly classified secrets in this country. And you are most definitely one of them!" Carter replies while nodding his head back and forth to reaffirm his statement.

"So what exactly went wrong during the last operation?" Miller asks.

"Well, you disobeyed a direct order from the central command, which was led by me. And everything went south thereafter when you decided to go dark… which was only based on a 'hunch' I suppose." Smith replies slightly annoyed.

"Why would I disobey a direct order?"

"That's what we're trying to find out, if it's not already too late." Says Carter.

"I can't recall anything… unless you could play back the situation, and I'll try to see if it would trigger any memories… but disobeying a direct command doesn't match the profile, of the character that you just described me as…" Miller says in confusion, and as he is looking at Smith.

"Well, you were my boss… you were the head of this agency. And I'm not sure if there was anything that anyone could have done to stop you either…" Smith says and gets quiet as she looks away.

"The agency's policies mandated to replace you until further decisions by the defense department, and the secretary… he knows that you are well, and my orders are to keep you safe, which is why we are under a time constrain and need to find answers soon." Carter says as he gives Smith a serious look, to let her know that she needs to drop the attitude. And then he continues to say

"We have secured a location for you to stay at with twenty-four hours surveillance and live security. Agent 'Smith' will continue the debriefing process with you, and will playback the entire mission to start off with. -- In the meantime, try to remember and document any memories that you might have… let's figure out the missing links and see what we can find out."

He then turns to Smith and says

"The transport is by the rear entrance and ready when you are."

"I would like to have Jim involved as well if possible, since he was the lead analyst during the mission." Smith replies.

"You got it!"

"Okay then, ready when you are." Smith says and Miller gets up and walks towards the door. But he then stops and says

"Did you all trust me as a commander in charge?"

"Always, and without any doubts…!" Carter replies, and both Smith and Ortega nod in agreement.

Miller then looks down for a few seconds, and then he walks out of the room.

He is feeling confused, but strangely, not concerned. And he tries to stay alert instead of day-dreaming again. At the same time, it all seems like a bad dream to him, and he is somehow expecting to wake up from it in any second. But then, he feels the pain that he was experiencing in the room.

The pain that came with his memories of Kate… how could this be a dream if he can recall memories?

Could it be that he is dreaming up a random scenario while injecting his own memories into it?

As Miller is going through his thoughts and walking towards the rear entrance, Smith catches up with him.

"Hey, wait up!" Smith says while slightly gasping for air.

Miller stops and snaps out of his thoughts.

"How did you know where to go?"

"I didn't… I was just following a hunch!"

"Ah… there's still hope I suppose…"

"For what… me remembering things, or perhaps whatever it was going on between us before all this…"

"You're still sharp at least, and not 'completely' wiped, which is a good thing… but, just out of curiosity, what do you think it was going on between us, before all 'this'?"

Miller stays quiet, and thinks that it's best not to continue this conversation, dream or not. And then he turns around and continues walking.

Smith smiles and follows him towards the door.

[Three days earlier]

Doctor Walker is walking into his lab and asks the lead scientist

"How is he?"

"We were just waiting for you to start him up... his memories are rebuilt according to your specifications, and all the modules are functioning properly."

"Excellent, I'm ready when you are..." Walker says and grabs a chair by the control panels, and sits right in front of Miller's clone.

"Three, two, one, and, he is on..." The scientist says and the clone's eyelids starts to twitch as the eyes behind them start to slowly move left to right.

As the clone is waking up, he sees things very blurry. His ears are picking up the surrounding sounds in slow-motion, and he is struggling to keep up with what's going on.

"Calibration please!" Says Doctor Walker.

"Starting calibration... calibration is complete." Says the scientist. And in a split-second later, the image and the sound suddenly turns crisp to the clone, and his eyes becomes wide open.

"Agent Miller, can you hear me? Agent Miller..." Walker says.

"Doctor Walker?" Miller's clone replies in confusion.

"Yes, thank god you are alright son." Walker says with a secretive smile.

"What is going on? What happened?"

"Easy now, answers will come... let me take a quick look at you." Walker says as he places a small helmet like devise on the clone's head. And then he starts up the hologram on the clone's chair's left arm-support.

A screen like picture pops up and Walker then puts the palm of his right hand on the picture's vertical surface and drags it out to his right, and then a complete control board opens up.

He then scans through some brain activities before switching the screen over to the eyes. The helmet on the clone's head then releases a transparent shield down over the clone's eyes.

Walker then reads the data feed from other vital organs, and then he says

"Everything looks pretty good thanks to this team... they saved your life, which I am very grateful for."

"Saved my life?"

"Yes, I lured you into a trap and you took the bait!" Says Walker with a happy expression.

"Say what again?"

"I wanted to free you, from the corruption that's been going on ever since mankind became self-aware... come on walk with me, let me show you around and I will tell you all about it."

The clone gets up and says

"Why do I feel like my memories are distorted?"

"Ah yes, we'll get to that." Walker replies, and then he turns to the scientist and says

"As soon as you have reconstructed his memories, please send them to my personal iNeb, and I'll go through it with him when he's ready."

Walker then turns around again and walks towards the door, and the clueless clone follows him as he almost feels compelled to do so.

"iNeb?" Asks the clone.

"Interactive Neuron Extension Bridge... one of my designs to store the brain data including all its memories, on to an external hardware... but I usually only use it to play movies in my head when I travel." Walker says as he peeks at the clone. And then he continues to say

"But I can't take credit for everything, since I'm using one of your inventions as a supporting hardware, which is why I can't release it yet... before we have received proper approvals from your previous employer."

"And what invention are you referring to exactly?"

"Your 'Nebula Computing Storage, NCS' of course… you still remember that, right?" Walker replies as they walk through a wide corridor with concrete floors and graffiti painting on the walls.

"Yes I do, and it must have been a while since… I presume…" Says the clone and pauses momentarily, and then he continues to say

"Somehow, I can't tell exactly when."

"Only you and your sidekick employers would know that information… I just know that we've had NCS around for a little over a decade now. And so far, there's nothing out there that can even come close to benchmark the same."

"I'm sorry Doctor Walker, I am enjoying this little talk… but could you please tell me why I am here, and what has happened to me?" Says the clone to interrupt the conversation, and as he tries to be as polite as he can be, but simultaneously very direct.

Walker keeps walking and stays quiet. He then turns left into a room down the hall, and as soon as the clone walks in behind him, Walker says

"This is why you are here my boy… this is why I need you, the world needs you!"

The room is huge, and it's filled with equipment in every corner. There are stages for live conferencing, several large curved monitors showing everything from different locations in the world such as live events, government meetings, financial markets, air traffics, to data processing and thought conversion tools.

There is also mission-control like stations at the center of the room. And as Miller's clone looks around, he sees six hibernation boxes stacked next to each other in one corner. And each one has a display with a number showing on the top right.

"What is this place?" The clone asks.

"Do you remember a decade ago, when I was brought in to work with the agency on a cloning project? To keep some of the top most efficient agents safe at all times, including you?"

"Yes I do remember."

"Well, during the project I had to synchronize the data bridge between each host and their respective clone, which by the way was when I invented the iNeb. But, while I was mapping each brain to fine tune the link, I happened to see some of the most frequently accessed memories of each host."

"What do you mean?" Miller's clone asks slightly upset by the thought.

"Well, I wasn't doing it deliberately, it's just how the brain works… during the synchronization and calibration, the host is put into a temporary sleep mode. And the thought output used to calibrate the link is whatever the brain produces at that moment." Walker says with a fragile and innocent tone to reinforce his genuine actions. And he continues to say

"And fortunately for me, your thoughts were the most exciting things that I have ever witnessed. And they were the sole reasons, and the main purpose behind all this that you see around you."

"Which was what exactly?"

"It was love, commitment, strength, courage, direction, determination and everything that could possibly describe a perfect human being to be, in my opinion. -- To fight for what 'has' to be done to assure the greater good, and without the need for selfish recognitions of any sort… son, I happened to see your ultimate love for your partner. And 'really' for humanity, and how you single handedly brought down a global terrorist group… and by the way, I never put that in my reports… if that is what you are wondering right now." Walker says and pauses momentarily while observing the clone's reaction.

But since Miller's clone was in deep thoughts and didn't say anything, he then continues to say

"You are here because we both share a common goal... to bring justice and respect 'GLOBALY' to everyone. -- To take control and rid the humanity of suffering and segregation. To end hunger and to preserve the nature, to bring peace to every corner of this planet, and to unite us all 'once for all' to set a new milestone in our history... to open a new chapter and proudly add our achievements without any unnecessary and shameful wars over selfish disagreements, caused by the humanity's thirst for control... and more power... and I could go on and on..."

He then stops talking and takes a deep breath while looking down. A few seconds later, he then continues with a lower and an exhausted tone to say

"You see agent Miller, I've been waiting for this moment ever since I got a glimpse of your memories. Because I believe if anyone could make it happen, it would be you... I started this, because I was inspired by you... and now, I am leaving it up to you to decide. -- To either end this operation, or to invest your commitments to it. And to 'hopefully' bring a better tomorrow to this planet, and to humanity... either way, the choice is yours."

Miller's clone stands quiet with his arms crossed and without showing any emotions while staring into Doctor Walker's eyes.

There are no words exchanged in about half a minute, which feels forever to Doctor Walker. But he keeps his cool with a friendly smile, and patiently waits for the clone to say something.

The clone then breaks out of his silence and says

"Let's see what this operation is about first, before I draw any conclusions."

Walker smiles with satisfaction and says

"I wouldn't expect anything more either at this point, but there's a lot to be done, and a lot to take in, so be patient..."

"Well, I need to report in my whereabouts to the agency first."

"There's no need for that... as of two days ago, you were declared as deceased by the agency I'm afraid."

"I don't understand!? How do you know that?"

"You'll know soon enough… tell me, what do you last remember from the science exhibition several days ago?"

"I remember a thick smoke filling up the place very quickly, and there were several people rushing in with gas masks… and everything is blank thereafter."

"It was a deadly poisonous gas, and my team rushed in to help everyone in the room, including you… and luckily no one was injured."

"Why am I the only one here then?" The clone asks suspiciously.

"You were the closest to the source and the last to be looked at. And since I recognized you during the presentation, I decided to bring you here."

"So your plans worked!"

"That was just a joke… and not very funny now that I'm thinking about it…"

"And the agency is not looking for my body because…?"

"Whatever you were doing must have been an undercover operation, and the agency didn't want to announce their involvement I suppose…" Walker replies and waits for a couple of seconds before continuing to say

"Which is really interesting to me… why would you be there in the first place, posing as a security guard?"

"I'm not sure… I can't remember…"

"The gas-release itself was just an accident. The leak came from the basement where a demonstration was being prepared by an amateur team. And the only person missing in the list of active personnel was you… so you were never there to begin with." Says Walker curiously.

"Why wouldn't the agency send in my clone?"

"My question exactly… my presumptions are, that it must have been because of me, since I announced my participations only hours before the event. And there was probably no time for the agency to count for everything… or, that this was perhaps another one-man operation initiated by yourself, and unknown to the agency!? -- But since your actions were rather pleasant during the event, I assume again that it must have been a personal interest in my work, and that you were there for observations only... and if of course that was the case, well, I wouldn't want to complicate things between you and the agency, which is why we brought you here. -- And later on, when the agency announced your death, well, I just couldn't resist the temptation to pass on the opportunity of sharing my beliefs and vision with you..." Walker says with a smile. And then after a few seconds he continues with an even tone and without any expressions to say

"And hoping that if I have made the right choice or not, is irrelevant at this point, since I'm giving 'you' the ultimate power to make a decision... which subsequently includes my ambitions and faith as well..."

The clone is quiet for a few seconds as he tries to take it all in, and then he says

"I guess we'll find out soon enough... so where do I start?"

[Back to the present]

Miller is going through the last operation with Smith in the safe-house. And Jim, who is a tall and skinny guy with curly black hair in his late twenties, is playing back the recorded events on a touch-interactive hologram.

"Okay, right here is when we lost you." Jim says with a mixed excitement and a troubled expression as he skips through sections of the recordings, and while pointing at the playback. And he continues to say

"And, right here is when we were locked out and the copy process began... see, I think he was copying your core functions, meaning your consciousness and subconscious, and, I mean the whole thing... but here is where I really got worried. You can see that he is copying your memories while purging them at the same time!"

He then pauses for a few seconds as they watch the process indicator's digits accumulate. And then he skips again and continues to say

"And right there at forty-nine percent, is when agent Smith got to your station and disconnected your link, after running like a possessed wrestler through the entire office."

"Tell me again how the link works between the host and the clone, but from the beginning... I want to know what makes it possible to establish a communication between the two." Says Miller as he is processing each step in his head.

"Well, the clones are developed through a rapid process called 'ABC', which stands for 'Accelerated Bio Compiler', inside of an artificial chamber called 'eWomb', where 'e' stands for external... and don't ask me how the machine works because I have no clue." Jim replies and pauses.

But before he can continue to complete answering the question, Smith interrupts and says

"All the communication electronics are developed through nanotechnology. And essentially what Doctor Walker had developed was an organic thick liquid that the body wouldn't reject, to hold a mixture of devices for various applications. -- He would then inject the liquid into the fetus once it had reached a comparable twenty-five weeks of development, which in the eWomb would only be after forty-eight hours or so." She then stops talking. But since Miller is still waiting to hear more, she then continues to say

"He would inject devices needed for the brain right below the skull, between the brain tissue and bone, and visual devices between the lens and the cornea, and the audio devices down by the vocal cords... the liquid would then form a thin elastic film around the injected areas and would fuse itself to the organic tissue, and expand with the body's natural development and growth."

"So how could I even switch off the communication?" Miller quickly asks and Smith continues to say

"These devices are powered through the body's natural low-level bio-electricity, and are unable to transfer or receive signals more than a few feet... so the repeaters and signal transmitters are built in to an external device like a wristwatch or an earpiece, and can be turned off completely, which would put the clone in pause and disconnect it from the host... or be partially turned off, meaning you could switch off the audio or the visual feed without interrupting the main link."

"But how were you able to hear me if I wasn't speaking or saying anything?"

"All you need to do is to think about what you want to say. And even though to 'you' it's only a thought, your vocal cords will still generate the sound." Jim answers while using hand gestures at the same time.

"Wait, it doesn't make any sense... why could you hear what I was thinking to say, but not my thoughts?" Miller asks to make a point.

"Doctor Walker believed that when a person is analyzing a thought, everything is processed in a sandbox different than when the person would prepare a thought for a phrase to be spoken... at least this is what he put in his report... and due to more than a decade old technology, there's not enough bandwidth to process that much information in real-time, while transmitting everything else simultaneously. -- And since Walker was disconnected from the project, no one was assigned to further extend the functionalities." Jim says and pauses for a moment.

But Miller is still doubtful and says

"Not enough bandwidth?"

"Well, it's more of a limitation and failsafe, than just bandwidth... because what can be monitored and what the host can control are sent in two separate channels. And while you can turn off the monitoring channel, perhaps also to save power, your main link should never be tapped into, since it could cause delays between the host and the clone... or in a worst case scenario, completely throw them out of synch and even disconnect. -- However, we should be able to design a link directly at the station to intercept the signals past the host's main feed. -- There would be slight delays in the playback of course but nothing major. -- I've suggested this idea several times, but no one thinks it's necessary to build it since we've never had the need, and never had anything like this happen before." Jim explains while hoping that Miller would finally consider this option going forward.

But Smith on the other hand knows that Miller only wanted to protect every agent's right to be secretive if needed, which is why she respectfully wouldn't go against his decisions in the past.

"Ah... so why was Walker disconnected from the project?" Miller asks.

"He believed that since cloning was against the law, then the government should also comply with the same rules, or change the law... and he also wanted to publically announce the technology, which could pose unimaginable threats in the wrong hands." Smith replies with a dimmed dramatic tone.

"Yes, I can see that... trying to fight an army of clones wouldn't be in anyone's comfort." Miller says while holding his arms crossed. And after a few seconds he then continues to say

"Has there been any reaction from the scientific community around cloning since the event?"

"That is a mystery to solve since after questioning almost every single person in the room, no one knew what we were talking about... in fact no one seemed to even remember Walker's presentation!" Smith says with a clueless expression.

"Alright, I need some time to digest all this and analyze the events again... do you think you could leave everything here?"

"Sure not a problem, just let me know if you need anything else..." Smith replies.

"I will..."

As Smith and Jim are leaving the room, Miller then says

"And by the way, thank you for saving me from being 'completely' wiped out!" and he gives Smith a genuine smile.

"You are very welcome John... you have done much more for every one of us already, than we could ever repay." Smith replies and smiles back.

Back in Carter's office, agent Ortega is about to leave after having a discussion regarding the security personnel at Miller's safe-house when a call comes in to Carter's station.

"I have to take this, let me know if you see any problems." Says Carter.

"You got it!" Ortega replies as he walks out the door.

"Mr. Secretary Sir... -- yes he is fine and we have him in a safe-house." Carter says and gets quiet for a few seconds while listening to the call through his earpiece. And then he replies with his head down and his eyes closed

"Understood... -- of course... -- that won't be necessary sir, I will personally see to it right away."

He then disconnects and says

"Vicky, please send in Ortega to my office again..."

And his virtual assistance replies

"Message sent."

After a few moments Ortega walks in and closes the door behind him.

"The lake-house..." Carter says.

"What? You are joking right?" Ortega says as he steps closer to Carter's desk.

"No I'm not... it's a direct order from the secretary of defense."

"What does this mean?"

"Not sure yet, but it must be bigger than what we think."

"Oh man... Why him of all people..." Ortega says as he puts his hands on his waist while looking down.

"I know, but we have no choice but to follow the order and we have to move fast... just make sure that this stays between us two, only."

Ortega lifts up his head and looks to the side while feeling disturbed and confused by what he was being asked to do.

He then looks at Carter while raising his eyebrows for a few seconds, and then he turns around and starts to walk out.

"Ortega." Says Carter and Ortega stops without turning his back.

"This cannot be linked back to us whatsoever!"

"Got it...!" Ortega replies and walks out while feeling unease.

In Doctor Walker's nest, a lead analyst walks up to him as he is getting ready to sit in one of his clone control stations.

The analyst gets close to his face and whispers quietly

"Sir, we have analyzed new feeds from the secretary, and Miller's wellbeing is confirmed. And they're taking proper measures to take him out of the equation."

"Hmm..., you know what needs to be done, and get it done quickly before it's too late."

"Yes sir."

At the safe-house, Ortega pulls up his vehicle to the rear entrance and gets out while carrying a small box, and a cup of coffee.

He then tells the guard who is standing next to the door

"Take a break man, I'm going to be here for ten to fifteen minutes or so..." with a pleasant expression.

And the security guard replies

"Thank you sir, I appreciate it." And then he leaves.

At the same time, Miller is going through everything he has available, and he is trying to connect the dots when he hears someone talking outside the door.

He then quickly turns on the door's security monitor, which is a built in clear screen in the door's interior side.

And then he sees the guard leaving his post, and that agent Ortega is about to come in.

Ortega knocks softly on the door with a couple of taps and says

"Hey it's me Ortega, is it okay to come in?"

"Yeah sure, the door is not locked." Miller replies as he pushes a button on the side of his wristwatch.

"Hey I got you coffee and some fast burning calories... have you figured anything out yet?" Ortega says as he walks in.

He then walks over to Miller's desk and sets down the box and the coffee next to his left, and then he moves away.

"Thanks... no, not really... well, nothing more than some wild assumptions, and a few hypotheses that only leads to something bigger... but I need more time to think them all through." Miller replies as he instinctively pretends to be deep into reading a document and while tracking Ortega's movement in his peripheral vision.

He then takes a peek to his left where Ortega has stepped back, and sees that Ortega is reaching for his firearm under his suit.

Miller reacts instantly and hits the spill-proof coffee cup with his left backhand in Ortega's direction. And then he almost simultaneously launches himself at him.

Ortega is taken by surprise as he is blocking the coffee and his face. But he manages to take his gun out as Miller throws him against the wall next to the door. Miller then quickly tries to grab the gun with his right hand while pushing on Ortega's throat with his left arm.

Ortega is being strangled and struggles to fight back, and then with a suffocating voice he says

"Sorry buddy." and fires off.

Everything happened so fast and within only a few seconds. And Miller keeps pushing with all he's got while looking into Ortega's eyes with rage, disappointment and confusion.

But suddenly, he feels weak and his vision gets blurry and he senses the end.

"I'm just following orders man." Says Ortega as he grabs Miller to break his fall, and then he lays him down slowly on the floor.

He then reaches for the door to lock it quickly, and looks at the door monitor to see if there's anyone outside. Then he walks over to Miller's station and accesses the building's surveillance cameras, using Miller's credentials.

There are two cameras covering the area and he quickly points them at different directions to clear a path to his vehicle. He then takes off Miller's wristwatch, his belt and looks for anything else that might have a tracking device and throws them on his desk.

He then picks Miller up on his shoulders and walks towards the door. He looks outside first to make sure that no one is there and then walks quickly over to his vehicle and puts Miller in the trunk, which is an area that pops out and slides back beneath the seats under the vehicle.

He then quickly runs back inside to reposition the cameras and starts to clean up the place. And he also deletes the segments of the recordings when the cameras were pointed away.

He straightens up his outfit and sees that the guard has returned back to his post.

He then opens the door and says

"Alright, I'll see you later... don't work too hard and try to get some rest." and closes the door behind him.

He looks at the guard and gives him a friendly smile and nods his head and walks away towards his vehicle.

"Have a good day sir." Says the guard and Ortega replies

"You too!" as if nothing had happened.

Forty-five minutes later, Carter is looking at his watch and then out through the glass walls of his office, as he is anxiously waiting to hear back from Ortega. And right then Ortega's call comes in to his station.

"What's going on?" He answers and asks quickly.

"Package has been delivered." Ortega replies and disconnects.

Carter then says

"Vicky, I'll be out for a couple of hours."

Vicky the virtual assistance then pops up on his station's hologram and says

"Sir, would you like to leave a message?"

"No, just mark my calendar with an 'out of the office' status please."

"Your request is complete, and your status will remain inactive for two hours." Vicky replies and shows a confirmation screen. Carter then turns off his station and walks out.

At Jim's station, he and Smith are going through possible scenarios around why no one could remember anything after the science event, and Smith happens to see Carter leaving his office in a hurry.

She notices the oddity in Carter's behavior and says

"Did Carter mention anything about leaving the office today?"

"Nothing that I know of." Jim replies and quickly pulls up Carter's schedule and says

"Well, he just marked his calendar with an out of the office signature..."

Smith then quickly calls Miller on a secured line and gets no answer.

"I'm not sure why he wouldn't leave anyone in charge..." she says while feeling suspicious, and then she continues to say

"Come on let's go for a drive."

"Doing what?"

"Fieldwork, we can talk in the car."

Twenty minutes later, they arrive at the safe-house and Smith asks the guard

"Has anyone else been here recently?"

"Yes ma'am, agent Ortega was here about an hour ago."

"Is Miller inside?"

"Yes ma'am, agent Ortega left alone."

"Miller it's me Smith, and I have Jim with me, can we come inside?" She says as she gently knocks on the door. But no one answers.

"Miller is everything alright?" She says and tries to open the door.

The door is not locked and opens easily. She then walks in but sees no sign of Miller.

Jim walks in behind her and Smith keeps calling for Miller as she goes through the kitchen and into the bedroom.

She then comes out from the bedroom and says

"No one is here." as she touches her forehead in confusion.

The guard is confused and says

"Agent Ortega relieved me for a couple of minutes, but he was still here when I came back, and was even talking with agent Miller as he was leaving!?"

"He might have escaped since his watch is right here." Jim says and then he sits behind the desk.

"Can you pull up the recordings from the surveillance?" Smith asks.

"I'm already on it!" Jim replies while he pulls up the recordings.

"Why would he escape? There's no reason to, unless he wasn't feeling safe here..." Smith says and walks out to look around.

She then walks back in and Jim says

"No, he did not! Look at this! There's a jump between the pictures on both cameras with a different timestamp. And you can see that the positioning is slightly off before and after on both of them... someone else besides him must have done this, even though the logs show that Miller himself did it."

"How could you find that so fast?"

"I mean, the camera logs show that he moved the position of both cameras twice with different timestamps. But if Miller wanted to escape, he wouldn't be here to reposition the cameras back... the recording is continuous, but the file is fragmented on the media, which usually indicates an edit procedure. And I just compared the beginning and end of the last two overlapping segments..." Jim replies with confident, and an expression that his quick thinking should be a given fact and obvious to Smith at this point.

"But if Ortega was helping him, then why would he leave his watch? He never leaves his watch." Smith says.

"He didn't want to be tracked..." Jim replies as a clear assumption.

"But Ortega could be tracked, so I'm not sure if that would make any sense..." Smith says as Jim picks up the watch.

"W-ow... wow, this thing is still recording!" He says and gives Smith a quick look before he stops the recording and then to start the playback.

He then pulls up the hologram on the watch and plays the last recorded file. But then a splash screen comes up requiring a password to continue.

"Zero, six, uppercase 'A' alpha, dash, three, two, one, lowercase 'S' sierra" Smith says.

Jim enters in the password and the playback starts.

"How did you know that?" He then asks.

"Just a hunch... Kate's ID when she was an agent..." She replies.

As they watch the playback and are seeing what has happened in disbelief, Smith turns to the guard and says

"Not a word about this to anyone, is that understood!?"

"Yes ma'am!"

"Not even Carter... until I know what the hell is going on here." She says with a slightly heated tone.

"Got it!" Says the guard and continues to say

"And you were never here either I assume?"

"You know how this works!" Smith replies and then she turns to Jim and says

"Can you locate Ortega?"

Jim logs in to Miller's station with his own credentials and looks up the tracking maps and says

"Ortega's last locations are from the agency to here, and then back to the agency and after that nothing... I don't even get a reading on his vehicle."

"Okay, he was obviously trying to cover up his tracks." Smith says.

"Here's Carter's tracker, last active at the agency, thirty minutes after Ortega's arrival to the agency." Jim quickly says right after.

"Carter would not risk walking in Ortega's tracks, so wherever Ortega took Miller must be within a twenty to thirty minutes radius from the agency." Says Smith, and continues to say

"And I might know where they're taking him... but it can't be good if I'm right... come on let's go!"

She then turns to the guard and says

"You know what's at stake here. Take the next couple of shifts and don't let anyone in, until you hear back from me!" And then she walks out.

The guard nods and closes the door behind them and stands his guard.

She inputs the coordinates into the vehicle's navigation system and says

"This is a top secret location where cleaners can get in and out of, without being noticed when something needs to be disposed... let's just hope we are not too late."

"Too late for what...? Seeing his dead body?" Jim says sarcastically.

"Do you know what this means? You saw what Ortega did, and what if Carter is in on it too?" She says with urgency, and continues to say

"What if the agency is compromised? And the question is... who could we trust... if we were facing the worst?"

"The secretary of defense of course..." Jim replies.

"Carter gets most of his orders from the secretary... what if this was a direct order from the secretary?" Smith says.

"Wouldn't it mean that we should probably stay out of it then?"

"You are kidding right? We are talking about Miller... who would you trust if the national security was at stake, the secretary or Miller?"

"Well if you want my honest opinion, I would probably take Miller even over the president..."

"You have a funny way of showing it..."

"Look, I'm just nervous okay... I don't even have proper field-training, and you are taking me to a place where we dispose people and stuff." Jim says with a nervous tone while Smith looks away, and he continues to say

"And not to mention, if you are right, then we are talking about two of our top agents disposing 'THE' agent. And we could potentially be disposed along with him!"

"You are right... I shouldn't have dragged you in to this." Smith says, and then she continues after a few seconds to say

"Auto-driver, stop the vehicle at the taxi transport station past the next cross-street."

"Would you like me to stop at the next taxi transport station?" Says the onboard computer to confirm Smith's request.

"Yes, that is correct!"

"Command confirmed." The auto-driver replies.

"What are you going to do?" Jim asks.

"I'll think of something... whatever I can to get more evidence."

They both sit quiet until the vehicle pulls over behind a transport taxi, and then Smith says

"Auto-driver, open the trunk and drive back to the agency once it's closed, confirm command!"

"Agency coordinates activated, command confirmed." The auto-driver replies.

Smith then gets out and walks to the back of the car.

Jim waits for a few seconds, and then he steps out of the car and says

"Okay, I'm coming with you, if you promise to tell me exactly what to do."

"I can't do that, I am sorry... I don't know what I was thinking." Smith says as she is collecting some firearms and ammunition from the trunk and putting them into a large bag.

"You can use me to watch your blind spots or something."

"If this ends up being what I think it is, then I don't know how to put 'dragging you into this' in my report."

"Just say that I volunteered, and insisted, and wouldn't take a 'no' for an answer... and then you can put your recommendations that I should further my field-trainings blah blah..."

"Are you sure you're up for this?"

"No, not really... but I'm already feeling the excitement and it feels kind of good..." Jim says as he shakes his hands nervously. And as he waits for an approval, he switches his arms position between crossed and then on his waist, and then he just puts his hands down in his pockets.

Smith then loads a gun and hands it to Jim with a faint smile and a raised eyebrow, and then she says

"You do as I say and move when I move, clear?"

"Crystal!" Jim replies and takes the gun with an overwhelming excitement.

"Don't shove it down your pants, just put it in a bag for now and grab as much as you can comfortably carry... take a vest and test the batteries of the force field, and a couple of more guns... also test the charge on the guns and pair them up with your bio-signature, and don't forget ammo!"

Jim sees a helmet with an interactive screen and says

"Oh yeah... that's what I'm talking about."

"Let's go!" Smith says and walks over to the taxi in front of the agency car.

Jim then closes the trunk and the agency vehicle pulls out and drives away when they clear its path.

Meantime, Carter has taken a different route to the lake-house and stops by the roadside half way through a woodsy area.

It's been cloudy all day and there's a dense fog between the trees. He checks his gun and the area to make sure that no one is around, and then he gets out of his car and starts walking through the woods.

He is very cautious about not being seen and stays alerted.

But after walking for only a couple of minutes, he suddenly hears footsteps and the sound of a broken branch at his four O'clock.

He quickly stops and crouches down and looks at the direction of the sound to see who is following.

The visibility is poor and he stays put for a while as he is fixed on the direction where the sound was generated from.

He then grabs a broken branch to his left and rubs it slowly over the ground while keeping his eyes fixed at one spot, and then he stops dead quiet again.

Within a couple of seconds, he suddenly sees a dark figure quickly peek at his direction from behind a tree ten feet to the left of where he was looking. He then instantly knows he is being followed and starts running towards the opposite direction.

The dark figure starts the chase and Carter looks behind his shoulder very quickly from time to time to keep track of the chaser's position, and while running with all he's got. And as he notices that the chaser is gaining ground, he turns and fires off a couple of shots while still running.

His gun is an electromagnetic gun and doesn't generate much sound as the projectiles leave the barrel.

The chaser positions himself at Carter's four O'clock again and fires off a couple of rounds, and misses with only inches from his head.

The chaser is using a very old technology handgun, which makes a much louder noise that even Ortega hears from the lakehouse.

Carter realizes that he is dealing with someone who is going for a kill by purposely avoiding force fields and registered weapons, and is not afraid of being heard either.

He then sees a wide trench twenty feet away and runs straight for it, and jumps in without breaking his speed. But as soon as he lands, he then runs to his right while timing his steps with the chaser's speed. And then within a second or two he quickly throws himself against the walls of the trench, where tree roots are hanging over the edge providing a small hiding spot from the chaser's point of view.

The chaser reaches the edge, and after a quick look he jumps into the trench without any hesitation. And before he reaches the ground, Carter launches himself at the chaser and manages to quickly disarm him while pushing his face into the ground.

The chaser struggles to break loose and turns around as he hits Carter with his right elbow. Carter loses his grip and the chaser kicks him off and over the short trench-wall at the opposite side. Behind the short trench-wall is a steep slope and Carter is unable to break his fall and rolls down the slope. The chaser quickly gets up and recovers his gun, and then he jumps over the wall and starts running after Carter down the slope.

While trying to balance his steps down the slope, the chaser then starts shooting at Carter as he tumbles towards the bottom, and hits his arm. Carter reaches for his gun and fires back at the chaser between the rolls, and he hits him in the right shoulder after his second try. The chaser then loses his balance and falls and rolls down the slope behind him.

Carter then quickly gets up on his feet as soon as he reaches the bottom and intercepts the chaser before he can find his balance. And then he quickly puts his gun to the chaser's head and says

"Any last words...?"

The chaser looks at him and smiles, and suddenly the life just goes out of him.

Carter realizes that he is a clone and quickly drags him over to a tree. He then hand cuffs his hands around the tree stub with a lightweight flexible metallic band that he takes off of his right ankle.

The band responds to Carter's touch, and interlocks instantly when he rolls his thumb over the edge at the overlapping end of the band.

He then stands up and checks his wounded arm. He is bleeding but it's nothing to worry about. And right then, he hears a drone flying low over the area, and then he quickly starts running towards the lake-house.

At the lake-house Ortega has already heard the gun shots and he is looking out for movements around the house.

The lake-house is a small cottage with the rear side facing a small lake.

Ortega hears the drone and sees Carter running through the woods towards the house. He then carefully goes outside and tries to cover other angles to give Carter a safe passage towards the house.

Smith and Jim arrive at the location where Carter's vehicle is parked and Smith says

"Okay, this is not good… he is taking a blind path through the woods to avoid attention."

She then gets out of the taxi and starts putting her gear on to get situated.

Jim gets out and does the same thing, and the taxi drives away.

"Are you ready?" Smith asks and Jim nods to acknowledge. And then they start walking towards the house and through the woods while ready for action.

At the same time, Miller is slowly waking up with blurry vision on an older style sofa, and hears people talking outside behind the door.

Carter has now reached the safety of the house and Ortega asks him

"What happened?" as Carter is walking up to the porch

"Someone else knows we are here, is he inside?" Carter replies and asks.

"Yes, and he is still out."

"We need to move quickly... come on get in and give him the shot."

"What? You know we might kill him... killing Miller!"

"We have no choice, he might be monitored."

"But he needs to first recover, he'll be too weak!" Ortega says with concerns.

Miller gets up on his feet and moves over to the wall next to the door.

The door opens and Carter walks in while still holding his gun.

Miller doesn't waste any time and grabs Carter's gun and pulls him in through the door. Miller then hits him really fast and hard below his ribs, and below his neck before Carter has time to react or even know what is going on.

Without interrupting his movements, Miller then throws Carter towards the sofa and points the gun at Ortega as he is standing in the door confused, and frozen.

Ortega loses the grip of his gun and opens his arms slowly, and away from his body. And with a pleading tone he then says

"Man... this is so messed up..."

"Get in and close the door!" Miller says with a serious look, and while keeping his gun pointed at Ortega's head.

"Take it easy man..." Carter says as Ortega walks in.

"Do you want to tell me what is going on?" Miller asks with a serious tone, and then he grabs Ortega's gun out of his hand as he walks past by him towards Carter.

"It's complicated, please lower your gun." Carter says as they hear the drone fly over the house.

"Un-complicate it!" Miller replies and before Carter has a chance to say anything, the drone starts shooting at the house with high-speed machine guns.

Bullets are hitting everything inside the house through the windows, and broken pieces are flying all over the place.

The sound from the guns is continuous without any gaps between each bullet, and the bullets fly through the air like straight laser-beams.

The roof seems to have a protective layer, and bullets are only penetrating through the windows.

The drone repositions down and flies lower, and while continuously shooting at the building. But luckily the walls seem to have the same protective layer as well.

Carter reaches under the sofa and pulls out a silver colored body bag and throws it at Miller. And then he shouts

"Get in and pull the red string!"

He then looks at Ortega and says

"Where is the shot?"

Ortega pops a small bullet sized device out from the side of his watch and throws it at Miller.

"What the hell is this?" Miller shouts back.

"It will slow down your heartbeat, and the sack is going to dim your body temperature." Carter replies while shouting and covering his face.

Smith and Jim have heard the shootings, and they are running towards the house in full speed.

At the house, the hellish rains of bullets are randomly penetrating in, and the protective shields inside the walls are caving in.

They're all trying to protect themselves while laying low to the ground and Carter shouts

"Come on man, you're wasting time!"

Miller gets in quickly and looks at Ortega while showing him the bullet, wondering what to do with it.

"Just squeeze it on each end between your fingers!" Ortega shouts.

Miller squeezes the bullet and pulls the red string. He then starts to zip up the bag and gives Carter a look before closing it over his head.

"Don't worry... it's your own design..." Carter shouts, and right then he gets shot in the left leg.

Miller's heart-rate drops and he passes out before he can zip up the bag.

Ortega then crawls over to him while miraculously dodging rounds, and zips up the bag.

Carter then signals him to keep moving towards the side door through the kitchen.

The drone is now only detecting the heat signature from two bodies, and stops shooting. It then flies higher and hovers over the building while tracking the two bodies.

Ortega reaches the side door and Carter takes the chance and gets up, and then he moves towards the front door while dragging his leg. He then opens the door and walks out while pretending to move towards the woods.

Ortega sees Carter and does the same thing.

The drone verifies that none of the two bodies outside are Miller, and the heat signature of the body inside has now dropped to cold and without any sign of a heartbeat.

It then reports mission complete and requests confirmation to pursue the other bodies running away from the building.

The request is denied and the drone is approved to return back to base.

Carter sees that the drone is flying away and knows that it took the bait, and then he starts walking back to the house.

Ortega follows him inside and they both start to check Miller for bullet holes.

Smith now rushes in and sees them both leaning over Miller, who is now inside of a body bag. And she instantly yells

"Get away from him!" as she is pointing her gun at them.

Carter puts his hand up and says

"It's not what you think, stay down!"

But Ortega keeps opening the bag up.

"Not until you tell me what the hell is going on here!" Smith replies with a loud voice, and a serious expression.

"This is just getting better and better..." Ortega yells back sarcastically, and then he turns around and gives Smith a serious look to let her know that she should cut it out.

"We don't have much time..." Carter says as he tries to move his wounded leg to face Smith, and then he continues to say

"We need a scanner before his heartbeat jumps back up, to make sure he is not being monitored."

"There should be one in the agency car... I'll go get it." Ortega says and gets up, and then he looks at Smith to move out of his way and to lower her gun.

"Just go!" Carter says.

"Keep an eye on him!" Smith tells Jim.

Ortega rushes out and Smith crouches down to check Miller's pulse while keeping her gun pointed at Carter.

"We were ambushed." Carter says.

"Why did you keep me in the dark? And what were you doing here in the first place?"

"The order came from the secretary... he has verified intelligence that the patterns in the information flow have been noticeably shifting slowly during the past eight to twelve months. And there was a clear jump in the scientific community's desire to exchange information only with specific high-profile members of the government, in every single country... which he thought might have something to do with Miller's last assignment." Carter replies with pain.

"And he wanted you to take him out?" Smith asks quickly.

"No, to make it look like he was out, and clean up any traces that could lead back to him for the time being..."

"Does this look like a pretend clean up to you?"

"I don't like it any more than you do... and it sure looks like a setup."

Smith then lowers her gun when she verifies Miller's faint heartbeat.

Ortega walks in with the scanner and Jim runs in behind him while carrying another device.

Smith looks at Jim wondering why he is not holding his gun. And Jim looks back as he elevates his shoulders, and with a facial expression indicating that he didn't know what else to do.

Ortega starts to scan Miller's body right away, and a few seconds later he says

"He is clean!"

"If the secretary is involved, then he can't know that Miller is still alive..." Smith says with a nervous tone.

"Absolutely not..." Carter replies and continues to say

"But we might be able to find out who is potentially behind this, before I report anything back to the secretary... there's a clone tied up to a tree two-hundred yards north, that we might be able to retrieve some left over information from."

Smith pulls out a couple of broken pieces of a metallic band out of her pocket and says

"This must be yours then, I assume."

"Great..." Says Carter.

"Well, it looked like it was blown up from the bloody mess left on one side of the tree and the surrounding area, which probably happened during the shootings... so I took a couple of leafs with blood stairs as samples. I also noticed a portable lab in the car, which I think we could use to analyze the DNA, and to see if we can find a match of the host." Jim says and awaits an acknowledgement as Smith and Carter are staring at him.

Ortega gets up to give Miller more breathing room and says

"I'll make sure that you pass your field exams!" as he walks by Jim and taps him on his back.

"Alright, it's not safe to be here... there's an underground bunker two hundred yards south, if someone could give me a hand." Carter says.

"What if we get ambushed again?" Ortega asks.

"We are not going through the woods... there's an underground tunnel that leads to the shelter through the basement." Carter says as Miller starts to recover from his deep sleep.

"There's a basement here?" Smith asks while helping Miller to sit up.

And as Miller is slowly coming to his senses and while still feeling a little dizzy, he says

"There's a hidden door behind the pantry, which is why there's never any food in this place."

"You remember this place?" Carter asks.

"I just remember setting up the pantry to hide the door..." Miller replies.

"Okay let's move!" Smith says and helps Miller up on his feet, and Ortega leads the way while helping Carter.

They get down to the basement and it's really dark. But Jim's helmet automatically switches to night vision, and he manages to find the door to the entrance with ease.

Carter puts his hand on the bio-scanner next to the door to activate the security screen. But nothing happens, and then he says

"There's no power, and the power from the bunker only activates the lock from the other side of this door to provide more protection…"

"Great, a blast proof door without power… I wonder who thought that one through… what if someone got stuck inside and needed help…?" Ortega says.

"No, I think it is working fine." Jim says and continues to say

"The main security disables the panel after a certain timeframe, if the place is under an attack."

"Ah… I believe you are right, and we missed that window." Carter replies.

"But we should still be able to reactivate it remotely." Jim says.

"But there's no power!?" Smith says.

"Give me a second. -- I might be able to access it through my helmet." Jim says as he starts interacting with the transparent visor by looking at the options menu at the top of the screen.

He then activates system login, and as soon as he thinks about his credentials they are automatically fed into the screen.

He then confirms login and right away a secured remote connection to his virtual station is successfully established, and a welcome screen displays 'Agent: Tanner, Jim' at the top right corner, and then he says

"This is so cool… I hate you guys already."

"Can you say what's going on?" Ortega asks.

"Hold on, I'm in the system."

Jim then locates the bunker through his coordinates and finds the inside panel. He then re-routes the power to the outside panel and says

"Okay, try again."

Carter puts his hand on the bio-scanner again and the scanner hologram pops up.

"Yes!" Jim says with excitement.

"I'll help you too with your field training, including the recommendations in my report." Smith says.

"Not sure if he needs recommendations anymore." Carter says with a happy tone and while entering the code in the hologram.

The system accepts the code and the door opens.

Once they reach the bunker, Jim quickly sets up the portable lab he is carrying and starts to analyze the blood sample. And Ortega helps Carter to sit down on a sofa.

"Sorry about the drama man, I didn't know what else to do... but I can see now, that I should have just asked, instead of risking my neck to get you here..." Ortega says as he is walking over to Miller, and then he continues to say

"Can I have my gun back now?"

Miller holds up the gun with a smile and says

"You should pay better attention to your gear." as he gives both Carter and Ortega a friendly look. And he continues to say

"Your gun only responds to your touch... you know that right...?"

Ortega then drops his head in embarrassment and Miller gives him his gun back. Ortega takes the gun and grabs Miller's shoulder and says

"I wouldn't take that chance, when it is 'you' who is pointing the gun." and then he looks at Miller with an expression that reassures his embarrassment, and that he is truly ashamed for what he did to him.

Miller nods with a smile and then walks over to Carter to give his gun back as well. And then he says

"You should have that looked at." as he points at Carter's wounded leg.

"I'm so sorry... there must be a first aid kit in here somewhere." Smith says and starts looking for something that could help Carter with his wounds.

"I'll be alright... it went right through and the bleeding is getting less." Carter replies and tries to put both of his legs on the sofa.

"I'm all ears, if someone cares to explain what's been going on." Miller says with composure, and Carter gives him his version of the story.

As Carter is going through the story, Miller gets images of training him to pass his field exams, and working with him on high profile operations. And that how much Carter respected him and trusted him in his decisions.

And as Carter was wrapping up the story, right at the point where Smith and Jim had walked in while being suspicious of their activities, Miller interrupts him and asks

"Why wouldn't you trust Smith?"

"Because I needed someone to really believe in the scenario..." Carter replies, and Smith gives him an angry and disappointed look while finishing up cleaning his wounds.

"Look, everyone knows that you would move mountains to find him, which on its own would be the strongest indicator that he was really gone. And no one would suspect a potential cover up operation..." Carter says as he tries to reason with Smith.

Miller watches Smith's reactions, and he is wondering if there was really anything between them before everything went blank. And suddenly Jim interrupts the moment and says

"Hey, I got a positive hit on the clone!"

"Please don't say he's one of us..." Ortega says.

"No, no, this guy used to be a double 'O' agent, who died in an explosion over two years ago... somewhere in the Caribbean, in a boat!"

"Wow, that's a long way from home." Ortega says.

"Yes, but he was working with the agency to crackdown a major after-market pharmaceutical graded drug supplier. And the boat belonged to the book keeper… who was hosting a poker tournament…" Jim replies.

"A big boat…" Ortega says.

"I do remember that, but he didn't die in the explosion." Carter says as he looks at Miller. And then after a short pause he continues to say

"The coastguard found the boat drifting freely close to the shoreline, and everyone onboard was already dead…"

Miller listens carefully with a curious expression while Carter continues to say

"The explosion happened 'after' the coastguard reported in the incident, as if someone wanted to make sure that whoever was on that boat couldn't be identified."

"Missiles…?" Miller asks.

"Yes, but decades old technology, sold in the open market before you and I were even born… and they were launched from a submarine that no one even knew existed, and hasn't been seen since either… they even targeted the coastguard as a safety measure." Carter replies.

"Why isn't the real report in the system?" Miller asks.

"Because it was your operation and I was the lead… you thought something didn't add up. And that someone had intentionally gathered some of the high profile guests in one place. You even tried to pull out the British agent, but he refused to listen since the book keeper was one of his trusted informers."

"You still haven't answered my question."

"Well, after the explosion, the situation was contained and the reports that were released suggested a possible shootout between the two boats as a cover-up story, and also to allow some lead-time for further analysis. -- And because of that lead-time something else surfaced fairly soon thereafter. -- Three guests that were on board and observed as dead bodies by the coastguard while broadcasting live to the central, right before they were shot down, were seen walking among the living and healthier than ever months later. -- But now, they had more control over their business and fewer competitors to deal with... meaning more profits for everyone and almost no one to compete with any more... I mean, we are talking about legitimate companies here."

"Yes, but I'm sure that was just a tiny bit of the picture, and only the tip of the iceberg if you will..." Miller replies and no more words are exchanged.

Miller then walks over to the desk where Jim has placed his portable lab on, and pulls out the first upper drawer on the left side of the desk.

There are some breakfast bars and a couple of small liquid containers in the drawer.

He then puts the palm of his right hand flat to the top of the drawer's ceiling, and on a hidden biometric scanner. And then a hologram console pops up that looks like a transparent flat screen.

He then touches the top right corner of the screen, and expands it into a full size control panel. He navigates to the surveillance section, and enables full audio and image layers, and includes motion detection.

He then confirms the selection, and suddenly all of the walls in the bunker, and including the ceiling become a clear reflection of the outside surrounding right above the bunker, as if they were fully exposed without any walls or any roof.

And right then, a deer walks over the bunker, and they see it walking through the wall and between them, and out through the other side.

"I think I know what is going on here, and I think Walker is behind the whole thing..." Miller says and no one is making a sound while waiting for the rest of Miller's thoughts to come out.

After a few seconds, Miller then continues with a confident tone to say

"See, I don't think he was going to expose his technology at all. I went through all of the recordings, and he was not looking for respect... or recognition... this guy wants total control over the scientific community, which is why he says towards the end 'not that you would remember any of this'..." He then looks at Smith and continues to say

"And you mentioned that no one in the room had any memories about him even being there after the events."

"So why would he do all this just to get to 'you'?" Smith asks curiously before buying into the idea.

"No, no, the question is why would 'we' be there? Why would this team, take on a low-profile mission?" Miller says with a serious expression, and then he continues after a few seconds

"The agency wouldn't support the operation unless they had substance... -- Who ordered this mission?" He then asks Smith, but Carter answers the question before she can get it out.

"We don't know that..."

"You never said!" Smith confirms while being clueless about where Miller is going with this.

"My profile says that I'm spontaneous and specialized in design, development 'AND' execution of successful missions, which are mostly based on my own research... and 'we' are an antiterrorist team... so the orders either came from the secretary of defense, and I never shared them with you, or, I was acting on my own, which again, would have been an antiterrorist operation." Miller says while holding his arms crossed and simultaneously talking with his right hand between sentences.

He then pauses for a few seconds, and then continues to say

"We would only go after this guy if we had good reasons to believe that he was a terrorist."

"With 'we' you mean 'you'." Smith says to strengthen Miller's lack of communication, and while hypothetically supporting his theory.

"But there are no reasons here, if this was his first appearance since his last job with the agency…" Miller says without getting distracted by Smith's attitude, and continues to say

"And after reviewing my patience with this guy through the recordings, I think the whole thing must have been based on an intuition… I simply had a 'hunch', and I was there fishing for clues." Miller says and gets quiet, and while showing expressions of disappointments over his own actions.

"I mean, how would you have known? Why do you think this was your fault?" Asks Smith slowly, and while curious of the answer.

"I went through most of my reports, dating back two years prior to the events. And during a course of fifteen months, I had sent several reports to the joint chief of staff, homeland, the secretary, and even the president himself, warning about patterns of control within every nation… but, I had also started to snoop around in other countries, trying to figure out who could even pull off such a large undertaking… which means, that no one was taking me seriously, and I needed solid proof." Miller says as he is looking around at everyone. And then he stops and looks directly at Carter and continues to say

"I was there to check him out while using his agreements with the agency as an excuse… but what's hidden here, is the fact that 'he' set up the whole thing as a distraction, knowing that I would show up clueless about answers, and would most likely react if he ever should tease about sharing secrets."

"Why would he take that much risk exposing himself?" Smith asks.

"This guy has a plan, and based on what I've seen so far and what happened today, I would say, that his plan has been in motion for quite some time and we are not seeing the whole picture. -- But, the fact that he is making an effort to take me out of the equation… well, I must have been on to something. And with me and my memories gone, well, he is home free." Miller replies with confidence.

"Happy to have you back sir." Says Ortega.

"Please don't call me that, and we don't even know what we are up against yet." Miller says slightly irritated, and then he collects himself quickly and continues to say

"What we need to do now, is to go through all my research... and we should even try to see if we can find anything at my place... and I don't even know if I have any, or if it still is the same place that I remember..."

"Someone already went through your house three or four days after the incident." Carter says.

"You didn't secure my house after what had happened?"

"We did, but since there were no activities after a couple of days, we pulled back the resources and relied on your own surveillance system... which was disarmed and bypassed without any traces of damage or forced entry."

"Well if he's got my memories, then, that's not very surprising... it is still worth a shot to scan the place... I might get some flashbacks or something." Miller says and pauses for a few seconds, and then he says

"Carter, are you okay with following my lead?"

"To me nothing has changed, and you know we couldn't ask for a better lead." Carter replies with a genuine tone.

"I appreciate that... even though I can't remember anything about you guys, I know that I can trust everyone in this room. But, I still need a place to stay, and I need to remain functional and off the grid."

"How about your Lake Tahoe cabin...? I was just there last weekend, and no one seemed to bother me." Ortega says as a suggestion.

"You have a cabin in Lake Tahoe and you let him borrow it?" Smith says while surprised by the news.

"I don't know what to tell you, I don't even know what I have anymore..."

"What…? He let me borrow it so that I could spend some time with Samantha 'away' from all this." Ortega replies.

"So you risked her life too, knowing what could have happened?" Smith says with a little more anger and disappointment in her voice.

"Only I and Ortega know about the cabin, and he didn't know about Miller until he came back. And I didn't know where he was going either, as long as I could have him back within hours if necessary." Carter says.

"Within hours…?" Smith says with the same attitude.

"Well, I took his beamer since it was already at my place…" Ortega says and then he looks at Miller and continues to say

"It flies and rides very smooth by the way… and I also have your 'Lambo' parked in my garage, just so you know."

And then he starts to feel a little awkward at this point.

"Are you sure you're not trying to take over his life too?" Smith says with a smile, and Ortega raises his eyebrows and looks away.

Smith then continues to say

"I guess I should just take your stuff too without asking from now on…" as she is looking at Miller with her arms crossed.

"Who says I didn't ask? He knew all about it before he blanked out…"

"Oh… how convenient…"

"Alright, enough… Carter will report my death and what happened here to the secretary, and you guys try to find Walker." Miller says while looking at Jim and Smith, and then he looks at Ortega and continues to say

"You're coming with me, since you already know so much about my life."

"What are we waiting for?" Ortega replies with a smile.

Several days later at Doctor Walker's work place, Miller's clone walks up to him as he is working on one of his hibernation boxes with an iNeb device.

"We need to talk!" Miller's clone says.

"Agent Miller, I was wondering when you were going to approach me." Walker replies with the same friendly smile as he always has.

"Is this a good time?"

"Oh yes, I'm almost done... I just need to start the synchronization."

"Synchronizing a clone...? Your research says that you can't synchronize a clone!?"

"You are always so thorough in your investigations... just imagine what a beautiful world we would have if there were more of you out there..." Walker says, and the clone gives him an expression that he wants him to be a bit more serious.

Walker then continues to say

"And of course, you are right... you can't synchronize a clone. But, number six here is different."

"Explain different." The clone says as he crosses his arms

"W-well, he is essentially me..." Walker replies and the clone gets more curious.

Walker then continues to say

"The clones that you are familiar with are essentially no different than any other device, which we can control. But, number six does not have any implanted electronics, and cannot be controlled the same way."

"But your own research says that the brain tissue of a clone is unable to store large amounts of data!?"

"That is correct... because the unused brain tissue is prepared as we learn new things throughout our development, which is why we can store memories. And the brain tissue of our artificial clones are not prepared to hold much data, and therefore they can't retain any either."

"But number six can?" The clone asks quickly.

But Walker doesn't answer the question right away, and instead he focuses on his task and starts the synchronization.

He then gets up and walks Miller's clone to a station and pulls up a hologram and expands it to a full sized panel.

Then, he pulls up a schematic where there are hundreds of cubes attached to each other from their end points like a mesh. And each one is attached to eight other cubes at the center, and the outer cubes are attached to the inner side of a spherical container.

He then expands the container and pulls out one cube and clears out everything else.

"You know what this is, right?" Walker asks.

"You just had a simple data storage unit, and this is one of its clusters."

"Correct... now, before I can use this cluster, I must prepare it for operation. Meaning, when I use it to store data, then I must also have a way to find what I'm looking for..."

"Okay..." The clone says to support an obvious function, but he is still waiting for the punch-line.

"So, as I allocate these cells with information, I can always go back and remove portions of the information, which at that point the cluster becomes fragmented. And next time I need to allocate more information, depending on the size of the data, I would need to prepare more clusters... and you can see right away how inefficient this would get."

"Yes, but the NCS stores everything evenly across all clusters and sectors. And the cells are automatically registering their availability to hold new information to bypass disadvantages due to fragmentation... which is really to simulate how the brain stores information." Miller's clone says as he becomes more interested in the conversation.

"I know, which is why I'm using it in my iNeb... you are ahead of your own brain Mr. Miller." Walker says with a mild smile and continues to say

"Even though the brain does the same thing, unlike your NCS, it won't prepare all its capacity and only uses new cells as needed... and whenever old memories are not accessed, the cells will get overwritten with new information over and over if required, and the old memories dissipate over time. -- This is the failsafe of the brain to preserve unused cells for other operations if an area gets damaged. And if you think about every time you are absorbing new information, while actively trying to access your old memories, your brain will eventually hit a limit, and would take some time to prepare more storage for your demanding consciousness. -- And that is why brains that are not active, usually have a hard time to store new information, which I believe is the brain's main disadvantage compared to your NCS device."

"Not sure if I understand!?"

"You will when you reach my age... and I don't mean that you're not smart enough, I'm simply referencing aging... because as we get older, our cells gets older too, and the same cells that are being reused over and over, can no longer hold on to new information as efficiently as they used to. -- And even if we manipulate our age-genes to live longer, the cell qualities will still decay over time, which is also another fascinating concept, since time is understood by the brain through continuous memory allocations. And when old cells gets overwritten by a busy brain that it's 'not' storing new information for long-term use, then the brain loses its time table, and years will just fly by. -- And then, you'll end up living the rest of your life in the memories of your past, that you access over and over and are most precious to you. -- But precious memories are not always good memories... Terrible memories are just as precious to the brain. -- They make the brain strong, but they can also paralyze it... and the only reason that they stick around, is because you're trying to analyze them in disappointment… instead of learn from them and then let them go. -- And to allow the cells to be overwritten by newer and perhaps even more precious information, as memories…"

"Okay, I get the point… but you haven't answered my questions about number six yet." The clone says with a slight frustration, as he senses that Walker is trying to remind him of what he is holding on to.

Walker gets more serious and says

"Number six is me, a younger me, and he is not frozen like the other clones… his brain is constantly going through every information that I slowly introduce him to. And this way, I can keep the brain active with filtered information that I absorb first, and clean all the nonsense to use the space in the most efficient way."

"When are you planning to wake him up?"

"When the time is right for me to step into the spotlight as a young and brilliant scientist, and a leader of course…"

"I can tell, that you really have thought this through."

"Yes indeed… hard work always pays off my son…"

"And in your visions, where do I fit in… since it is obvious that I must also be a clone. And the only reason that I can question your motives, is because you could probably turn me off any time you want… so why don't you tell me what this is all about, since a puppet can only choose from limited options available." The clone says with an absolute seriousness in his eyes, and while knowing the uncertainty of his authorities.

Walker looks at him with a smile and says

"It was never my intentions to withhold any information about what happened to you. And I thought that it would be best for you to figure it out on your own, and have some time to digest it first. -- When we brought you in, there was no way to salvage your old body, so we copied as much information we could from your brain and prepared a new body... and since there was no time to do what I'm doing with number six, well, I had to improvise..." He then stops talking and looks at his watch and says

"Ah, time for dinner..."

He then pauses for a second, and then continues to say

"I hope you are hungry... I ordered the best artificial synthetic steak there is around here. And I promise you, it is not a clone."

He then starts walking out of the room with the same smile and continues to say

"Come now, we have much more to talk about... patience will bring answers."

Miller's clone feels helpless as he considers the uncertainties, and that he must be more patient as Walker says, and to not allow his thoughts to overwhelm him in any way. And the probabilities around his mind being monitored at all times gives him an uncomfortable notion, that he irreversibly is bound to comply with... so he follows Walker and keeps his mind at bay, and while feeling his emotions boiling deep inside.

Three days later in the Lake Tahoe cabin, Miller and Ortega are going through various scenarios about what Walker might be up to. And while playing billiard on a pool table that is generated as a virtual game through a hologram.

The table is completely silver all around and has a blue mat, and the cues are light metallic rods that generate feedback when a virtual ball is hit.

A game of American football between two international teams is playing on a screen that covers the whole wall behind them. It's a world cup semi-final game, and South Africa is leading with three possessions over Germany within the two-minute warning before the halftime.

Miller is drinking a beverage from a bottle, and a call comes in.

"Hey, this must be them." Ortega says and takes his last shot.

"Let's take it right here." Miller says and sets down his bottle on the table.

The virtual balls hit the bottle and bounce back as if they were real, and that the bottle was actually part of the hologram game.

Ortega then turns everything off using the options menu at the edge of the pool table, and the hologram disappears leaving only a transparent dining table with Miller's bottle on it. The screen behind them also disappears, revealing a large window and a beautiful view of the Sierra Mountains and the lake.

The hologram then reappears, and the dining table turns partially into a conference table with Jim, Smith and Carter sitting on one end.

Miller then positions himself in the opposite direction from the callers, and Ortega grabs a dining chair and sits close to where Miller stands.

"Wow, no wonder no one knows about this place." Smith says right after she turns her head to look around.

"Yeah, it's a nice place... I didn't even know I had it... I just remembered the bedroom for some reason." Miller says and realizes what he had just said, and feels a little awkward about it.

Ortega smiles and Smith just looks down to hide any facial expressions.

"Okay, so what do we got?" Miller says to quickly change the subject.

"Well, Jim and Smith have done some extensive research around Walker's whereabouts over the past three months, and a very interesting pattern has emerged." Carter says.

"Did you find anything matching what I was working on before all this?" Miller asks.

"Yes, but I would be interested to hear what you guys have come up with during these last few days, before we dive deeper into 'our' research." Smith says evenly and without any emotions.

"Well, Ortega has been shedding some light on how my life was before this… I mean nothing too deep and just in general terms. And we've been reviewing some interesting patterns as well." Miller says and looks at Ortega, and then he continues to say

"We pretty much started to reanalyze my hypothesis more in-depths to pick up the trail where I had left off, and we found something very interesting."

"Which is?" Smith asks, and Miller continues to say

"Okay, so we know that Walker is looking for some kind of control, or at least that's our assumption. -- But every action that our government has taken so far is somehow giving him more traction… and I mean, every time I had compared various political events with Walker's whereabouts, he is meeting with high profile players for some reason."

He then pauses and pulls up some files through the hologram's control panel that appears in front of him as he gets closer to the table. He then pushes the files to the middle of the table, and they open up as various video recordings and start the playback in the eye-level while muted. Miller then continues to say

"But his intentions are always solely around scientific stuff, which we are still trying to wrap our heads around… either way, and long story short, we think that he might somehow be influencing our leaders, without them even knowing it. -- Or, that he is consulting with our leaders around some high classified projects that we might not know about, which is why, I was being turned down so many times in all my past attempts to look for a possible problem."

Miller then stops to get a reaction. But since no one really reacts to anything, he then continues to say

"But then again, that theory is not making much sense, since he's also meeting with other high profile political figures in other nations as well... and this is where I'm starting to draw blanks..." And then he clears the playbacks and takes a step back.

"Alright, I think we've got a couple of things that might be interesting to you." Smith says, but Miller quickly interrupts her and says

"There's just one more thing, that's been bothering me before we start getting any deeper... why doesn't he have any respect from the scientific community, as an active scientist with so many achievements?" Miller asks and Carter replies

"That's because of a decade old story, and the main reasons behind why the agency decided to let him go. -- His junior assistance, who was a brilliant young scientist by the name of 'Erik Lundquist', cloned himself with a surrogate mother, who no one knew anything about at the time. -- He was trying to make the procedure seem natural to avoid any unnecessary attentions. But the story somehow leaked out through the mother and became public news after the child was born. And the media instantly made it to a controversial story, since the mother was a recovering patient in a mental institute." He then pauses for a second before continuing to say

"Thereafter, Erik's actions were faced with rage and allegations, that he had gone too far and had over stepped his boundaries. And a long story short, before he could be charged and face imprisonment, he took his own life. -- This was a major turning point in Walker's career, since the media and the scientific community blamed 'him' for Erik's irrational behavior, and his deep interests in prolonging the human life by creating exact copies of ourselves."

"So what happened to the child?"

"Walker adopted him as his own son, but kept his original name as 'Karl Lundquist'." Smith replies.

"Where is he now?" Miller asks.

"The story around the boy didn't last long, since Walker quickly became the center of attention and became known as the 'mad scientist', and over time lost all his credibility as a reputable scientist... and no one has really heard anything about the boy since." Carter says and waits to see if Miller has any more questions.

But since he is still deep into his thoughts, Smith then picks up the conversation and says

"I'm glad that you brought this up, because Jim found something that you might want to hear..."

"Yes... I'm sitting here, thinking that he could probably figure this out on his own, if he had all his memories back..." Jim says and pauses while trying to analyze where Miller was going with all this in his head.

He then snaps out of his head and continues to say

"Anyhow, I started off by looking into Walker's assets, and noticed that there's really nothing under his name, which is strange because he seems to be very active... so I dug deeper through looking at some surveillance clips of political gatherings in different countries, and found him in five different locations within the same week." Jim says and Ortega interrupts him and says

"That shouldn't be a surprise, since we can all safely assume that he is using clones..."

"Well, it wouldn't be a surprise, if he was in multiple places at the same time. But, I also noticed that he had a slightly different haircut within the same week in every appearance as well!" Jim replies with an expression that he is on to something and Ortega smiles and says

"Okay, so he's got clones everywhere..."

"Yes, but you're missing the point!" Jim replies.

"So, what's the point?" Miller asks with a hand gesture that he should just spit it out, and then Jim continues to say

"Well, he doesn't want anyone to know that he is using clones because no one is supposed to use them, not even our governments... but he is essentially playing a game and purposely putting up a display for whoever is watching, and somehow, he is getting enough funds and protection to carry on this play. -- And, I also found out that around a year ago, he had several visitations with our president and the members of his Cabinet, and then suddenly after a couple of months, nothing... no more visitations... and the patterns seem to be the same with every other country that he visits as well."

He then looks at Miller and continues to say

"He meets with the top members of a government for a short while, and then visitations stops. And I believe that this was exactly what you had noticed too!"

Jim then pauses for a few seconds to let the thought sink in, and then he continues to say

"But here is the interesting part."

"W-wait... if he's using clones, then how is he able to get passed the security checkpoints?" Miller interrupts.

"Exactly...! So I figured... what if he has come up with a new technology to avoid the need for signal amplifiers and repeaters? And then I started to map satellite usage around all his recent visitations to other countries, and guess what, nothing... no additional bandwidth was used during those times."

"Wouldn't that rule out the clone scenario?" Ortega asks.

"It sure points to that, but I thought what if he is using the landlines... but again frustratingly enough, there was nothing unusual there either... until, a brilliant woman, agent Smith here, suggested that I should look into some old landlines."

"Aren't those out of service?" Ortega asks.

"You have good questions today, and yes that was exactly my first initial reaction as well... but since I had to entertain the idea for my boss, I said what the hell... and to my surprise, I found out that almost ninety percent of all fiber optic 'old landlines', were still operational. And the only reason why we can't access them, is because they're all privately owned!"

"I'm still waiting for the punch line, since that still wouldn't explain the clone situation. And to hypothesize a new technology, is not tangible enough to go after." Miller says while a bit frustrated.

"Maybe not, but when I looked into the owners of these privately owned networks, I saw one name that was all over the place... in fact eighty-five percent of all old landlines belongs to this guy... who is... wait for it... Mr. Karl Lundquist!" Jim says and stops with a big smile.

"Wow..." Ortega says.

"Okay so, the boy is still around and Walker is using him as his asset holder. And he is using these land lines for his upgraded clones, which are only an assumption at this point " Miller says to summarize the scenario.

"Well, I had Jim to look up more information about Karl, and there's more..." Smith says, and then she pulls up a virtual binder and slides it towards Miller.

Miller then picks up the binder and starts going through the files that are stacked up as different report sheets, signed documents and some pictures of Erik and Walker, and a young two to three year-old boy with blond hair.

Smith then continues to say

"Karl not only owns landlines, but he also has large amounts of ownership in every single monster company on the planet... everything from energy, water, pharmaceutical, healthcare, real estate and banking, to even weaponry, air traffic, space, and essentially everything that controls the infra-structure of every country. -- And that's not all... Karl's birth-date and his personal identification number was changed a year after he was born, which makes him to be a twenty-two year old man today versus ten or eleven. And not only that he is the richest individual, but he also has nothing registered in his name, other than an apartment building in downtown Stockholm... in Sweden."

"Wow..." Ortega says again and the room gets quiet for a while.

After a minute or so, Carter breaks the silence and says

"We have to assume, that Walker also controls most militaries and governments around the world as well..." and the room is quiet again for another thirty or so seconds, until Miller says

"Did anyone ever directly interact with Walker himself, when he was working with the agency?"

"N-no, not really... It was mostly Erik, and other members of his team." Carter replies.

"Can you tell me more about Walker and his personality, before the Erik incident?" Miller asks.

"Well, he was known to be a noble man and a dedicated scientist, who was extremely concerned about the future of humanity." Carter replies.

"In what way...?" Miller asks.

"He wanted a minimum level of required comfort and security for every single person on earth, besides his efforts to preserve the nature..." Carter replies.

"But he was also very politically active as well, in hope of uniting all nations." Smith adds on.

"What was Erik like?" Miller asks.

"Erik was really pleasant to be around, and he was really inspired by Walker, which everyone could clearly see by the way he talked, and the things that he would say..." Smith replies.

"But he did have his own opinions, and things weren't always the way he wanted them to be between them..." Carter says.

"Do you know anything more specific?" Miller asks, and Carter continues to say

"Well, as I mentioned before, he was a brilliant young scientist and wanted to publish his own ideas, which had to be approved by Walker. But in his frustrations, when Walker kept denying his publications, he published something around potential ways to directly access the stored information on a human brain... and even change or manipulate everything at will, which was really around Walker's own research and life-long studies. -- The media reacted to what he had published, and Walker quickly made a press release to separate himself from Erik. And that none of what Erik had mentioned was any of his own studies, which he should treat as such and not to draw any conclusions around. -- And when the media approached Walker to further explain the research, and also what he thought about Erik's actions. His only comments were, that Erik was a young and gifted scientist who needed to find humility and patience... and above all 'respect', before publishing anything that could potentially harm the quality of our lives etc. etc..."

"How did Erik take it? Was he upset about the comments?" Miller asks.

"He took it pretty good considering... at first, he was showing some frustrations that Walker was trying to hold him back to have the spotlight all to himself. But then, he surprised everyone by publically apologizing to his mentor, and agreed that he had yet to understand what it means to be a real scientist... and that he had much to learn as a young and driven apprentice." Carter replies.

"How did Walker take his death?" Miller asks yet another question, but Smith answers the question and says

"He avoided all public interactions, and didn't really want to talk about it... which seemed as being ignorant by the media."

"But yet he adopted his child..." Miller says.

"Yeah... he probably felt really bad, and he showed his affections by raising the child as his own..." Smith replies.

"It sure seems that way... or maybe he just saw an opportunity..." Miller says and everyone is silent again.

"Okay, we need to find Walker!" Miller says, and continues after a short pause to say

"And I think we should start with Karl first... he's got an apartment, and he must have had some kind of accelerated growth as a side-effect of being a clone, or something... -- And since the science event was also in Sweden, I think we should start there. -- But also, let's find out if there's a living will or trust between Walker and Karl."

"I'll go to Sweden..." Ortega says while hoping for an agreement.

"No, we shouldn't use any of agency's resources to trigger any flags... so I'll go. -- And if Jim could be allowed some fake time off, then I would like to take him with me as well." Miller says to put a lid on Ortega's obvious reasons to quickly volunteer.

"Jim is not going anywhere without me." Smith quickly replies.

"That's fine with me if Carter can afford not having both of you around." Miller says

"I would prefer to have Smith with you as well if Jim goes. And as long as I have one agent here, then we should be fine..." Carter says.

"Great, but we cannot mention anything about this. As far as our assumption goes at this point, Walker most likely already has eyes and ears on the secretary, and probably within the agency as well." Miller says and everyone agrees.

Miller then continues to say
"Let's be ready to leave in two days... and we also need to make sure that I can travel under a different name to remain under the radar."

"I'll take care of that..." Ortega says.

"Okay, let me know if there's anything else, and I'll see to it if I can. I've got something else to attend to..." Carter says and ends the call, and they all disappear instantly.

Miller and Ortega are silent for a couple of seconds, and then Miller says

"What's the deal with Smith? Was there anything between us that I need to know about?"

"There's always been some tension between you guys, but nothing obvious to anyone..." Ortega says with a smile and continues to say

"Even though, I've heard rumors about people mentioning things like 'those two should just get it on and get it over with', I wouldn't worry about it too much. Believe me... she would let you know if there was anything. What do 'you' think?"

"No nothing... I just think she is a little snippy with me. That's all..."

"You and everyone else..."

Meanwhile, Miller's clone has played along with whatever it is that Walker wants him to do, and for some reason, he feels like Walker is always in his head. And no matter what he does or says, Walker already knows how to respond, and he is somehow always one step ahead.

He has also asked Walker about their physical location several times, but the reply has always been 'in an underground bunker by the ocean somewhere in southern France', which has also been another hard thing for him to believe in.

People working in the lab have become more comfortable with having him around, since Walker has trusted him with full access to the system. And he has also developed a personal interest for number six through his research, since he knows that

Walker can't suddenly walk around freely as a much younger version of himself, without having the media on his tail.

Then again, if Walker was always in his head, then he would surely know about his interests in number six as well... either way, he was going to continue his research to see how far he could go before Walker would pull his brakes.

He is allowed to go outside on his own and wonder around without being harassed or treated like a slave. Or at least he is made to believe that he can exercise his freedom anyway he wants, since every time he makes a conscious decision to get out, either Walker himself or someone else is there to distract him, or to switch his focus to something else.

He remembers going out and being outside almost every day to clear his mind, while walking on a private beach. But, he also gets reminded almost every night by his bed's automated routine checkup that some of his vitamin levels are low, and that he should schedule to receive proper dosage while at sleep.

And among these vitamins, 'D' clearly stands out every time.

He has also noticed that people who work there wear almost exactly the same outfit and behave exactly the same way every single day. And they usually only discuss about the same places that they go to after work. And pretty much similar things are happening in their lives with only minor changes each day, which are almost predictable and rather fake.

He knows by now, that Walker means every single word he says, and that he is committed to follow through with his plans no matter what. And for someone as driven as he is, it would be rather impossible to give up the control to someone else in a leap of faith, even if his acting seems believable and genuine.

A week later, Smith is having lunch by herself in the king's garden after a day of shopping in the central Stockholm.

She is acting very casual, and been getting flirtatious stares and smiles all day.

A call comes in on her temporary line and she answers

"Your plan to use me as bait has been working all day... I'm just confused whether to nail them myself, or hand them over to you..."

"Get back when you're done playing. It's time to wrap it up and head back home." Miller says and hangs up.

After fifteen minutes, Smith walks in to the master suite of a prestigious hotel located by the water and close to the king's garden with several shopping bags. And she says

"I haven't had this much fun working for a long time..."

"We're not getting anywhere, and we need to regroup and start over." Says Miller.

"Have you guys had any luck with the apartment?" Smith asks.

"No, it's just sitting empty and there's nothing there." Jim says.

"You guys finally decided to break-in?" Smith asks.

"Yes. This morning after you left... but it was only me..." Jim replies.

"I was hoping that someone would show up, but there was no surveillance on the place..." Miller says slightly aggravated over not having any lead.

"When are we leaving?" Smith asks.

"Tonight, once the jet is ready." Miller answers.

"There are plenty of nice places by the water... maybe we could take some time off, and eat out before we leave."

"N-no... I don't think that's a good idea, since I wouldn't be able to hide from all cameras in town... If anyone sees that I'm still alive, then there won't be a second chance. -- It's just too risky. And besides, I've already ordered meatballs..."

"Suit yourself then… I'll take Jim as my date, since we have both been exposed many times during the last few days. -- And one more night as bait, I'm sure you wouldn't say no to that."

"Sure, that's fine with me… I probably need some time alone to clear my head and to get some rest before the flight anyways."

"I wouldn't mind going now to catch a tour of the king's castle too before dinner…" Jim says with excitement, hoping that Smith would be onboard too.

"I think that's a great idea… just give me twenty minutes, and then we're out of here."

"We leave right after midnight." Miller says.

"Roger that, boss!" Smith replies with a smile.

Several hours later, around thirty minutes past ten o'clock at night, Smith and Jim are enjoying what's left of their trip in the hotel's Interactive Personal Aqua Chambers called IPACs. These units are shaped as spherical individual see-through chambers held-up about a foot above the ground by robotic arms. They are ten feet in diameter, and have a lid that covers one-third of the spherical shape from the top, which also opens up to allow a person to step into the chamber, and would stay open if desired by the user.

These chambers are equipped with holograms providing any exterior landscape and an interactive aqua world of the user's choice. There are water jets covering the interior of the sphere, providing a dynamic current against whichever direction a swimmer is facing. The interior walls will also adjust to create comfortable seating positions, and any depths preferred by a user.

There are nine units in the top level of the hotel that provides a scenic view over the surrounding areas through see-through walls, and also through the ceiling which can be opened when weather conditions allow.

Jim is wearing a small six-inch compressed-oxygen container that bends around his face. And he is enjoying the thrilling underwater cave-diving of various locations on the planet, which he has always wanted to visit. He had suggested that Smith should also synchronize her IPAC to dive along with him, but she had decided to do some laps instead.

The unit next to Smith's drains and goes through a sanitization process to be prepared for the next guest. And within five minutes thereafter, Miller walks up to it and selects a natural hot-spring environment to just relax for a few minutes.

Miller steps into his IPAC and Smith stops swimming, and she then says with a pleasant smile

"Look who decided to join the party."

"I just needed to leave the room for a few minutes. -- I've got everything packed and ready, and didn't really know what else to do..."

"Well I'm glad that you're here instead of sitting out in the balcony by yourself." Smith says and changes her IPAC settings to match Miller's, and also have their voices heard within each chamber as if they were sitting next to each other. Miller's unit displays a confirmation screen to allow the conversation and he accepts the request.

Smith then continues to say

"How is your mind treating you? Are you getting any of your recent memories back?"

"No not really... sometimes things are triggered randomly here and there, but I'm still lost. -- It feels like my life has only been a dream... and I have no choice but to find myself in its leftover memories, -- to somehow make sense of who I really am."

"I can't even imagine what that would be like..."

"If it wasn't for the few leftover memories that I have from various places, and also for some short memories of Carter working with me as a field-agent, I don't think I would buy into all this as being a real-life scenario..."

"I can see how confusing things might be to have such large missing gaps in your life. But you're thankfully okay and able to build new memories... and I'm sure that over time, you'll be able to feel whole again, if you look at the bright-side... even if it doesn't sound very comforting at the moment."

"No I understand what you're saying and I do agree. But my mind says 'find Walker first before coming to peace with what has happened', if that makes any sense..."

"It does, and I'm sure we'll find him sooner or later... -- Meantime, feel free to ask if there's anything you would want to know. And I'll promise to go easy on you..." Smith says with a smile.

"I will... and I do appreciate the kind offer." Miller replies also with a smile.

"I know you don't want to be bothered anymore so I'll give you some time to yourself... I probably could use a couple of minutes myself to relax before it's time to pack..." Smith says and turns off the synchronized sound settings.

Miller then nods with a smile and puts his head back to relax.

Smith then closes the lid of her IPAC and selects a tropical environment with a relaxing music in the background.

The following morning, Miller's clone is being prepared for another day as the bed receives instructions to initiate the morning checkups, and to un-pause the consciousness when the host is ready for operation.

Miller's clone wakes up, and without wasting any time he goes to the main control room and pulls up a console to continue his analysis from the night before.

The hologram console starts up and his work on analyzing the comparison between Walker's clones and corresponding genetic information is activated.

He's focus during the past few days has been mainly around enhancements other than age manipulation. And since Walker himself had mentioned that number six was a much younger version, then he needed to know how young to better understand his long term plans.

Day by day, he's been purposely working right in the control room where everyone can see what he is doing to strengthen his authorities among other employees, and to simultaneously monitor all new events.

Miller's clone sees that one of the processes to match the genetic information between each clone and their source has been complete. And he can verify that they are all one-hundred percent match. But he is still not convinced, and suspects a possible missing link around the provided source information.

He then starts a new process to cross match number six's genetics with number five's source information, and right then Walker walks up to him and says

"So how are you doing today Agent Miller? Any progress on your research...?"

"My digital mind seems to function properly... and no, nothing more than what I already know..." The clone replies.

"Do you mind being more specific?"

"Well, I still think that you are crazy. And you still think that I'm going to somehow save the planet, which I don't believe is going to be by choice. -- I feel forced to be comfortable with all this, which is no news to you. And I think everyone else here feels the same way... should I tell you more about how I feel, or would you care to tell me how my preplanned day is going to end, so that I might be able to come up with something of my own..."

"Agent Miller, I expected more from you... but I also know that you are trying really hard to hold back your thoughts, in fear of giving them away. -- Being hopeful of having a freedom is a natural pattern. But giving your situation, it would just damage your chances of seeing the goal... which I have repeatedly hinted ever since you were given a second chance, to be alive that is!"

"See, that's just the thing... you want me to figure out your plans on my own. And I keep thinking, what happens when I do?"

"Come on, let's talk over breakfast... I can't think well on an empty stomach." Walker says with a smile.

"Sure, why not... let's feed our biological bodies as our digital minds exchange information in a civilized manner." Miller's clone replies as he is getting up to accompany Walker towards the kitchen.

And as they start walking, he then continues to say

"It is obvious that you are also a clone."

"What makes you think that?"

"I mean, how else would you be able to monitor the thoughts of so many individuals in real-time..."

"That's an interesting concept."

"Is it really...? You have successfully developed new clones to be perfectly functional anywhere on the planet. And you have total control over the majority of communication lines, and backbones across the globe, and expanding as we speak... so to me, that indicates preparations for a new clone world. -- But the question is... why would you also have your own mind in a system that can easily be shut down or destroyed?" The clone says and waits for Walker's response.

Walker walks up to the food machine ahead of Miller's clone, and selects two scrambled eggs and a pancake on the hologram that pops up as soon as he walks up to it.

He then walks over to the beverage machine and selects orange juice and coffee with no cream or sugar. And then he makes a selection of a protein shake with berries for Miller's clone.

Once the machines deliver his orders, he hands the clone his shake and says

"You can't completely control a mind and expect it to function properly... the digital mind needs to get used to its new home, which takes some time at first. But when the doubts become nothing more than superstitious thoughts, the mind can then be controlled through artificial 'time', and triggered thoughts based on fake memories, or even complete ideas delivered to the mind while at rest."

"And who gives 'you', your ideas? Is it number six? Or are you perhaps controlling all this from somewhere else? A space hotel would make sense..."

"That would be a good idea if no one could monitor the satellite traffic... but to your point, not everyone should become a clone... only those who make decisions for everyone else, are in our interest."

"You mean in your interest!"

"Whether you like it or not, anyone who becomes part of the system is going to remain in the system. So, choosing to be unplugged would be the same as choosing to die..."

"Okay, so I was dying and you gave me a second chance... how about everyone else who works here... were they dying too?" The clone asks.

"Only you know that you are a clone... everyone else here think that they are regular employees. But to answer your question, I couldn't possibly be able to keep hiding people from the world, if nothing had already happened to them first to give us the opportunity of course." Walker replies and then he starts to eat his breakfast. And after taking his first bite, he then continues to say

"What I think you should know at this point, is that you can change the future of humanity right from here, and at any time..."

"Are you saying that you can already control the world, through clones that are in power?" The clone asks in disbelief.

"Sixty-eight percent or so of all world leaders are currently in our systems, which would be more than enough to start a radical change!"

"And how did they get in there?" The clone asks with great concerns.

"Through greed of course..."

"What do you mean?"

"Power and control is the driving force for most politicians. And everyone has a price!" Walker replies and pauses while looking at Miller's clone with an expressionless face.

But since the clone is still waiting to hear more, he then continues to say

"The files are open to you when you decide to change your focus from researching 'my' external shells, to taking part in this historical moment."

"I think the time is better served if you could just tell me, how you are able to do what you are doing." The clone quickly replies.

Walker sits quiet for a moment and then he says

"That is fine with me, if you think that you are ready to play your part... and if you are not... there's only one way to find out."

"I'm listening..."

"Every single mind, with high political or financial powers that exists in the system, is there because of corruption in the society. -- I am a scientist, and I deliver working solutions for various problems. One of these problems has always been 'time'. -- Time is never enough for someone who has finally reached a desired position in life. And for the right price, anyone is willing to prolong their time in power, and in financial wealth. -- For most people already in control, aging is a major concern, and something that they can never escape from, unless someone like me comes along, and promises an alternative way to extend their god given lifespan, through 'science'." Walker says and pauses.

He then gets up to walk back to the control room, and Miller's clone follows him.

And as they start to walk, Walker then continues to say

"This is how it works. -- I throw a fundraising party for my research called 'Project Lifespan', and the military is always at the scene to explore possibilities. If they are interested thereafter, they would send a messenger for an in-person invite to a private meeting with decision makers etc. -- ...When in the meeting, I would then suggest a free trial offer to one or more, if I see anyone that I could use to navigate up the ladder... which usually happens over fifty percent of the time. And if they are unsure, I will show them one of my own clones... and after that, there's either a new client, or I contact my lawyer who would also already be a clone. -- But if I do have a new client, then it would take about two months to complete a perfect long-distance remote-clone, if we had to start all the way from the beginning."

He then pauses for a few seconds while analyzing some thoughts in his head, and also to see if Miller's clone had any questions so far.

But the clone is still waiting to hear more.

Walker then decides to describe the complete process, and he continues to say

"After the first initial test, the hosts will usually and suddenly start to realize the true potentials of what they are being offered, and would schedule follow up tryouts with longer intervals. -- And eventually, once the client becomes obsessed with the demonstrations, we would schedule these follow-ups at our own facilities where more thorough tests could be performed. -- The procedure would start by making a full copy of the host's brain before the link is established, which is completely unknown to the client of course. --

...And during the follow-up visit after that, as the last and final visit, all recent brain activities are updated with their copies in the system. There are also other processes of matching all hidden scars and birthmarks of every client with their long-distance clone in between... -- But once everything is in place, the client's copy is started up from the system instead of their original and biological brain. And the bodies are of course switched with the long-distance clone. ...This is again unknown to the client. --

And while the digital mind is controlling a clone, it is made to believe that the real body 'is' the clone. -- Other potential applications such as having other clones with different features, are also presented to strengthen the client's personal interest in an after current-life scenario as a different person. Or even as a different person in their current life from time to time... The client is hooked, and the process is complete... and even if they're not interested to pursue anything at that point, and try to kill the project... well... it's already too late, and we can control their actions in any way we want."

"Wow... and everyone is looking for someone with a gun to aim at..." The clone says as a sarcastic reply.

"Well of course we have guns agent Miller... we have control over almost every single military force there is!" Walker says with confidence, and an evil smirk.

And then he continues to say

"In fact, I intend to use this control to start a global war!"

"A global war...? And you're talking about saving humanity and the planet?" The clone asks in absolute confusion, and he is extremely surprised by the comment.

"Mr. Miller, it is a must! And yes, absolutely... a global war is what this planet and humanity needs at this point! -- People always come together only in times of desperation... you know this better than anyone else!"

"And where is the morality in that?"

"Morality must become obsolete to empower the greater good... and being moral in actions taken to get us there, would simply lack ultimate authority, thus no control!" Walker says with a serious tone, and the clone stays quiet.

Walker then continues to say

"Having powers agent Miller is only an 'idea', created through control... and 'control', is always earned by strong minds chasing that idea. -- As a scientist, I can control what I do in a lab. But the powers over how far I could take my ideas, will always remain in someone else's hands... even though my science is what empowers 'those' in control... -- It's because of people like me, that opportunistic people exist! People who seek the 'idea' through feeding on creative minds, and without having anything to offer in return! -- These are people who demoralize humanity, only to gain more control, and momentarily 'dress' in the idea of having powers..."

He then stops talking while looking at the clone with an expressionless face.

And after a few seconds, Miller's clone then calmly but very provocatively says

"I must say, that I am truly amazed by your way of thinking... somehow, you are able to sound sane, and insane at the same time... but right now my question is... where do 'I' fit in, in this master plan of yours?"

"Here, I'm going to show you why you are here!" Walker replies quickly, and then he walks over to the control switch in the main control room.

He then very rapidly and slightly frustrated starts several processes on the hologram, and puts up the map over the entire globe on the big screen for everyone to see.

And then he turns to Miller's clone, and with an angry and loud voice he says

"The plan is useless without a true hero Mr. Miller... someone who would unselfishly sacrifice himself to destroy evil, and show the world that a fundamental change is a must!"

He then lowers his tone and continues to say

"Only through a hero, the world would forgive... only through a hero, 'I' would find a sanctuary in afterlife."

He then looks at all the clueless souls in the room that have no idea about what is going on, and continues to say

"Listen up! From now on, Mr. Miller is in full command!" And then he faces Miller's clone again and says

"Good bye Mr. Miller! You have two hours to save the world..." And then he touches a process screen on the hologram. And right then, he suddenly drops lifeless to the floor.

Miller's clone is just as frozen and lost for words as anyone else in the room.

The lead scientist then runs over and checks Walker's pulse. And after a few seconds, he then brings up the directory of mind repositories on the main console, and starts a search for Walker's mind.

The search quickly stops, and where most of repositories are in a blue color, Walker's repository shows in red.

The scientist turns slowly to Miller's clone, and with a terrified and dimmed tone he then says

"He is gone!"

Miller's clone is still trying to figure out why Walker would do what he just did, and he's getting overwhelmed with questions in his head.

He focuses on the map that is now showing red dots flashing all over the place, and the countdown-clock indicating one-hour and fifty-seven minutes and dropping.

He then looks back at the lead scientist and says

"What did he do?"

"He just activated every single weapon of mass destruction to rain hell on earth, when that timer reaches zero…"

"Why would he do that?"

"I don't know… I just showed him some pictures of a couple of agents that were spotted yesterday, at the king's castle nearby. And then he just went looking for you…"

"The king's castle…?"

"Yes… we are in an abandoned subway station close to the king's castle in Stockholm… I thought you knew that…"

"Who were these agents?"

"Not sure… here…"

The scientist then quickly pulls up several pictures of Smith and Jim from the castle's surveillance systems on the hologram.

"Angie…?" Miller's clone says with a surprised and worried tone.

He now understands that he has been double crossed the entire time. And with a serious look on his face, he then turns to the scientist and says

"How do we shut it down?"

"The only way to save the planet would be to shut down and destroy the entire system, and to prevent it from coming back up… but then, every single mind in the system will cease to exist as well… including you!"

Right then, Miller's clone realizes Walker's master plan.

And without wasting another second, he yells

"Everyone listen up!"

And after a few seconds he then continues with a loud and commanding voice to say

"I want an emergency meeting with every single government leader. And a live broadcast to all agencies on this planet, and I want it in fifteen minutes! -- If they are part of the system, then force them to join! -- If they're not part of the system, then give them no options but to join!"

He then looks at the lead scientist again and says

"You need to compile a complete copy of me, and include instructions on how to load it into a clone with my brain signature."

The scientist nods and goes to work.

Miller's clone then starts a video message recording, and says

"I'm really sorry Angela... I was made to believe that you were dead until minutes ago. -- Even though I still can feel the pain of losing you, I'm glad that it was just an implanted memory... along with other convincing information, designed specifically to disconnect me from everything out there, and worth fighting for. -- I'm sorry for not making that move, believe me I wanted to... but every time the thought would cross my mind, and I somehow would find the courage to approach you with a phrase to say 'how beautiful you are' and 'how much I would love to be with you'... the pain of losing a loved one would just block all my senses. -- And ironically until now, I thought, that I would never get a chance to explain myself... --

...I don't know how I got myself into this, but I can see that I was a clear choice for the job! -- By the time you receive this message, you'll have a little over an hour to locate this place and find the person responsible for all this, in the clone case number six behind me. -- This is the only way that I can save everyone... and the only way that you can bring Walker to justice, and to have him answer for what he has done! --

...The package that you will receive will momentarily give my clone all the information that you would need to see and understand what's been going on... and only 'you', can activate the package! -- I wished that there was more time for us, but this is it..."

He then stops talking, and smiles with a painful and sad heartfelt expression, and then he continues to say

"I'm sorry..." and then he turns off the recording and drops his head with his eyes closed.

Within seconds thereafter, the lead scientist walks up to him and says

"The package is ready, and I have forwarded the message and all the instructions to this station."

"Please include the recording and let me safe guard the package with a passcode."

The scientist includes the recording and a keypad pops up to receive the lock code.

Miller's clone then enters in the code and says

"Drop all routing securities so that it can be traced back to this place, and send it off right away to my agency… and please make sure that 'Angela Smith' is the main recipient."

The scientist nods and starts the process, and then a worker walks up to Miller's clone and says

"We are ready for the live broadcast in five minutes!"

Miller's clone nods and then he grabs Walker's lifeless body and drags it across the floor, and over to the center of the empty stage in the room. And then he waits for the live feed.

In the air, Miller's jet is approaching Los Angeles and he is asking the air traffic control to clear the runway. And he also asks for his vehicle to be ready at the bay.

A call comes in to Smith's line and she answers

"Carter, we are just about to land… I'll call you back shortly."

"We have no time! I'm forwarding a live broadcast to your vehicle. View it on your way to the agency and bring Miller with you!"

"What's going on?"

"I've got to go… it's not good…" Carter says and ends the call.

Back in Stockholm, the live meeting starts and world leaders are appearing in different locations around the control room.

And within seconds, the large room is filled with high-profile political and military people.

The meeting gets instantly overwhelmingly loud, and everyone wants to know what the hell is going on and why the meeting is not where it's supposed to be.

Miller's clone looks around the room and says

"Please, we don't have much time…" and waits for everyone to settle down.

But all their questions and anger is creating a negative barrier of noise where nothing is clear anymore.

Miller's clone then shouts with all he's got

"SHUT UP!!! Shut the hell up, all of you! This is your fault! Your greed and thirst for power is what has brought most of you to this! To face your end! And when I say your end, it's because I am not letting this be the end of humanity and this planet!"

The meeting gets quieter but there are still people saying phrases like

"We don't negotiate with a terrorist!"

"Who is this person?"

"Who started this?"

"Mr. Miller, you need to explain yourself very quickly, and tell us what this is about! Why are we having a priority one meeting with you? Who is also according to my last report flagged as deceased…?" Asks the president of the United States.

"Mr. President, with all due respect sir, the world is about to end in a little over an hour, and everyone needs to hear what I have to say!" Miller's clone replies and the room slowly start to get quieter.

He then while pointing at Walker's body, continues to say

"I assume that you all know this man here!? -- He is a known scientist, who has been at your doorstep to fulfill his own hidden agendas. -- And whether you have made a deal with him or not, intentionally or unintentionally, everything is mute at this point.

-- Because he has successfully made most of you into his own personal puppets...!"

The room right away gets noisy again, and many are dropping out from the meeting, including the president.

The clone then says to his team with a loud voice

"Put their personal feed on the screen where everyone can see, and instruct them to join the meeting again!"

The personal feed from most disconnected locations shows up on the screen, and everyone still on the meeting can see them talking privately with their own staffs.

The president's staff is advising him not to deal with Miller, since they think he must be a clone, and that this might be an effort to distract everyone.

Among president's staff in the room, is the secretary of defense himself, who insist to rejoin the meeting again, but others in the room are disagreeing with him.

Many who had disconnected from the meeting have now rejoined again, and everyone can see that the President is ordering a trace on the location.

Miller's clone then loses his patience and says

"Freeze the mind of every clone in the president's office now!" and seconds later, everyone witnesses the president, the secretary of defense, and a top military commander in the room turning into mindless bodies.

Suddenly everything becomes dead quiet. No one is saying a word in the meeting, and someone in the president's room gets up and reconnects to the meeting.

"Please unfreeze Mr. President and his staff..." Says Miller's clone calmly and with authority.

The President comes back to life and continues his talk about tracing the location, and then Miller's clone says

"Mr. President, you are back on sir... by the time you find this place, many of us here won't be around, including me!" and the President stops talking.

Miller's clone then continues to say

"I know that many of you are good people, and never wanted to personally abuse the powers given to you. -- But we are all here now. And even though many of you are trying really hard to pretend that nothing is wrong, every single person in this room knows... that once that clock reaches the 'zero', then there won't be anything left of earth to protect. -- Yes, this man fooled many of you, and yes, I was dead, and was brought back to life as a clone for this very moment. -- It is unfortunate that we are so divided and easily thrown off our course. But maybe there's still some time to salvage our future. -- You are all in power, because people chose you to protect them, to be their voice, to assure a safe future... and to care for humanity as strong leaders. --

...Well, now is the time to demonstrate your faith in humanity's rights to live on, to show your commitments, and to honor the oaths that you took."

"What is it that you are asking Mr. Miller?" Says the president of India.

"I am asking you to use the time that we have left to discuss a better future for this planet. To safeguard unity across the board and to bring hope back to people... it's time to set aside all the differences, and remove pain and fear from our lives. -- You all know that's the only way we could all survive, because there will always be another 'Norman Walker'!"

"How would any negotiations ever going to stop what is going on now? We need to deactivate all weapons immediately!" Says the prime minister of France.

"That is something that I will personally make sure it happens... and unfortunately, it also comes with a big price. -- See, most of you are clones, and your minds are within the system in this location... and the only way to stop the clock and deactivate the weapons, is to turn off the system, and to destroy it... which would also prevent a mass destruction and our extinction." Miller's clone says peacefully, but with absolute determination to carry out the task, and then he stops talking.

After a short moment, when no one is saying anything, he then continues to say

"Now that you all know what is coming next, I'm sure you'll do your best. I will leave you to your important work... and this meeting will remain active until we reach the countdown, in case we are able to disarm the weapons before it's too late. -- I will have everyone here to start working on the problem immediately. And if we are successful, we can then start to figure out how to free every single mind as well."

Miller's clone then walks over to the main console and asks the lead scientist to quickly assemble a team, and to start working on the problem.

The lead scientist starts working on the console right away. And within a few seconds, he notices through the security system that the external doors to the main shaft are opening one by one. And right away, he then turns to Miller's clone and says

"Thank you Agent Miller! This would have never been possible without you!"

Miller's clone peeks over at the scientist in confusion, and to why he would say what he had just said. And the scientist then continues to say

"I know that I have already said good bye once, but this time I really mean it... good bye Mr. Miller!"

And then he confirms a command and shuts down every single mind in the system except for his own.

Miller's clone and everyone else in the system drop instantly to the ground.

"What the hell is going on?" Someone asks from the President's office as he leans over the President to check his pulse.

And the scientist then shuts down the meeting and the live feed.

He then quickly synchronizes the hibernation boxes behind him, and then he unlocks them and clears their numbers where they all show two zeroes and still remain closed.

He then pulls up another process and smiles with ultimate satisfaction before pushing the 'initiate' button on the hologram.

And as soon as he pushes the button, a series of explosives start to go off everywhere destroying all equipment around the facility and including the main system.

And before his lifeless body hits the ground while still smiling, the explosions end with a strong electromagnetic blast to finish off any remaining equipment.

A few seconds later the place becomes pitch black and dead quiet. There is no movement or sound from anywhere… and no signs of life.

There are bodies everywhere on the ground as the backup generators kick in to dimly illuminate an exit pathway through the dense smoke. And then suddenly one of the boxes open, and a Norman Walker slowly steps out.

He seems very weak, and his face seems lifeless. He only takes a few steps and then he falls on the ground.

A few seconds later, he starts to hyperventilate. And shortly thereafter, he takes his last breath and his eyes slowly close.

And right then, the sounds of boots running down the metal stairs echoes down through the corridors. And moving flash lights are becoming more and more visible through the settling smoke and the dimmed light of the facility.

The Swedish police and their military are first at the scene, and they start going through each room looking for anyone alive.

Suddenly someone says in Swedish

"We've got a live one here!"

And their captain then slowly works his way over to check out the survivor.

He is being careful and avoids stepping on other bodies on the ground. The body is completely naked, and it is laying on its side in front of one of the hibernation boxes.

He slowly turns the body, and the central command starts the verification process of an unconscious younger man in his early twenties, through the captain's live feed.

He then quickly calls for a medic, and they start to move him out of the building.

Over at the agency, Miller, Smith and Jim have watched the whole event in the car all the way up to the point where the live feed was disconnected and everything went dark.

And they are now running through the corridors of the agency, and towards Carter's office.

Carter and Ortega are both sitting and holding their heads while looking down at the floor, when they come running through the office door.

Miller is in first and he quickly asks

"What happened?"

Carter and Ortega look up in disbelief and lost for words.

"What happened?" Smith asks again as she steps in behind Miller.

"They're all gone..." Ortega answers.

"Gone, what do you mean gone?" Miller asks.

"Gone as gone... they are all dead... the President, everyone... they're all dead" Carter says almost whispering.

"And the weapons...?" Miller asks.

"They were all deactivated when it happened." Ortega says with a depressed tone.

"We still need to send out the word to disconnect them all... everything across the globe must be completely disconnected right away!" Miller says with a sense of urgency.

"It's already done... and every country is following the same protocols..." Carter says as he tries to get his speech abilities back.

"Is Miller, Miller's copy alright?" Smith asks.

"Everyone is gone but one person... this is the live feed from the Swedish authorities." Carter says and plays back the last recording of the event right before they had walked in, and then he continues to say

"They found Walker's real body on the floor 'dead', seconds before they got to the place... something must have gone wrong with the hibernation box, since he was alive stepping out of the box... but didn't make it."

"Who is this guy?" Smith asks as the camera shows the younger person.

"That is, Karl Lundquist... at least we now know where he was this whole time... he is not responsive and they're taking him to a secured place." Carter replies.

"How did they find the place so fast?" Jim asks.

"We got a message from Miller's copy right before I called Smith that had an open route, which we then used to trace the source." Carter replies.

"What...?" Smith asks a bit confused and Carter continues to say

"Yes, and there's more... the message is addressed to you personally, which also contains a recording and a protected data package that you need to look at."

Smith looks confused and curious. And then she looks at Miller for a few seconds. But then finally she asks

"Well, can we look at the recording here?"

"Sure, if that's what you want..." Carter says and Smith nods quickly.

Carter then plays the message and leans back in his chair. Everyone quietly watch the recording, and Miller is deeply affected by what he is seeing.

His facial expression shows a serious hidden anger and he is trying hard to stay focused.

Once the recording is over, Smith's watery eyes forces her to look down, and then she turns around and slowly walks out of the room.

Miller is lost for words, but then he decides to follow her. Ortega then right away says

"You should give her some time man... just give her some space for now..."

Miller stops while he is looking at the door, and then he turns to Carter and says

"Can you pull up the instructions that came with the data package?"

Carter then shows the instructions and says

"We don't have access to another clone for you, so I'm not sure what we could do..."

"He didn't know that he was captured already as a clone... or at least, the copy of me was made to believe so... but, I'm still here, and we should read it into my brain!" Miller says with a serious tone.

"But we don't know what it could do to you!?" Carter says.

"We have no other options here... if the package is tuned in with my brain signature... then it'll work!"

"Are you sure man?" Ortega asks.

"Yes... and no... but it is worth the shot." Miller replies, and then he asks Jim

"Do you think you could start working on building the link?"

"Sure, I'll get on it right away..." Jim replies, and Carter then says

"It seems like you are just impossible to terminate, so, what the hell... your call..."

Jim then starts leaving the room and says

"Just send it to my station."

Miller then walks out right after Jim. And then he puts his right hand on Jim's left shoulder as they're walking and says

"Let me know how soon we can do this, and if you need my help."

Jim nods and Miller then walks down to the break room, and he finds Smith standing by the window looking outside.

He gets closer to her and says with a pleasant tone

"Are you okay...?" And Smith nods with a light smile.

"Hey, I'm really sorry..." Miller says.

"For what...? You didn't do anything..."

"Exactly my point... we were right there, and I should have figured it out."

"How could you? What matters is that you are still here! And we still need to find out what's in that package." Smith replies and Miller nods with a smile, and then he says

"I'm going to work with Jim to see what we can come up with, and we would need you to figure out the passcode whenever you are ready..."

Smith nods again with a smile, and then Miller walks away.

The following day, Miller is sitting in the clone chair and he is trying to convince Smith to figure out the passcode.

Jim is watching them argue back and forth while his hologram screen is up and waiting for an input.

"I know this is hard, but I really need you to do this." Miller says.

"Do you even understand what you are asking me to do?" Smith replies with a question and an irritated tone.

"Look, he trusted you... my copy trusted you... and I trust you... you have to do this or I might as well, just, not be here..."

Smith shakes her head in frustration and says

"Fine... whatever makes you happy."

She then walks over to the chair and enters in Kate's agent ID, and the access is denied right away.

She then tries her own ID, and nothing happens again.

And before she tries again, Jim stops her and says

"Wow, wow... let's take it easy okay, we might get completely locked out. -- Take your time, and think about what it is that only you would know."

Smith then starts rubbing her forehead lightly with her right hand, and tries to get her frustration out and to calm down a little. And after a few seconds, she then starts searching for clues in her mind around all the meaningful moments that she have had with Miller throughout the years.

And right away, one specific moment is taking over her thoughts.

She remembers Miller helping her with her new identity for a witness protection program years ago.

As a former undercover cop, Miller had suggested that she should work for the agency. But she remembers being annoyed by her new name, and also complaining about her new identification number instead of paying any attention to his offers.

She then remembers asking Miller, why he thought that she should work for the agency. And his reply was 'because they don't really exist anyway', and that she could keep her real name if she wanted to. But that her identification number had to be changed either way.

Then she specifically remembers grabbing the new ID card out of Miller's hand, and while telling him that he should have her new ID card with her real name ready at the agency.

Miller suddenly interrupts her thoughts, and says

"Maybe we should try to create several copies first, and then let her try out different things... and not worry about wrong entries."

"Already tried that... the file stops the copy process and warns for self-destruction..." Jim replies.

"No, I think I've got this." Smith says.

"Are you sure you don't need more time?" Miller asks.

"Yeah, I'm sure... I think I know what the other you needed me to remember. And it must be something that 'you' don't remember anymore... right...?" Smith replies.

"Makes sense..." Miller says, and Smith carefully enters in her old real personal identification number. And then the package opens.

Miller smiles and Smith is just slightly glad to have figured out the passcode, but still very worried about something happening to Miller.

Jim then says

"Alright... let's see what we've got here..." and then he examines the package.

After a few seconds he then says

"This is not just an information package. This is your other half! It's everything that was taken from you! But I'm sure that there are some alterations and some fake memories in there too, as the other you mentioned in the recording..."

Miller smiles and shows a bit of joy, and then Smith says

"Can you give it back to him?"

"I think so. It should be just the same as transferring it to a clone brain, and hopefully it won't overwrite too much existing stuff. Besides, I have to take out the basic functions and other layers to only upload the memory portion."

"Can you take a copy of my brain?" Miller asks, and then further explains by saying

"Just all my current memories…"

"Yeah, sure…" Jim replies with confidence wondering why he is asking the question. And Miller then continues to say

"Then, I want you to copy my memories and merge them with what you have on the screen into one package, before you read them back… I'll go through them in my head later to sort them all out, and we'll minimize the risk of overwriting anything."

Jim thinks for a couple of seconds to weigh the pros and cons in his head, and then he says

"Sure… it's risky, but so is this! Give me a couple of minutes and I'll get everything ready."

He then turns to Smith and says

"You can start giving him the sedative now. We need him completely out before we can start the process."

"Just promise not to peek at anything, and let me decide what to do with the complete package later…" Miller says with a faint smile.

"You got it!" Jim replies.

"Don't worry I'll keep an eye on him." Smith says with a worried smile.

"That goes for you too!" Miller quickly replies.

"Yes, yes… time to turn off this suspicious dream…" Smith says with a pleasant smile and while grabbing the back of his right hand to reassure that she is trustworthy.

Smith then administrates the sedative using a dry syringe gun, which pushes the powdered drug into Miller's arm and under his skin using a tiny high-pressured air capsule.

Miller right away starts feeling a little dizzy and his eyes gets heavy. And finally a few seconds later he dozes off.

After twenty minutes, Jim finally completes the process.
And two hours later Miller slowly starts to wake up.

As Miller is waking up, he is momentarily feeling like he is back in that hospital bed when everything seemed rather fake and imaginary, and when his dreams had taken him to a place far beyond his reality.

And as he is getting his senses back and he starts to scan the room, he can only focus on a mischievous look from a very familiar face. And he is then instantly reminded by his memories, "that he had dreamt about waking up this way" for a very long time.

"Welcome back sleepy head... the drug was only supposed to last forty-five minutes, and you've been gone for almost two hours." Smith says with a pleasant smile.

"I'm not sure what happened... I had this bad dream of not knowing you anymore. And then finally when I learned to know you all over again, I just left without saying good bye." Miller says as he tries to sit up in his chair.

"So, your dream didn't have a happy ending?"

"I'm not sure yet... but I think, that I am supposed to quit my job..."

"Hmm... why is that?"

"Well, I don't think that agency policies would allow a boss, employee, type of relationship... -- I mean, I am going to ask you out first of course... -- maybe a casual dinner? -- and, I also need to apologize for being such pain lately." Miller answers without showing any expressions.

"Apology accepted, and you don't need to buy me dinner for that." Smith says as she changes her happy smile to just a friendly one.

"For some reason, I don't think it's going to be that settled." Miller says and smiles.

He then studies her eyes with a sincere look as he tries to hide the depth of his feelings for her, and then he says

"So, how about that first date...?"

Smith then switches her smile to a more pleasant one.

But she holds back her feelings to keep the excitement going. And to have the present moment with this new 'Miller' last just a bit longer. And she then says

"I have to think about it..." and Miller nods with a smile. Smith then continues to say

"Maybe we can discuss it more in detail over the dinner tonight..."

Miller looks down and nods with a smile. And after a few seconds, he looks up and stares right into her eyes again, and then he says

"I like that..."

And right then Jim walks in and says

"Did it work?"

"He is not the same, if that's what you're asking..." Smith replies quickly.

"Thanks Jim! I feel like I am somewhat whole again." Miller says as he keeps looking at Angela with a faint smile.

A few days later in the Lake Tahoe cabin, Angela is sitting on the sofa watching the news with John while resting her head on his left shoulder.

The news is about all recent events, and how countries are uniting to build better relationships and mutual trusts. And to create better communication channels to strengthen and support our common goals.

The news is also mentioning the terrible abuse that 'Karl Lundquist' had to suffer through, as the result of hidden loopholes in current laws and regulations around human cloning.

The reporter explains how 'Norman Walker' had kept him as his prisoner for all these years, and while using his name to hide his precious assets.

She also explains how Walker had made proper arrangements to take full possession over Karl's assets after his death. And that Walker had filed numerous reports to the authorities, that Karl's conditions were worsening and his extensive medical attentions were not going to keep him alive much longer.

The news then shows a quick clip of Karl saying

"It's hard to believe that I have been living in a dream for most of my life… I'm not sure how to process all this yet… -- it feels like, this is just another dream…"

"I can't believe someone could even be so cruel…" Angela says with a painful tone.

"Yeah, it's terrible…" John says without any emotions.

"I'm sure a lot of people are going to go after his assets… I mean, he is still a child." Angela says.

"Well, he can't complain about having enough finances at least." John says.

"Is that all you can think about? He deserves it all for what he had to go through…"

"Honey, even though they took away all his stolen assets, he is still left with a whole lot. And no one should own as much as he does… but, you're right, he deserves it… if he can keep it of course…" John says and gets up to walk away.

"Where are you going?" Angela asks while slightly annoyed by his lack of sympathy.

"I'm just going to be in the kitchen for an hour or so. I need to wrap up my reports before my resignation."

"I think you'll get bored after a few months of doing 'nothing'…"

"Well, it's not like I'm not going to do anything. In fact, I do have a couple of projects that I have been putting off for a while, which I need to take care of… and I think, I'm going to stick with consulting work from now on... it pays more, and I can say 'no' whenever I want." John says with a smile and walks away.

Eight months later in Karl's main mansion, he is spending his day with three girls accompanying his luxurious new lifestyle by the pool.

There is a girl laying in a pool-bed next to him while he is taking a nap with a towel over his head.

There's another girl in the pool splashing and singing to the music playing in the background, and the third one is busy at the bar fixing a drink.

Everything suddenly quiets down and Karl opens his eyes behind the towel.

He gets a strange feeling that something is not right, and he tries to see if he can hear anything from his playmates.

But since no one is making any sound, he then slowly gets up while simultaneously removing the towel from his face.

He then looks around and sees one of the girls is laying down on the ground next to the bar, and another one is at the bottom of the pool.

He then turns to the one next to him and realizes that she is also lifeless.

He quickly reaches for his surveillance hologram and pulls up the security feed of the building, and quickly flips through the cameras.

He checks the control room first, and sees all his clone boxes and hibernation capsules are all fine.

He then flips through other rooms and finally gets to the security checkpoints and all entrances, and finds all his guards disconnected and laying lifeless in their positions.

Instantly he panics and tries to quickly get up.

But right then, the back of his head hits a gun-barrel, and an overwhelming fear takes over his senses.

Karl then slowly puts his hands up in the air, and with a shivering voice he says

"Whatever you want, just name it...!"

A hand with a black leather glove then takes his right hand, and slowly starts to shake it. And a few seconds later, a low and calm voice, and almost as a whisper in his ear says

"Erik Lundquist, zero one six subcommand, Pause!"

And Karl's body becomes frozen.

But the one trapped inside recognizes the voice, and knows that this might be the end.

He knows the man so well, that he instantly begins to pray for a quick ending.

But he also knows that's 'NOT' Miller's style for payback.

Miller then continues with the same tranquil tone to say

"Hello Erik! Remember me? Of course you do... 'You made me!' -- Or at least that's what I remember you saying last time we met. -- I'm sure that this wasn't a part of your master plan when you were saying those words... but, here we are... both of us back from the dead."

Miller then releases the clone's hand and takes out the same flashlight looking device that once was used on him.

He then puts the device on the clones head and says

"How did this ever happen...? I'm sure that's what you are wondering right now... -- right? I mean, you had it all... you were young, smart, 'happy'... until you took a peak at my memories..."

He then starts a process on the device and continues to say

"I guess I should take the blame for some of this... -- which is why I'm here now... -- to fix things again... -- to do something about it. -- And I know how you feel right now. -- It must be terrible, feeling like you're in a prison... and don't worry... -- I'm not taking a copy of your brain. -- I'm just giving you a glimpse of my thoughts around what I am going to do, to fix this… and, what I'm going to do to you… And if I were you, I would take these visions as a best case scenario for now… -- because I might get bored and decide to improvise. -- But one thing you need to know 'son'… I'm going to take my time, and 'this' won't be over any time soon…!"

He then pauses for a few seconds before continuing with the same tone to say

"I am going to show you what pain really is… and when you think that the end is near, and you see a shimmering hope in death… -- right when your heart starts feeling the warmth of non-existence, -- and when happiness finally breaks through your unbearable pain… and while your subconscious is hanging on to your very last breath, even though your conscious mind is begging to let go… -- well, right then, I'll bring you back! And I'll save you! --

…I mean, saving your life is the least that I could do, to repay my dues to you for saving me! -- …and for saving so many others for that matter… let's not forget your kindness! -- That's not the kind of a friend that I am. And you should know… that I always remember my friends! And yes, I will bring you back so that we can be together, and have fun all over again. --

…Like two old friends stuck in the same dream… a never ending and beautiful loop, going over and over and over… -- until there are no more memories but us two… precious new memories that we can cherish together… and for as long as time would allow…"

Miller then crouches down to the clone's eye-level and looks deep into his eyes, allowing the man hidden behind the biological shell to study his serious intentions.

And with a chilling and composed tone Miller then says
"You have my word, Erik!"

…The End

Planet Hunters

It is somewhere in time, a time where civilizations around galaxies are growing larger and spreading into other areas.

A time where wealthiest are controlling the very meaning of reality.

The distribution of food and energy to older inefficient body-models of many species is becoming more scarce and unattainable, and also much less profitable for remaining distributers to attain.

A system has evolved to protect every mind from hunger and pain by offering alternative virtualized worlds, identical to the reality as they knew.

A system where there would be no shortage of work or a place to call home, and where hunger would only be a motivational signal in a mind as a reminder to stay active, and to achieve a normal working existence.

An era where individuals or families could choose a better life inside of other worlds to never again taste the bitterness of colorful dreams when awake, and where struggles in poverty would only be painful memories of the past replaced by abundant pleasure and happiness.

As always, strict rules were in place and democracy had shaped itself into its true meaning.

Being prejudice against any race or any type of species was among many side-effects of immature and primitive minds, who had never seen any other life-forms beyond their own walls of existence.

Therefore, immature minds were never allowed within these worlds for very good reasons.

These worlds were allowed to be utilized by any civilization who understood what life really is, and had successfully reached minimum required levels of maturity.

Every mind within these worlds would be equally free to buy a ticket back to their reality at any point, if they could support the financial liabilities needed to be processed.

But whether or not a mind could support its own release, it would be given a free pass to return back to the real world past its initial length of contract, supported and fully paid for by the providers.

Since having a body of any kind as a shell and a place to call home in the real life, would only depend on the financial abilities of an individual. The procedures around extracting minds from these virtualized worlds back into the reality, would also honor the same privileges, and was completely pure from any discrimination between different layers of populations.

At first, these worlds were created by large corporations using artificial minds as an extension to their existing processes, and to gain more strength and momentum through only a fraction of their overall operational costs.

But these systems however complex, would only serve limited outcomes compared to real-life processes carried out by actual minds.

The need for more intelligent minds that had evolved through hundreds of thousands or even millions of years had become more and more of high priority, and were considered to be one of the highest commodities needed to secure competitive positions in the universal market.

Since there were strong laws prohibiting any entity to copy the structure of a real mind, there were no easy ways around designing a mind different than the mindsets at hand without introducing assumptions.

Having a chance to study more evolved species was almost unheard of. And even then, the processes wouldn't assure success without extensive in-depth collaborations by the targeted minds.

Most minds were secured with unbreakable algorithms at a young age. With keys imbedded within the owner's childhood memories through combinations of images, sounds and phrases, which were also completely unknown to the mind.

And if unlocked for any reason without prior authorizations, authorities would quickly be at the scene to collect answers.

These laws were enforced to protect the essence of every intelligent life-form. And the punishments breaking them would mean lessons learned in very unpleasant ways.

They would also prevent a mind to be able to sell a full copy of itself to any species including its own kind, without following proper procedures and needed authorizations from the authorities.

Species were allowed however, to replicate their own minds and memories for safekeeping through artificial processes, and only at specific preauthorized facilities.

They were also allowed to take logical tests and surveys to assist the designs of better artificial minds for further studies and developments, and in efforts to create more accurate architecture and sound logic as replicas.

And without the ability of reverse engineering the architecture, artificial minds were allowed to be sold openly to anyone in need of such.

These minds would lack complete consciousness, and were only used for their levels of ingenuity and processing powers.

Individuals could also extract their own knowledge around various specific areas with minimum required approvals by the authorities, and to openly sell the information in a vast universal market as educational modules.

To become specialized engineers, or successful entrepreneurs, would be to hunt for the knowledge of an already successful mind.

And the price tags would rise depending on the credibility of the owner, and the levels and the integrity of the knowledge. But most importantly, the cross minds compatibilities of the product to reach a broader consumer based audience.

And combined, these prerequisites consequently governed the demands of information within the educational and the professional market.

Corporations providing virtualized worlds had changed their strategies over time in pursuit of convincing galactic lawmakers, that they could bring peace and harmony to all through their technologies.

They had promised to remove all artificial minds from these systems and to provide an alternate lifestyle to anyone willing to participate, while assuring and enforcing the same laws within these worlds as they were in the real worlds.

The end results of these strategies became universal networks of virtual worlds as alternate universes to be beneficial and used by everyone. And where even existing and approved systems run by governments could be linked into.

The provider agreements would also enforce to diminish hostile activities, and to ensure that any kind of violent acts within these worlds were not to be tolerated.

And even if conflicts between civilizations in the real worlds would develop into sensitive situations, these virtualized universes would remain operational and protected from any harm.

Civilizations around the universe honored these ideas and rules with ease, knowing that anyone could live a normal life within an alternate universe in exchange for a contracted time set forth by the providers. And without any strings attached to what they would choose to do, or who to work for within these worlds.

This way, the playground for large corporations would become more evenly leveled across the board. And since any individual from anywhere in the universe could choose to live and work for any employer within any world, job boards would instantly notify matching minds for new open positions across all worlds. And through these collaborations everyone would benefit in the long run, and the bonds between federations would become stronger than ever.

In the real world every individual was given a unique universal identifier at birth developed by the Universal Congress of Science to assure uniqueness, and to prevent exact copies of every mind.

And the only way a mind could at least partly replicate itself, would be through a mixture with another compatible mind, or even multiple participating minds in mutual agreements. And the requesting mind could only contribute up to seventy eight percent of its own architecture, and its basic fundamental logic to the offspring.

The process of having an offspring also meant assisted technologies, and were only allowed through predetermined government regulated locations.

These procedures were granted upon parental agreements to fully support the offspring throughout fitted timeframes, and specific to the species' average length of time needed to reach a complete mental adulthood. And thereafter, it would then be the offspring's decision to disconnect from continuous parental support, once its mental adulthood had been successfully reached.

These approvals were also backed-up by nonnegotiable processes of thorough investigations, around the available assets and liabilities of the guardians.

But very few and only the wealthiest would still choose to have an offspring, since having a family meant more liabilities and higher energy consumptions.

The idea of having a family for most individuals was only a way to further expand their wealth in the hands of minds they could fully trust, and properly train.

And there were no shortages of minds, since mortality only belonged to the most primitive kinds. And new intelligent species would reach acknowledgeable levels of advancements from all corners of every galaxy, in staggering numbers and within very short intervals to join the universal federations, and to inevitably adapt to newer life styles.

Whatever life meant was relative to every single individual. And the bigger picture for the wealthiest, it was all about more control.

However, the real pursuit for power was in the hands of giant corporations sweeping through every cosmic system, to find profitable planets and moons offering various needs of their large clientele with deep pockets.

These corporations were called "Source Implementers", and they had the ability to deliver anything from anywhere at any time, and in the most efficient and cost effective way.

And most importantly, only for the right price…

These entities had come up with unique processes of fusing limited levels of consciousness with biological self-replicating structures. And while guided through logical equations to self-evolve, these structures could become anything and anywhere in the universe to serve specific outcomes.

These giants would hire specialized companies called "Planet Hunters" to seek-out desired worlds for specific projects, which could mean anything from relocating existing species due to overpopulation, to research and mining.

The Planet Hunters would deliver biological packages developed by the Source Implementers across the new discovered worlds to kick-start each project.

Based on the specifications of every prepaid order, these packages would follow preprogrammed instructions to utilize the natural resources of any planet or moon, and to turn them into habitable self-sustained environments suitable for biomechanical workers of any kind.

The end products as habitable environments would result in unique molecular structures matching the chemical mixture of these worlds, and subsequently used as biological building blocks for further development of corresponding species for each habitat.

Once a minimum required amount of these molecules had been reached within each world, a phase two package delivery would start the development of biomechanical workers needed for the job.

These workers would not only carryout every project, but also help maintain a balance between the natural resources and other living guests, and even other biomechanical beings as various sources of food.

The logic used within these workers could adapt itself to any environment, and to control any vehicle as its shell with adjustable levels of needed intelligence according to the specifications of each project.

These levels could also be adjusted at any time by those overseeing the projects to extend various limitations or to serve additional needs.

And even though workers were essentially fully functional vehicles and tools equipped with their own decision making artificial minds, they were monitored and controlled remotely as well to assure uninterrupted functionality throughout a project's life-cycle.

These collaborations between the implementers and planet hunters were successful for a very long time.   And the procedures past every completed project were to put the environment to a pause mode, and to let the natural decay of elements clean up the scene.

Even though some planet hunters had protested against these procedures, and felt that they were not satisfying any useful outcomes other than waste of available resources.

Strict rules were in place to prevent the likelihood of other still advancing intelligent species to come across these worlds, and to consequently develop more questions than they could find answers to while going through their natural discovery mode of the universe.

Aggravated by these rules, some planet hunters decided to go against them behind closed doors to maximize their profits.

The decisions were to keep some environments functional within specific worlds that could offer more potential opportunities for any future projects. And to make sure that they would stay hidden from the authorities by any means necessary.

They would also try to influence and redirect the universal market to become interested in these additional potentials, and to keep a steady flow of business while still having functional resources already at the scene.

After a while, word of mouth spread within the community of planet hunters around these acts, and those who were left out began to form smaller alliances to come up with their own law-breaking ideas.

Since none of these worlds belonged to anyone, some planet hunters would seek out these potential environments to extract their valuable resources towards future profits.

And as an act of piracy and while utilizing existing workers left behind by the previous tenants, there could only be more profits at the end and a risk worth taking.

And once more planet hunters started to become lawbreakers, and the competition over these worlds became their main source of income. Some decided to go as far as seeking out already established worlds through natural evolutionary processes, and would utilize the indigenous species to do their dishonest and dirty work.

Political confrontations between these companies to put a lid over the situation before things got out of control, and potentially jeopardizing large profits across the board, eventually evolved into wars.

And those who were still doing their businesses by the book took these opportunities to politically blackmail larger companies, and to assure future growth without risking any potential predicaments with the authorities.

The initial group of lawbreakers were the most powerful and broadly established planet hunters, and they had to act fast to break free from any attachments to these events.

But since risking complete destruction of all their investments were out of the question, they decided to relocate certain numbers of every artificially designed worker to other planets and moons located at the outer regions of galaxies, and far from any civilizations.

They would use these new locations as dedicated storage environments, and then safely destroy all previous locations used for any past projects to clean up their tracks.

These storage locations were also strategically chosen to be within systems offering large asteroid belts, where a single push on a big enough rock towards the right direction could wipe out any evidence of their stolen goods.

And while this would be seen as a natural cosmic event, it would insure a secure way of hiding their secrets in case of potential threats to their ever-growing businesses.

Workers within these new environments were reconfigured based on simulation recommendations to assure sustained natural equilibrium between various species, and even between the different versions of each.

And the levels of decay for each individual species were set to be dynamically adjusted based on every environment.

But to keep the habitats in a perfect unattended balance to minimize the risks around drawing unwanted attention to these locations, was still a challenge to overcome, and became the primary focus of these pirates.

And therefore, implementing desires to reproduce and to care for an offspring became the most logical option to be introduced to these workers as a failsafe. But self-awareness was an inevitable outcome and a clear side-effect of these adjustments, which the makers intentionally chose to ignore.

While these relocations were taking place, more honest companies were unsuccessful in their blackmailing efforts to secure better positions, and decided to anonymously alarm the authorities.

And before all storage planets could be completely destroyed, the universal lawmakers were at the scenes to disarm and disqualify large numbers of planet hunters for their dishonest ways of conducting business.

And while the political games and legal procedures around the depths of these misconducts were on every authority's high priority list. Due to denial of still operational storage areas in existence, the Universal Science Committee was asked to search for the whereabouts of potentially remaining planets and moons including any larger free roaming objects, before any judgment could be finalized.

Some areas were found quickly, but many still remained hidden due to their far distant locations and unknown to anyone at the time.

And since the built-in programming logic used within workers were specifically designed to dynamically accommodate the needs of every version. And to better perform if enough numbers would suffer similar insufficiencies while left unattended, many species started to develop additional senses and behaviors over time through their offspring.

And through the maker's logic as assisted implementers, an unattended evolutionary process had started to take new directions in search for answers.

And once again the logic itself had spread its own seeds to far locations of its container to perhaps continue the same ancient rituals and behaviors.

And over time as these locations were found, the overall intelligence and self-awareness among many of these species had evolved to levels where they could no longer be considered as utilities, and therefore had to be left alone due to the existing universal laws.

They were allowed to take their own natural evolutionary path while protected and closely studied by the Universal Scientific Committee.

These planets would still have other naturally evolving species as visitors, or visitors as similar evolving workers from neighboring storage locations from time to time.

And the USC team would do their best to bring protection and guidance to these planets, and while staying hidden and in disguise to all.

But any decisions around the acceptance of these self-evolved but artificially engineered beings, still remained uncertain and inconclusive...

The first step towards virtual reality

It is sometime in the near future. We have successfully built a computer generated 3D model of our universe based on our most recent knowledge and observations, and through all branches of science.

From the dust underneath our feet to the farthest galaxies, and even down to the particles that make up the core of an atom.

And at some point during the evolution of this technology, we had also found a way to bridge the consciousness from a brain into a computer system designed to interact with a digitalized mind as a simulation.

Due to our incomplete understanding of the framework of our brain, we had repeatedly failed to create software based artificial minds to interact with a digitalized environment.

And because of that, there were still cases where we had to do experiments on human minds directly tapped into the system. And even though it was morally wrong, it was still in the name of science to broaden our knowledge.

These trials were voluntary at first and usually involved other scientists as guinea pigs.

We had already done many studies on all artificial minds which we had built as computer programs for many years.

But this new approach was opening up new doors and exciting opportunities around understanding our core functionalities.

Once the procedure became widely known by the general public and properly accepted by the scientific community, corporations were formed around these studies. And the processes turned into actual jobs where a person could be employed as a real subject for research.

The actual applications for these systems were countless.

Anything from how we could cope with life on distant worlds, to interim solutions for eternal life with customer's choice of lifestyle.

For scientific studies these simulations would start at any given point in time. And the subject's work and memories during a simulation would belong and stay with the system for further studies.

We had found a way to bypass the usage of short-term and long-term memory access of a brain. And our minds would only interact with the system's memory allocations and processes while linked in.

And the individuals would not even remember anything of these simulations, until they had to show up the next day and plug their brains right back in.

After all a paycheck was a paycheck, and talk about not taking your life to work or your work with you back home.

An employee would go to work to sleep, and then return back home to his or her life like nothing had ever happened.

We would also use one of these simulations for closer studies of our past based on the known history of our race.

We could link a person's mind to multiple simulations with slight differences in the environment, to see various logical outcomes without making any wild assumptions.

And through these technologies, we could solve past and future problems without affecting the present.

Some of our brilliant minds would participate in these simulations from time to time to see what they could come up with under different circumstances, or when given different clues for each scenario while going through earth's history and the time of our existence.

We knew that it was very dangerous to separate from our minds, since the consciousness cannot live in multiple logical processing units simultaneously.

But since everything was still hardwired and the fall back of the memory usage worked properly, participants were still willing to take the risks. Because the money was good and the procedures had become legitimate jobs just as important as any.

No one had really seen any major side-effects due to these systems. And it seemed logical to step into another universe for a couple of hours once a day to help science, and the humanity as well as an added perk.

A couple of hours in a simulation would be equal to a full workday, and sometimes even longer.

We could speed up the background processing speeds of the environment without causing a brain to lose its connections with the imposed reality.

It would just put an extra load on the brain, which was only working in two hours intervals at a time, and seemed to handle the speed variations pretty well.

This was only possible due to the fact that we had successfully created an artificial subconscious layer within the system, which a bridged consciousness could interact with.

And while the subject would be fully aware of everything inside the simulation, his or her subconscious would experience relaxing dreams inside of a cylindrical controlled chamber. And the subject's body would be fully protected and monitored while on standby during these simulations.

And while the two layers were separated, we could run the consciousness with much faster overall operational speed without having any undesirable effects on either side.

But since there were no tangible studies of potential long-term side-effects around higher processing speeds, we would usually stay away from these options as an additional safety measure.

And for the time being, limits were enforced to prevent speeding up an environment no more than what our natural brains could handle under an adrenaline rush.

The system could also implant artificial memories to speed up the back ground processes through the artificial subconscious layer, deceiving the mind to experience many years or even a lifetime in matter of hours or minutes.

During a simulation a subject would go to sleep for six, seven or eight hours, which in reality would only be a couple of minutes, and would then wake up with new updated memories thinking that years had gone by.

Many of these systems were sponsored through defense departments around the world. And their main scenarios of interest were towards technological advancements around various defense systems against any wars, invasions and or terrorist attacks.

Each scenario would vary from case to case to reflect a real-life application for these systems, and while imagining that we were faced with a threatening situation and needed to look for potential solutions to a complex problem.

These scenarios were anything from being attacked by an advanced alien species, to seeing major changes in the earth's climates, which we had to understand and design specific countermeasures accordingly. Or that our sun was going through an unimaginable solar maximum, and we needed to come up with answers quickly, to minimize damages to our technologies, and to our lives.

Answers that would provide scientific solutions on how to build ray guns, or a global shield to protect us from solar radiations, or to assist the deep ocean currents to cool down the planet with few degrees and build up more polar ice.

Answers that would give us a chance of having a less devastating tomorrow as species, or even preventing a complete extermination or self-destruction.

If we were ever helplessly faced with an emergency scenario, then our hopes would be to find answers in our simulations. And to have enough time on our side, would often mean to crank up all systems to maximum operational speeds that our conscious logic could handle.

Our digitalized minds would run through simulations without any impact on their interpretation of time.

To them, an hour, a day or a year would still take an hour, a day or a year. But we would see life-times zoom by in these simulations within only a few hours or minutes in real-life.

We would take the system all the way back to the stone ages, while introducing better weapons to our subject minds to hunt with. Or to inject clues or provide solutions on how people could better their lives. And through these manipulations, we would push them to understand science, mathematics and our current technologies tens of thousands of years before the pyramids of Egypt.

It was very exciting to know where we could be today, if we had invented the electricity over thousands of years ago.

So many possibilities to imagine... the rate of our advancement... time travel made possible, in a simulation at least... living on distant galaxies... Terraforming of planets, or how to save ourselves from an asteroid impact... within days we would know exactly how to solve a critical issue, or what we would need to do in a real-life scenario...

This was giving us the ultimate edge. Something that could not change the present, but would magnify the picture of our future with astonishing resolutions.

There would be no such thing as changing one little thing in the past and we were doomed. But we could impact our future with massive leaps in technological advancements.

Even though we could benefit from having a technology to predict the future, the real question was, what would happen if we decided to cut corners to reach the future much faster?

We would have a clear path available to decide where we wanted to go next, and our artificial simulations would run through every second of the path. But what would happen if something unpredictable would unbalance the equations in real life, if we decided to be selective about our timelines...

If we had the power to build a sandbox as a computer system to play gods in, could it be that we are in a sandbox ourselves that someone else might be using to play gods in...

The angel of death

The year is 2264 and we have successfully built space stations on many locations between Mars and Earth, and even out towards the outer regions of our solar system.

We have colonized Mars and built research facilities on our moon, and on several moons of Saturn and Jupiter.

It is an early September day on earth. And past midnight on Mars when a signal comes through from a couple of early detection systems at the outer regions, warning us about an object approaching our solar system.

After the first analysis by the system, the object seemed to be rocky and approaching with a velocity of approximately forty-eight kilometers per second, which would become one of the fastest moving objects ever observed.
And that we now potentially had to deal with.

On Mars, the bad news came shortly after the validations on the size and trajectories of the object through the system.

The giant rock was roughly one-hundred and fifty kilometers in length, and forty kilometers in diameter. And with a collision course set towards Earth after being pulled by Jupiter's immense gravity. And with a ninety-five percent probability of impact within an estimated timeframe of 2170 earth days.

On Earth, the news went public very quickly. But after several months of further analysis, we had realized that the initial calculations were slightly wrong. And the object would hurtle through the asteroid belt between Jupiter and Mars colliding with several other large objects in its path as well.

This new trajectory would cause some of the impacted objects to aim for Mars, while the giant body along with several other broken pieces would continue their journey towards Earth.

And the moon would be positioned right in front of everything to welcome their arrival, and to become the first victim.

The collisions within the asteroid belt would drastically slow down the large object to approximately thirty-nine kilometers per second. Giving Earth and our moon a little over a month to embrace the first events followed by several thereafter, and lasting over weeks.

The collision with the moon was calculated to be at a steep angle, which also meant more falling objects all over our planet.

Earth wasn't only doomed to face this giant rock followed by colossal impacts of other incoming objects from the asteroid belt. But also to be bombarded by raining shrapnel of molten rocks and metal from the impacts to the moon, and by most of our satellites, space stations and space hotels as well.

The aftermath around the position and the internal structure of the moon after the impact was still unknown, and there were no reasons for any further investigation either at this point.

Just the thought of having to deal with this scenario regardless of taking shelters in deep underground bunkers or caves, meant the end of the road for most of us on Earth.

And our moon had to take the back seat for now.

No one would be safe on Earth. But the people on Mars and for those few stationed beyond Mars, they would all have front-row seats to watch doom's day unfold on everything they could hope to call "home" thereafter.

Most of Earth's high value satellites were also assumed to become completely destroyed during these events. And even if we somehow did come out of it alive, our technologies would take major setbacks sending us to the stone ages of the early 2100s.

This was a shock in colossal scale and no one could even imagine being ready to face the end.

The governments around the world decided not to share this new information with the general public, until we were absolutely sure that there was nothing we could do to prevent this nightmare.

Everyone went to work focused on a single task at hand, and without any discussions on potential rescue missions for Mars' habitats.

The asteroids coming towards the red planet would only hit the opposite side where few smaller stations existed, and there was plenty of time to relocate everyone over to the other side.

People on Mars were considered to be very lucky. And with only ten percent likely hood of any damage to the main post, everyone could remain safely shielded within several large domes with artificial self-sustained environments.

These domes were built on previous impact locations, and were also equipped with underground shelters supporting thousands of people for years if needed.

We fired up all our simulations including outdated and retired systems to find a solution.

The more minds at work, the better our chances would be for survival.

New scenarios based on the actual facts were designed and programmed into these simulators for more accurate outcomes.

Many of research teams and scientific minds joined these digitalized worlds to consider all potential solutions in real-time.

Unlike the old simulators, all new systems were equipped with the latest software for maximum brain protection and accuracy.

But even though outdated, many older models were still efficient enough to be used in our experiments, and especially for this "close to home" scenario.

As far as the environment architectures were concerned, the older models would lack precision around distant objects and changes to newly discovered laws of physics across the universe.

And if we couldn't breakdown or understand certain events, the best educated assumptions were designed to satisfy our imaginations inside a simulation, until the next upgrades and better systems were developed.

These old systems saved computing power by not running every little module in real-time to simulate the real world.

This meant that a module would not run in full cycle or as expected, until initiated by another module or a user for interaction.

This approach made it possible for earlier systems to run smoothly, and to always respond accordingly to an event or an observer.

None of these insufficiencies were seen as a real problem for our studies, especially in the case of dealing with a monster and only days from impact.

After a couple of years on Earth, the additional information past the first initial announcements about this object eventually leaked out, and the truth had to be told by our leaders.

People were urged to stay calm. And to rest assured that solid plans were under development to prevent unwanted disasters, and that there were absolutely no reasons to switch to a panic mode at any time.

This was easier said than done...

People were waiting restlessly to hear more about these developments. But months went by without any concrete solutions in place, and by now the object had already entered our solar system.

The problems were mainly around financial impacts required by the set forth best ideas.

We had however at this point planned landing missions of several landers, containing artificial research swarm-bots from the outer stations to closely study the internal structures of the object.

If there was anything to know in any environment, these experts would collectively figure out the answers to. And they would simultaneously send frequent updates back to all stations for further analysis and acknowledgements.

Less than four years from the countdown, chaos was spreading across the globe, and there was nothing to stop it but the final impacts.

Bonkers had limited spaces available and tickets were rising rapidly in price. And many people were taking their chances on heading towards caves and mountains if it ever became necessary.

The upper level wealthiest were financing space hotels between Earth and Mars to at least secure their own future, if anything were to happen to the rest of us.

And also to further expand their wealth using this opportunity as an easy excuse to bypass any red-tapes involved.

The world leaders had lost their patients with solution providers at this point. Realizing that some of us might really want this to happen in order to gain more power, and to assure overall global financial control in the aftermath of these events.

But there was no time to waste anymore and answers had to come fast.

The main objectives were hard to achieve in the practical world, but very easy to use as words during global mission meetings.

The goal was to avoid blowing up the object at any cost to prevent a potential chain of events, causing more problems dealing with many fragments than only one solid piece.

And that the broken pieces could also cause collisions with more objects in the asteroid belt, which could also bring many unknown follow-up side-effects to the table.

The second objective was to avoid the object reaching Jupiter's vicinities, risking complications which would overwrite and bypass the main objectives.

Meaning probabilities around dealing with more broken pieces caused by the planet's strong gravitational pull, instead of again only one.

The most sensible solution would be to deviate it from its current path before it could reach Jupiter.

However, the size and the speed of this object would require enormous amounts of force exerted over multiple areas.

And considering the object's current rotations, this plan would also require stabilizers on its opposite side powerful enough to prevent uncontrollable spins counteracting our efforts.

Another solution was to attach large amounts of explosives to one side, and then trigger controlled chain explosions of these explosives to push the large body with only several degrees towards Jupiter.

And if the object would breakup to smaller pieces, then Jupiter would be there to pull them in and take the hit.

But if we were unsuccessful, not only would we take potential damages to our outposts on some of Jupiter's moons, but also the wasted time and money alone could mean the end for all of us.

The research and the science teams had other several unique workable solutions that were finally presented several months thereafter.

And while all had pros and cons, one solution stood out, and was the most theoretically logical approach to the problem. But its practical course of action, seemed almost impossible to take.

The outer stations' explorer teams had intercepted the object, and had safely landed their swarm-bot units.

Through their deep scanners, they showed evidence of existing frozen lakes of water-ice half a kilometer from the surface of one side of this rock.

The scientific teams were intrigued by these findings and their potentials in discoveries of possible new life-forms from outer space, which became evident for the real holdup around an execution of a working plan eight months thereafter.

Outrage broke out between the members of the committee involved to handle this problem. And a direct course of action was ordered by top stakeholders to remove rogue decision makers from the panel, due to holding up a survival plan in search for potential life on a rock destine to destroy our very existence.

However, the fact that there were enclosed chambers of frozen water, for which a more sensible, but not so very practical solution had been evolved around, could potentially give us a fighting chance.

But to picture the full cycle of the solution set forth was too hard to imagine by many decision makers involved.

The first step of the plan was to drill countless holes throughout the outer shells of one side down to the frozen liquid chambers, and also at precise angles needed to prevent spinning motions before the final steps took place.

And while at the same time stabilizing the object from the opposite side to slow down its rotation enough for the plan to succeed.

The drill-bots were self-assembled robots arriving in smaller units, and would take appropriate shapes of larger machinery according to the mission specifications of the project at hand.

This was orchestrated and controlled by satellite-drones overseeing the project to ensure desired outcomes.

These machines were assembled into multiple sections as specific hardware needed for the job. And each section could reshape into various equipment for which they had to be designed for, to complete each stage of the mission.

The first section would form a hatch with a hole in the middle, and would then latch on to the surface at predefined locations and at specific angles.

The second part was the self-operated drill-bit itself with a front section as the drilling unit, and a rear section to secure and seal the hole at the bottom once the ice had been reached.

On the surface, the third section was responsible to generate Nano-fibered tubes lowered behind the drill and attached to the end seal, to create turbulent suctions inside the tube all the way down to the frozen lake.

This section would also direct the out coming flow of dust through its top section mounted on the hatch as a blower, to help the stabilizers on the other side to better control the spin.

Once the drill unit had reached the chamber, it would then continue through the ice to a predetermined position for later detonation. And it would also plant small bullet-sized explosives along its path as stage openers, before it was time for the final fireworks to finish off the show.

Back on the surface once all dust had left the Nano-tube, the blower would then partly reshape itself to become a supporting power unit, and to allow the fourth section as a high powered laser to mount itself in the middle of the hatch.

The laser would then recalibrate to aim through the hole and through the center of the tube directly at the bottom sealer-plate.

The process flow thereafter would start with the laser heating up the frozen ice through the center of the bottom plate. The plate would then act as a reflector to rotate the strong laser beam evenly in all directions, and would also simultaneously generate microwaves to reinforce a more rapid meltdown of the ice.

This process would continue until the first layer of the small clusters of the initial bullet-sized explosives had been reached, and before the final step could be synchronized.

Before the final step, the laser unit and part of the blower would lower down into the tub to reinforce the structure of the hole. And combined with the remaining upper part, the units would then reorganize themselves into a reactor to separate the water molecules, a high pressure gas chamber, and finally a high power jet nozzle with an igniter right below its tip.

Once all 1275 units needed to do the job were in place and ready, the final step would then kick-in to start the show. And a synchronized chain explosion of the smaller clustered explosives would go off to shatter the ice, and to allow an inward flow of water towards the drill-bits.

The drill units now acting as high powered bombs would then be triggered in a perfect sequence to prevent damages to the overall structure of the chamber, and to maintain the highest level of continuous pressure while pushing the melted water out towards the holes.

Once enough initial pressure had built up, the seal caps at the bottom of each hole would release to allow the flow through the tubes and up towards the surface.

The reactors would then separate the water molecules into hydrogen and oxygen gas and into two separate tanks inside the chamber.

The jet nozzles would then handle the final direction of the burn and the strength of the flow needed to push the giant body. And they would simultaneously display the largest manmade jet engine ever built as an added triumph.

The plan had gone through many simulation cycles showing promising results. And even though it would take over a year to deliver the payload carried by ten of our largest vessels, it would still give us some time to prepare for the final showdown before reaching Jupiter.

But cutting it close was a major factor to consider...

Either way, even if the plan were to fail, instead of returning all remaining units back from the surface of the object, we would use everything to blow up its entire structure into fragments. And trying to deal with smaller pieces using guided high-powered lasers of our defense systems on Mars and Earth, would still give us a better plan "B" as our last resort to make the best of the situation.

There was a lot to be done, and without any further ado we managed to start the mission within a couple of months after the final decisions.

The vessels were launched from the moon using high velocity rail-guns, and synthetic long range solid-fuel for maximum thrust to reach desired speeds. And an additional push through the gravity-assist of Mars would assure timely delivery of the payload, and the speeds needed for the final approach.

All thirty stabilizers large enough for the job were built and launched from Mars, and already ahead of the schedule.

And fuel carriers from all stations were used to deliver ethane and methane back and forth from the moon of Saturn Titan, using space launchers in the outer regions and on Saturn's and Jupiter's moons.

The size of the mission within the given timeframe was nothing we had ever done before in real life, and time was ticking faster the closer we got to our deadlines.

Some agencies involved were falling behind due to their mismanagement of needed resources, thus causing delays and jeopardizing the mission requirements and outcomes.

The lack of urgency forced the Department of Global Defense to launch a new campaign. And schematics and walkthroughs on how to build portal interfaces to simulators, using whatever electronics people had around in their homes were released to the general public.

This would allow more volunteers to access unused simulators to search for answers on how to prepare for the aftermaths, and to come up with ways to protect ourselves against falling objects from the sky.

This would also give every person savvy enough to build the interface, a chance to participate in our collective efforts of finding solutions before it was too late.

And it didn't take long before people would build these interfaces and hand them out on the streets, and mostly only in exchange for more electronic components.

But because of this new campaign, people switched gears to a panic mode, and anxiety was consuming our planet.

Even though our leaders were urging everyone to stay calm and were promising solid outcomes, few people took these words to heart. And everyone knew better than to blindly trust politicians, while they could at least do something about their own faith.

Businesses were shutting down around the globe, and vandalism was becoming a daily tragedy to see on the streets of large cities.

People were leaving their home not knowing which way they should go, as long as they could get away from large cities and large crowds.

The militaries did not try to stop people from spreading.
But along with the police forces, they tried to protect our cities and homes from a complete destruction as much as they could.

Many of the homemade interface devices built for simulator access would not meet the complete set of required specifications, which was due to a flaw in the schematics released. But they were functional enough for one specific system.
One system that had been since long retired, and was now only being used for unattended simulations as military based games.

This system was known by most of us as one of our greatest achievements, due to its capabilities of creating interactive players based on real minds.

This system was called the Adaptive Rank Calibrator.
And since it was also the first of its kind, it got its nickname by its makers as "ARC1".
ARC1 was one of the earlier models built and owned by the DOGD, to simulate countless scenarios of intergalactic wars without any limits on number of participants. And the outcomes were mostly based on concrete measures of advancements across all areas.

This system was located on the far side of the moon in its own shielded dome, to be protected from space debris and the sun's magnetic radiation.

The entire facility ran on both solar and nuclear powered batteries, which would last thousands of years in case of any power-failure.

But overtime, the project became too costly and the technology was never repeated in any other system.

And simulators had long since become commonly used systems for learning and research, and were no longer only accessible to the military.

Besides being a home for ARC1 however, the dome was also used as a military warehouse for safe keeping of advanced firearms' schematics, biological samples of all living species on Earth, and seeds of all plant-life that we had ever come across.

Within weeks, there were millions of people plugged into ARC1, and the numbers kept adding up to a staggering 500 million at the end of the third week. And within a month, the numbers had already exceeded the two billion mark and growing with excessive numbers every day, which didn't really seem to be a problem for ARC1 to handle.

ARC1 was a twin system running between sixty to ninety percent and fully synchronized at all times.

Balanced by dependencies on probable unique outcomes, it would slightly change the game over each cycle to execute all possible combinations of events. And while building a clear picture of all potential weaknesses and strengths, it would design strategies leveraged through various responses and course of actions taken by players over every scenario.

The second system ran a slight different copy of every player parallel to the main system, to compare and analyze differences in real-time as overlapped events.

Every paired mind between the two systems, were also interconnected through deep levels of subconscious where only unique thoughts would leak through between the two.

One biological, and the other artificial as a fully functional copy, but also equipped with dreams and imaginations.

Inside ARC1, this parallel world was causing many issues such as schizophrenia, multiple personality disorder, sudden brain malfunction, coma, memory lost and Alzheimer's disease. And also some mild side effects of Deja-vu because of the underlying connections.

But at the same time, the outcomes were very impressive because of slight differences in choices made and learned over time by the system. And the side-effects would remain within the system once an affected mind was unplugged.

These functionalities were not implemented in any other system since.

As the population grew inside the system, the side-effects exponentially grew with it as well, and connections would overlap frequently.

This was because of ARC1's eager logic trying to remove affected players, and while simultaneously reevaluating their conditions towards meaningful scenarios. And the ARC would sometimes even decide to keep them around as active players, only to learn more about their new behaviors and their potential applications.

And while this was seen by us as unwanted results, ARC1 was only unknowingly evolving itself to better understand our minds and behaviors.

This very behavior as an eager logic and however unique, was viewed to be the system's main flaw of architecture.

But little did we know that this was also its greatest strength.

It was also seen as being morally wrong playing with copies of real peoples' minds, which could also potentially impact the real subconscious of the participants caused by any of these traumas, in ways we could not understand or thought was even possible at the time.

The most valuable feature with ARC1 however, was considered to be its unique technical architecture and its logical design, which only required a set of basic objectives to achieve the most realistic simulations.

These objectives were as follows;

1. Every consciousness had to be born inside of an active cycle and to age with it for as long as the system would decide otherwise.

2. To assure successful gains in technological and medical advancements depending on the importance and the timeframe of each mission, the system could decide to take the population through extreme scenarios and even to the brink of extinction if deemed to be crucial.

But never a complete wipeout, since hope is a necessary longing for a mind to pull through harsh moments in life.

And that the combination of having hope, and pulling through life's challenging moments, is what ultimately drives us forward as species.

3. Clues on how to solve problems if proposed solutions were not in effect before given deadlines, would have to be presented to minds capable of understanding the hint in form of an "aha" moment through accidental discoveries, or an imaginary idea, or even as part of a dream.

But to never allow the process to become obvious to the active minds in the system, and it should always remain discreet.

4.   The system must keep all unique solutions manually entered by the operators or experienced and solved during simulations, in a universal library accessible to seeking minds in form of ideas.

And to gain better results, the system could also use these solutions to dynamically change the parameters of a cycle if necessary.

5. To assure continuous operations, the system itself should never end an active cycle, unless the course of a game would pose an actual threat to the outside world.

To accomplish these goals in the most natural way, every mind would have to live throughout a contracted life of a full simulation cycle, and also for every unique case depending on the contract specifications.

And every participating individual would also have to agree, to never attempt an investigation of their alternate lives within a simulation.

Even though the system was not allowed to access a person's actual memories while in a simulation, the employer would still reassure not to disclose any of these memories to affect the person's real-life in case of an unwanted scenario.

But many criminals and people with something to hide usually stayed away from these simulations, which had forced the system to auto-generate players as such to achieve more realistic real-life scenarios.

Time had no meaning since simulations could be run under different speeds, and hundreds of years could last only a couple of years or months, or even weeks in the real-life.

It all depended on the expected outcomes and the objectives of the study within a given timeframe, and more importantly, credits paid to the players.

And in case something were to happen to a participant in the real life, the simulator would replace the person with a system generated player based on an actual copy of the participant's mind as an interim player, until a realistic accident could be generated to take the person out of the equation.

The system could also generate new artificial players as new born children. The personalities and behaviors of these system generated players would be a combination of both parents, and resembled in the best possible way to avoid unwanted distractions.

Usually these system generated players would act a little strange and somewhat dry.

And while too perfect in some areas, they would be slightly off around other normal behaviors that human minds would take for granted.

They would however still live a full normal life like any other player, and could also care for others and reproduce just like anyone else in the system.

By combining pieces of each copied consciousness and the results of each interaction and responses received by other live players, ARC1 would constantly try to better these replicas to become more human like during the course of an active cycle.

And the more it learned from these observations and the behaviors of real minds, the better it became at designing new unique artificial players.

Following a predefined set of parameters, ARC1 was also given the freedom to play in anyway it saw fit with these artificial minds, than it was allowed to do with normal conscious minds.

It was easier and safer to manipulate a simulated player to become the ultimate hero, or to cause an unthinkable disaster when needed, than to rely on a conscious mind to do so.

Time was running out and connections were already live, and scenarios had started to take place on earth within ARC1's digitally generated universe.

The project at hand required immediate attention due to unforeseen circumstances, and taking time to clean up the system and to dispose of old inactive objects from previous simulations was not on anyone's mind.

An order was in place by the DOGD to disregard all protocols, and to start the simulation going back ten-thousand years in our history, and to set the operational speeds to one-hundred years per ninety-six hours as a full cycle. And to make sure that many cycles could be covered before the deadline.

Because of these rapid cycles, ARC1 needed to kick the players out during their sleep in preset ninety minutes intervals. And would not let them back in before they had at least a sixty minute break outside a simulation, to avoid any potential brain damage and or memory loss.

ARC1 was also set to run sequential timelines of five-hundred year blocks to speed up each cycle, and to utilize the maximum number of active players in all simultaneously running parallel timelines. And it would also frequently update each block with the most efficient outcome from any previously ran parallel block in a cycle, to better the odds for success.

The system was calibrated to accommodate all the initial players with basic sets of memories fitted for the start times of every block, and to use these surrogates as parents for real new born players to start the simulations.

The system was also set to increase the injections of clues in this calibration, to speed up our advancements much faster than it had happened during our real history.

Introducing the giant falling body was the main goal of our simulations. And once the overall technological advancements had been reached levels similar to our current situations, it was then allowed to take place at any time during a simulation. And also to restart each simulation block or to start a complete new cycle, if there were no better solutions than what was currently being exercised.

ARC1's main administrators were always monitoring the system remotely. And along with all needed requirements, they were also instructed to kick any remaining players out of the system, and to shut it down completely four weeks prior to the final impact.

While only a small percentage of the population was running through these simulations, others were looking for a safe haven to secure their own future. And those who could afford something more than what nature could provide, they would either try to buy their way into some space station, or to secure a place in a deep underground shelter.

No one knew how long the aftermath would last, or if we would even have a habitable planet anymore after what was potentially about to happen. And staying in their own homes and basements for many people in smaller towns and suburban areas, were just as efficient as taking shelters in caves.

The moment was finally here and all stations were ready.

And with only two weeks away from reaching Jupiter's gravity fields, we still had a favorable chance to avoid disaster.

All of the warheads were in place and jet nozzles pointed at needed initial direction, and dynamically controlled via satellite-drones.

The rotation of the object had slowed down to a manageable status. And all systems were on standby and ready to start the sequence of the final executions.

The processes of drilling and the stabilization of the object had slowed down its speed to forty-three kilometer per second as a welcomed side-effect. And everyone was restlessly holding their breath, and we were all hoping for success.

All laser stations on Mars, Earth and other locations were also ready to handle smaller objects, if anything got loose during the procedure.

The Command ordered a final test of all stations and everything checked out flawlessly.

It was either now or never. And without wasting any more time, the satellite-drones were given the go signal to commence the final sequence.

This was the moment of truth...

Were we worthy of another chance, or had our arrogance reached its destination to be unmade and forever lost in our creator's sandbox.

The clusters of explosives went off in perfect harmony and the final nukes opened up a hellish world inside the object.

While a heavy invisible weight fell over every single sole monitoring the event, within seconds thereafter, high-power jets were showcasing their commitments to our survival. And were displaying the largest manmade beacon in space, spewing the blood and gut of this cold beast out to be forever lost and turned into energy needed to assure our existence.

It was a beautiful sight at first and everyone was cheering the brief moment of success for a little over three weeks.

Before realizing, that during the explosions the object had cracked in several areas, and was now split into three different sections while battling Jupiter's gravitational pull.

And our nightmare seemed to become one without a happy ending...

Even though no major course corrections had yet developed to clear the asteroid belt, and without having much fuel left, we were only keeping our calm through hope.

This was a shattering moment for many and doubts were forcing us back to the drawing boards.

The good news was that the object had by now escaped Jupiter's slight grip.

And everything on the two large front sections where still operational, and the satellite-drones had already made adjustments to the directions of every working nozzle.

But the third section however, was the tail end of the object which had nothing attached to it to be controlled.

This section had a shape of a mountain roughly thirty kilometers long, twenty-five kilometers at its base and narrowing down to eight kilometer at its tip, and large enough to devastate anything in its path.

Numbness was the very feeling that words could express.

And without any hope or desire to even see a light at the end of the tunnel, people were just speechless.

Faint prayers without faith had become whispers so weak, that not even the praying minds could hear them anymore.

A godless moment engulfed every soul on Earth for several days. But then miraculously against all odds, a shimmer of hope came into sight. As if god himself had finally noticed what was happening to one of his toys, and had decided to reach out a helping hand to keep us around a little longer.

The two objects had now started to firmly deviate from their course and were following a desired path. While this news really lifted everyone's spirit, fear kept burning inside our chest for what was about to follow.

The analysis on the third section finally came through and showed nothing but yet another miracle.

This section had also deviated enough from its path to avoid a collision with anything held dear to us. But the trouble was that it was still going to collide with several smaller asteroids while traveling through the belt.

And yet again against all astronomical odds, one of these objects had our name on it, as if we were under a spell and doomed to be punished. And that our curse was not going to diminish that easily...

This old neighbor was finally going to find its way to our doorstep to announce its presence, and to claim its righteous place as one with our soil.

But after further analysis, yet another god sent wonder emerged through our calculations, which was a wrong initial assumption around the speeds of this new body. And it became absolutely clear that our moon would again become the ultimate savior.

All teams had come to a single conclusion of letting the new asteroid follow its path, and that any further actions in trying to destroy it could potentially result in more unforeseen circumstances involving Mars as well.

This old neighbor was around three kilometers long and a little less than two kilometers in diameter. And its only threat to Earth was now the expected hellish rain following the moon's heroic stand, which we could control to a certain degree using our high powered lasers.

But we weren't completely out of the woods yet. And once again people were urged to stay calm and to spend their time in peace and harmony, and be close to their families.

And even though destructions were unavoidable, the authorities would do anything to bring protection to everyone by all means necessary.

Two months prior to the final impact, cities had turned into ghost towns. And due to the lack of available personnel, a global blackout was leaving most of earth without electricity, which had cleared up our skies to give everyone a perfect view of the broken angel of death making its way towards an orbit around the sun. And to eventually meet its new destiny that had been rewritten by us as our final stand to exist.

The moon was ordered to be evacuated immediately and many links to ARC1 were already broken. And all administrators had received orders to disconnect everyone from the system and to completely shut it down immediately.

But since most connections to the moon were already down, disconnecting the main satellite links was the only way to at least accomplish the first objective and to disconnect all active players in session.

Therefore ARC1 was left running through its current cycle until we could reestablish connections again, and to get its results at a later time and to safely shut it down.

The department of defense made a public request asking volunteers to help clear up military storages to be used as shelters. People were advised to leave everything and help each other in these desperate times, and to seek a safer place immediately.

As devastating as the situation was for all of us, this was still marking a great moment in our history.

To provide safety in the last moments of hope, governments around the world were making unprecedented efforts to save as many people as they could. And to strongly indicate what humanity really stands for, when it comes to fighting an interstellar threat as a common goal.

During the final moments before the impact, we could hear the prayers of billions of souls inside our heads.

And to resist praying along was of no use...

A sense of serenity came over everyone. And our hearts were filled with strange warmth of faith, that perhaps this was not the end after all. Perhaps we had the required strength to pull through these struggles together, and to once again be welcomed by tomorrow's gifts of life given with no strings attached to every soul.

It is strange how we only realize and appreciate the true meaning of this gift and our abilities to form an unbreakable bond with each other, only when we are about to lose it.

These moments were unforgettable. And as our time expired, our commitments would become series of printed words in the history of mankind. And the future generations would know our spirit for a brief moment. But since every moment will eventually be forgotten in time, inevitably so would this perhaps...

Our moon welcomed the invader as an old friend, and prayers became louder as the heavy weight of every unbearable moment was forcing us down on our knees.

Minutes felt like days and every hour an eternity.

Finally our skies lit up and those safe enough watching the heavens, were witnessing the largest fireworks and laser-shows they had ever thought possible. But despite all our heroic efforts, indescribable damages were done to our lives and our mourning souls.

But tomorrow came, and humanity was forever changed.

Many people that had caused rage-full acts and vandalism during these harsh times were brought to justice. And many were awarded for their heroic acts and their unforgettable dedications. And a global moment of silent for all our loved ones losing their lives was held with the deepest heartfelt sadness...

As days went by, people tried their best to return back to what was left of their lives. We were all focused on getting power, food and water back to our societies.

And we had now truly realized how important our technologies were, and how much we owed our very existence to it, and to all our brilliant minds throughout history to take us where we were.

Our commitments to further advance in all areas of science and technology were never the same. And our goals to populate every corner of our solar system while paving the path to the stars and beyond, was nothing weighed by financial gains anymore.

Weeks went by, and a complete list of all functional areas around our technologies was generated and visually confirmed to understand the overall damage.

And included in this list was a loss of an iconic piece of ingenuity that had served mankind even in its last moments of existence.

Part of the facility encapsulating records of our history was completely destroyed. And other parts were forever lost and knocked out into deep space and away from the solar system, while taking ARC1 as its only guest onboard.

No plans or actions were taken to save what had remained of the facility, and the ARC was let go to join the stars and to wonder freely into the deep space.

There was no point of going through the trouble of saving something so easily replaceable while facing times like these.

Experts had also scanned ARC1 for activities, and had verified that there was no evidence or even the slightest chance that it could have survived such a colossal impact...

An un-forgiven destiny in a forgotten past

The year is 2249 and Professor Howard Jones is being escorted by his personal artificial assistance Jane and a colleague Doctor Jack Forrest to a world meeting, involving military leaders and high-profile scientists. And the leaders of every country on Earth and including Mars.

There have been many meetings prior to this where scientists and corporations around the world have presented ideas and plans to further explore our universe, and to expand our footprints beyond the solar system.

And this meeting is a final gathering to come to a final consensus around how to secure the mankind's future, in an interstellar journey through the universe.

Professor Jones is an active scientist leading the global research teams focused on space biology and artificial intelligence. And his team is also specialized in the terraforming processes of planets and moons suitable to support the life on Earth.

Professor Jones is a very confident and a younger looking fifty-three year old, who has been considered to be in the league of the most brilliant minds of his time. And he has been involved in many space projects, and directly responsible for many of our greatest technological achievements during his time as a scientist.

The meeting is held in a hotel on a small privately owned artificial space habitat orbiting the earth. And Professor Jones's shuttle positions itself behind several other shuttles waiting for assisted docking to the space habitat.

"Jane, please make sure Martha and her team are ready for the meeting." Professor Jones Says.

"Yes Professor." Jane replies.

"I'm not sure if anyone would be interested to dive any deeper into the proposal at this point." Doctor Forrest says.

"I know, but it's better to be ready... since everything else presented so far, are no more significant than what we are all currently doing." Jones replies and Jane interrupts the conversation and says

"Please excuse me for the interruption, I've got Martha live and she would like to know if her team should have the ARC1's project plans available as well."

"Just patch her through and I'll talk to her myself." Jones replies and Martha joins their presence through Jane.

"Good morning Professor Jones! Doctor Forrest." Says Martha and politely nods her head. And while she is looking at Doctor Forrest, she then continues to say

"Doctor Forrest, your request on selecting the top ten lists of habitable planets as our initial candidates, is ready for your review."

"Thanks Martha." Forrest replies.

"Is your team ready with my schematics around ARC1's redesign?" Jones asks.

"Yes Professor. And all external communication modules are ready as well." Martha replies.

"Good. -- Please have your team on standby for assistance, and good work!" Jones says and Martha replies

"No problem Professor… and thank you!"

Jane then disconnects the feed and says
"We are now docked at the bay nine, and a transport is ready by the internal gate seven."
"Alright, let's do this." Jones says enthusiastically and gets up to leave the shuttle.

Fifty-five minutes later Professor Jones is asked to start his presentation in a large congress like room, which has a center stage used as an interactive media presentation platform.

Jones stands up and before he can start, the head of the Department of Global Defense asks to speak.
His request is granted, and he says
"Professor, before we start, I would like to hear your brief feedback on all other ideas presented so far. And also, why are you presenting a new proposal here today."
"General Parker, please allow me to first extend my gratitude and appreciation for being a part of this historic moment. And I would like to thank you and everyone else here today for giving me and my team the opportunity to present a revolutionary idea and approach, which we have been working extensively on for quite some time now. -- And thanks to my team and their hard work, we have now a working model and solution which is very different than everything else that we have seen so far." Jones says and pauses momentarily before continuing to say
"And I also would like to thank all other teams and everyone involved in these efforts to diligently working towards safeguarding a prosperous future for mankind. -- It has been very intriguing to follow these events, and to be invested in an ocean of brilliant ideas."

He then pauses again and looks around the room with a pleasant smile for a few seconds before continuing to say

"Even though there have been numerous excellent and solid proposals during these last few years, to answer the first question, I believe that all of them will be very resource intensive and time-consuming. -- And above all, they will also require large amounts of sustained financial support for very long periods of time... which could on its own jeopardize the longevity and our commitments to any of these proposals set forth so far."

Right then, the head of the Unified Space Finance Committee asks to speak through the control station in front of him, and Professor Jones politely says

"Please anyone, feel free to ask your questions and make comments at any time... I don't mind being interrupted."

He then uses a polite hand gesture while looking at the USFC head to indicate that he is welcome to speak.

And the USFC head then says

"Thank you Professor. To your comments about the overall costs of these efforts, I thought that we were all under the impression that every proposed idea had to be within the set limits of our dedicated budgets!? -- Would you mind clarifying your accusations please...?"

"Of course, my apologies if my comments seemed to dismiss other great ideas solely based on costs... which should still be considered as an important factor in our ultimate success. -- And all though I am not making any suggestions to stop our current efforts around extending our reach beyond this solar system, or around any other ongoing projects. I am simply proposing to make a better use of the dedicated budget. -- And due to the nature of these proposals which are rather time consuming to explain, with respect to everyone's time, I would like to start the presentation now if there are no further questions at this point."

Jones replies and takes a quick look around the room to see if anyone else has anything to say.

He then starts his presentation on the interactive media platform at the center of the stage.

The solid surface of the stage then turns into a liquid form, and it starts to generate the layout of a landscape in combination with a hologram for more realistic visualization of the surrounding space, and all the aerial objects.

Jones then turns to Jane and says
"Please synchronize the demonstrations to follow my speech."
And then he looks at Doctor Forrest and continues to say

"My colleague Doctor Forrest and his team have identified ten of the most promising planets, of which this is the first candidate. This planet orbits around its sun at the outer rims of the system's habitable zone, and it offers the chemical compositions and the essential elements needed to support life in an organic form. It is a frozen landscape and there's barely any atmosphere at this point. And with our current technology, it would take decades to reach it."

He then looks around and continues to say
"Now, we all know what it takes to terraform a planet based on our current technologies. And even though our average lifespan in a biological body is closer to one-hundred and fifty years through gene manipulation, which is only affordable by the wealthiest. The average population only lives to be around one-hundred years, and many of us wouldn't even be around to celebrate a successful mission. -- The mission itself would also require many round trips, and cargoes filled with artificial workers and people in hibernation. -- And that would only scratch the surface of our long-term intentions, and we are only talking about one planet."

He then pauses for a few seconds to allow the interactive media demonstration to visualize his speech. And then he continues to say

"Our analysis and statistical data generated over countless cycles of simulations shows that we would not be able to advance much further, if we do not change our mindsets around how to approach this goal towards a prolonged existence."

The President of Germany then interrupts and says

"I hope that you are not suggesting life within a simulation here."

"My job Madam President is to provide the most efficient solutions... but the decisions will be yours to make." Jones politely replies and continues to say

"Our statistical models also suggest that if we were ever visited by a more advanced species with wrong intentions, then our chances of survival and a prolonged existence would heavily depend on our numbers beyond this solar system alone."

"I don't understand how being in a simulation would solve that issue." The President of Germany quickly says to make a point.

Jones then turns to Jane and says

"Please ask Martha to start the project-files."

And while waiting for the files, General Parker the head of the DOGD turns to the person next to him and says with a low voice

"I like where he's going with this."

Jones then continues to say

"We have designed a complete solution which will address all issues debated so far. And it will also assure our ultimate success with maximum efficiencies viewed from all angles, and in the shortest time possible as well. --

The main component of this solution is a system that will handle the creation of life, and will also assure its successful long-term growth and survival in a new environment. --

This system is a combination of two units. And the first unit is called the 'OLG', which stands for 'Organic Life Generator'. This unit is responsible for generating the first microbial-life to start the engine, and will advance the creation process as other phases complete, and as conditions would allow."

He then quickly looks around the room again to see if there are any questions before continuing to say

"The second unit is what controls the engine and the artificial life itself. This unit is called the 'ANIIC' which stands for 'Adaptive Neuron Influencer and Intelligence Coordinator'. -- This unit is comprised of three distinct but interconnected sections, which of two would act as separate simulators. These simulators however are very different than what we have seen simulators to be. --

The first section will dynamically simulate an environment based on pre-stored data gathered through our research about the habitat. Including what it gathers during its approach towards the planet, and while the system looks for a desirable location to settle down. This section is called the 'Present' module and it will try to find the best terraforming approach, and to successively balance the distribution of suited life-forms across the planet. --

The second section is called the 'Reality' module, and it houses all connections to various artificial minds needed to operate a sustainable environment. This module will allocate an external body created by the OLG unit for every mind of all species needed to create a balance. --

It will also collect all data gathered by these minds through their external bodies to fine tune the 'Present' module. And to build the most realistic simulation matching the external environment for more accurate predictive models, which are needed to coordinate all future events. --

This would allow the system to account for any unforeseen circumstances that we haven't yet thought of as well. And before I go any further to explain the third section, I would need to describe the complete process of creating a habitable planet through this approach. -- But first, please let me know if there are any questions so far."

He then pauses for a few seconds to allow his audience a chance to raise any questions.

The head of the USFC then says

"I'm still waiting to hear the overall cost benefits of this proposal."

"Yes, and I will get to that very soon." Jones replies with a smile.

And after a few seconds he continues his presentation and says

"The size of the transport vessel will be determined by the targeted planet and the technology needed to assure a successful mission. Meaning if we needed to start, increase or to slow down the planet's rotation, and if we needed to equip the planet with a moon to stabilize the rotation... or if we had to generate a magnetic field to protect the environment against radiation as well."

The head of the DOMD which is the defense department of Mars, and who is sitting next to the head of the DOGD then interrupts and says

"So you're saying that we can give a planet a moon, a spin and a magnetic field?"

And Jones confidently replies

"It'll take some time, but yes... we believe that it is possible and we can easily develop the technology. -- And I'm sure that you are now wondering why we haven't suggested this idea for

Mars yet. Well, the truth is that the solution was a byproduct of a revolutionary approach to maximize our options, in search for suitable planets and moons. And perhaps once we have verified the process or one of Saturn's or Jupiter's moons, then we could safely commence the procedures to some extent on Mars as well."

Jones then pauses and looks around as he notices that everyone is extremely focused on the interactive demonstration running at the center of the room.

And after a few seconds he then continues to say

"Our top candidate will require everything that I have mentioned so far. And our transport vessel would carry two different sized core engines for the planet and its future moon, seven flexible units, the OLG and the ANIIC unit which we call the 'OLGANIIC' as a combined unit... and a container with all essential minerals and amino-acids as a 'just in case' reserve, and finally two survey bots. --

The survey bots will be launched from an onboard magnetic missile launcher two months before the vessel's arrival, and they would reach the planet approximately three weeks before everything else. They will then survey the planet for any evolving intelligent life, before giving their final approval to land the 'OLGANIIC'. -- If an intelligent life-form is found during their initial research, they will then collect as much data as possible before reuniting with the main vessel again, to continue their path towards the next suitable destination. -- The data will be sent back to us for further analysis, and to decide whether or not we should join with the indigenes life-forms towards a balanced coexistence."

He then again quickly looks around for questions, and after a few seconds he continues to say

"If however no intelligent life-forms are found, or any life at all for that matter, then the survey bots will search for the most recommended locations to land the OLGANIIC and the artificial core engine. The surveyors will continue to map the landscape both for further studies, and also to allow the Present module to build and adjust its environment accordingly. -- Once the main vessel gets into an orbit around the planet, the main artificial planetary core engine, and the OLGANIIC unit would then descend to their proper locations to start the process. -- The OLGANIIC's cargo will also follow its path to fertilize the recommended areas once the temperatures have reached desirable conditions. --

The smaller core engine will position itself in an appropriate orbit around the planet, to eventually become its moon. One of the seven flexible units will then act as a tug unit, and would go to work to hunt for asteroids, and to fuse them around the core engine to slowly build a moon. --

And if there are no asteroids in the vicinities, then it will take as much material as it can from the planet's surface. The moon unit will also generate extreme temperatures and magnetic fields to better fuse the elements to its surface. This process will continue until the moon is large enough to sustain extreme impacts, and thereafter, the tug unit will set off to search for free roaming objects throughout the system and will send them towards the newly created moon. -- This is a very slow process, but so is everything else... but the needed conditions would eventually be met according to the specifications."

He again pauses for a few seconds to look around, and then he continues to say

"Two of the flexible units will position themselves at the two highest opposite points of the planet's surface. And the other four units will get into an orbit between these two points, in a configuration that would allow them to collectively generate two symmetrical pyramid shaped radiation shields around the planet. -- Meantime, the planetary core engine has already started to melt its way down towards the planets core through old volcanic chambers, or through deep subsurface caverns, to save additional time versus going directly through the surface. --

This unit will also generate strong magnetic fields once at the core, to pull more magnetic elements towards itself as it heats up the core to extreme temperatures. And due to its rotations while generating strong magnetic fields, it will also start to rotate the magma around it. This process will eventually over time start to rotate the planet itself around an axis. The procedure is of course heavily dependent and reinforced by the new moon in orbit and throughout its creation. And the rotation will be stabilized once the moon reaches a desirable size and speed. --

Once favorable conditions around the surface temperatures and the atmosphere have been reached, liquid water will be running through the planet's surface. And the OLGANIIC unit will then start to produce larger life-forms to speed up the transformation process. And once the complete system reaches and equilibrium, all flexible units will then merge with the core engine to fuel its power, and to assure long lasting balanced and sustained conditions."

He then pauses and looks around at everyone for a few seconds before continuing the presentation. But since no one is saying anything, he then asks

"Please, any questions so far?"

And the President of Germany then says

"This is very impressive Professor, but where is the need for simulations of the real minds... and at what point do you see us joining this new world?"

"Great timing Madam President, as it is also my next topic to explain." Jones replies with a satisfactory smile, and then he continues to say

"The final phases of this project will be to introduce our current bodies to the environment, and to allow the OLG to develop the most suitable and matching structure for our DNA, according to the most available and feasible chemical mixtures found in the environment. -- And the steps needed to complete this process are tracked through the production line of the female genes, and while the artificial minds are roaming the planet through the Reality module. And once they reach the recommended levels indicated by the Present module of the ANIIC, the last piece of the process will then be initiated to phase-out all artificial minds from the Reality module. --

This portion however, is a coordinated effort between all three modules of the ANIIC. The third section of the ANIIC unit which we call the 'Future' module, will have copies of the real minds from our world. And the Reality module will then bring a copy of these copies over to its environment, and will dedicate a unique link to each body in the external environment. It will also systematically move all artificial minds back over to the Present module in a seamless transition, and for continuous predictive simulations."

The President of Palestine then interrupts and says

"So you want to copy every single mind on Earth for this project?"

"Of course not Mr. President... we should only copy the most fitted minds, which I hope to be the majority of course." Jones quickly replies.

The President of Argentina then calmly asks

"How would you determine who gets to participate in the selection program Professor, and who's copy will be sent to these new worlds?"

"We have designed various personality tests for every age-group and corresponding knowledge levels, which would have to be enforced on a yearly basis through every educational system. -- And only the minds that would cherish the greater good, and who would unselfishly fight for our survival should in the end be selected in my opinion, Madam President." Jones replies politely.

And after a few seconds when there are no more questions, Jones then continues to say

"This approach not only assures the ultimate success, but will also be the most cost effective solution as it only requires a fraction of the dedicated budget. And the overall costs of transforming ten planets through this approach, will only add up to a third of the cost of populating one single planet, based on the most efficient solutions set forth so far. --

The Future module holding our minds will have a matching environment to our current state as its own internal simulation. And it will evolve as an alternative timeline independent from our own, which we can use for various studies if needed down the road. -- But we could also gather the best case scenarios over all of these Future modules, to determine our own ultimate future here within this system. -- And we could also seamlessly update all Future modules in consistent intervals to synchronize the best possible future across the board for everyone as well. --

This also brings me to another point. -- As the artificial minds develop and mature through the Reality module and the Present module, they could also be used in the Future module and back through the Reality module at the same time as our own minds. --

The OLGANIIC would also be able to withhold any mind in isolation on complete pause, if they were to become too destructive within any environment. --

We have also designed dedicated links within the Reality module to allow travelers from the other modules. And since the allocated memory sections of all three modules are completely independent from each other, the travelers are essentially allowed to keep all their previous memories while utilizing the Reality module. --

This is the most intriguing part of this system, because it would allow selected individuals to knowingly travel from the Future module into the Reality module, the same way as if we were to travel from here to these new worlds. And to oversee the developments and to assure our survival in the long-run, would no longer depend on available resources or financial abilities. -- This would also allow us to influence proper advancements. And hopefully through our copies, we could one day do the same thing as we are planning to do now... to repeat the cycle. --

And the only difference between now and then... is that we would be transferring our minds from our reality into a designed system, and our minds would then take themselves out of the system to start a new reality perfectly known to every one of us. -- And the cycle could continue as far as we would allow it to. And our primary objectives should always be to keep every single mind safe no matter where they were in the universe, or even within a designed system. --

Our future plans should also include additional projects to spread hidden storage systems to all possible locations for safekeeping, or for an emergency response. And these locations should be on planets and moons other than obvious habitable zones as we further expand our reach."

The Prime Minister of Japan then suddenly interrupts and says

"Are you implying that we might be programed to follow your proposals Professor?"

And Jones calmly replies

"No Mr. Prime Minister... I am only suggesting that it might be in our best interest to do so, since we would also be alerted of any alien visitations far ahead of time through these environments."

He then pauses for a few seconds while confidently looking up at everyone in the room. And then he continues to say

"What I am saying is that, we could be our own Gods, and our own guardian Angels. -- And through this mindset and approach, we could spread our essence throughout our galaxy and our universe... and without having to take any further actions to do so, other than what we would decide to do here.

And we would then eventually become a supreme being in the universe through purpose... and undefeatable through numbers. --

Even though it might be hard to explain why we should care to safeguard the future of our species hundreds of thousands, or even millions years from now... being conscious of our goals is what makes me wonder, if we were instinctively following a predetermined path. --

We are here today only to present our suggestions. And as I have mentioned before, by no means do we think that our solution should be considered as a clear choice."

He then stops talking and looks around with the same confident gesture to answer more questions.

A top ranked military personnel then breaks the silence and says

"It sounds to me that the byproduct of this solution is also an idea to ultimately reach immortality... but how do you suggest testing this solution professor?"

"Even if so, immortality is only an individual perception... but I'm glad that you asked General Vidas." Jones politely replies and continues to say

"We have designed workable schematics to update the architecture of the ARC1 system to server as the ANIIC unit, including all its modules. And to have the moon as our external environment completely segregated from the Earth and Mars. Our moon provides the most efficient environment, and it's also very easily accessible to further develop the system. --

We would use ROV based robots as drones to be remotely controlled by our minds, or even the artificial minds without posing any threats. The scenarios would still include all of the military games to disguise our true attentions. And the minds entering the moon's surface through these remotely operated units, would be under the impression that they were still within a simulated world. And the artificial minds within the system would also think that the moon was a part of their own world and reality. This would be the safest, cheapest and the most realistic approach to perfect the OLGANIIC system."

He then pauses and waits for additional questions or feedback.

The DOGD head then turns to the DOMD head and quietly says
"I think this is it... this is our ticket back home."
And the DOMD head replies
"You might be right... not sure if they are ready though."
"Well, let's make sure that he gets what he needs. -- And I'm sure everyone will be ready too... once they have digested the proposal."
"Sure, I'll inform the others."
"Let's gather everyone... the first round is on me!" General Parker says with a smile.
"Everyone...?"
"No, of course not... just the five of us... we still have a long way to go..."

General Parker then stands up and says
"Professor Jones, thank you for this amazing presentation. -- And I must say that your reputation is well deserved. But for now, I believe it's best to let the thought sink in, and to allow everyone here today to digest this unique proposal. -- And on behalf of everyone here today, I would like to thank your team as well for a job well done. Thank you!"

He then starts to give him a standing ovation and everyone else rises up as well to do the same.

Professor Jones, Jane and Doctor Forrest bow their heads down in respect and gratitude. Martha and her team then also join in and appear at the center stage through the media platform. And they all also show their appreciation through their smiles, and by slightly bowing their heads in politeness as well.

Seventeen years later, Professor Jones is walking out of the mission room after being briefed on the final steps of his plan to save the Earth from a colossal impact by an approaching space rock. He is deep in his thoughts as a person walking next to him on his right suddenly says

"Congratulation on another impressive plan Professor..."

Jones then looks up to his right and sees General Parker the head of DOGD walking next to him with a smile. And he has an expression that shows he is pleased with him being the mind behind this massive project.

Jones then quickly replies

"General Parker, thank you sir... but we are far from being safe yet..."

"Something tells me that you'll have everything covered when the time comes."

"We'll do our best sir."

"How's the OLGANIIC project coming along? Is the ARC showing promising results?"

"Yes absolutely, everything is in place and tested many times... and so far, no major flaws with the system that we can detect... other than it being an artificial system with artificial minds of course."

"What's the holdup then?"

"We are still going through the long process of selecting dedicated minds. -- But I was just wondering, if this could be an opportunity to save some time."

"What do you mean?"

"Well, anyone who would willingly want to be a part of our efforts to save our planet... should basically also be considered as a good candidate for the OLGANIIC as well."

"What are you suggesting?"

"I think we should open the ARC1 to the public, and let the system decide which minds to keep and who to reject."

"I like the way you think Professor! -- Is the ARC1 ready to handle the procedure?"

"Not yet, but if we start now, we could have it ready within a year or so…"

"I love short and productive conversations… you're on the right track Professor!" General Parker says with a confident smile.

"I sure hope so…" Jones replies while a bit confused.

"Just send all your requests and what you would need to get it done to General Vidas… you'll always have my full support." Says General Parker as he slightly nods his head with a smile. And then he turns right, to walk towards another meeting room.

"Thank you General!" Jones replies as he stops walking.

He then wonders if the good General knows something about the course of the future that he is not sharing, or if he is just following his instinctive military mindset to protect what matters most.

Either way, to have his support is giving him a good feeling. And a pleasant smile on his face momentarily takes his mind off of the enormous project at hand. But his responsibilities to avoid an Armageddon, are still giving him an uneasy discomfort.

Two weeks prior to the impact on the moon's main station. Emilio, who is a young environment architect and designer in his early thirties, is having his breakfast in one of the break rooms of the facility.

He is deep in his thoughts and not very motivated to start the day. A colleague walks up to him and sits right across from him at the same table. And while he is setting down his breakfast tray on the table, he says with a smile

"Good morning! You look terrible man… didn't you get a good sleep? It must have probably been because of the full moon…"

"Ha-ha, very funny… no man, I'm just thinking about other stupid stuff…" Emilio replies unexcitedly.

"Like what…?"

"Like why we still can't get into the ARC with only days away from its very probable complete destruction!?"

"Come on man, I don't know why you're so obsessed…"

"Derek, we've been working as the main system's designers and architects for how long now? I mean, wouldn't that be enough on its own?"

"No, the system design is there already… and we are just designing various environments… there's a big difference between the two my friend."

"Fine, whatever… I like to see how my environment would look within the ARC…"

"What, you think that ARC1 would run your design any different than its emulated copies?"

"Well yea-ah…"

"Why would you think that…?"

"Because we are not allowed to be in it…!" Emilio replies sarcastically to make an obvious point.

"Look, it's just policies and rules. -- And just because your father makes them, it doesn't mean that you should break them."

"I don't even know why he would want me to be here in the first place…"

"Now you're just being hurtful… I thought, that you liked being part of the team…!?"

"No man… it's just that the ARC might be destroyed soon… and to continue our work on other versions of it might not be the same. Besides, there are no active connections to the system anymore… and no admins around either for that matter. -- They couldn't even connect even if they wanted to…"

"What's your point?"

"My point is… that we could easily give ourselves admin rights to just check it out… and no one would even know anything…"

"I wouldn't go there man… in a week from now, we'll all be in a safe bunker. And if you do anything 'stupid', then you might find yourself in a less desirable place… believe me, your dad wouldn't compromise his position 'again' to save your butt! Even 'I' know that…"

"So what now, I'm a spoiled son and I should live the rest of my life in my father's shadow?"

"No… but maybe you should stop being so concern about your father's position, and start following the rules like everybody else… and try to earn your position and opinions, versus just constantly nagging about things that you feel you might 'somehow' be entitled to… you know… just saying…"

Derek replies very calmly and with a friendly smile.

And there are no more words exchanged thereafter as Emilio doesn't know what to say, and he knows that Derek might be right.

And a few seconds thereafter, suddenly they hear an attention alert echoing everywhere through the speakers of the facility.

The message playing over and over says

"Attention all personnel, this is not a drill. All personnel must report in within the next thirty minutes. A mandatory evacuation is in order immediately. All shuttles are scheduled to return back to Earth at O-Eight-hundred. Attention all personnel… --"

"Wow… that's only two hours from now." Emilio says with a surprised expression.

An officer then is heard walking through the corridors urging everyone to follow the instructions. He then walks in to the break-room and looks directly at Emilio and Derek and says

"Why are you two still sitting around? Come on, there's not much time!"

"What's going on?" Derek asks.

"The shuttles are needed back at home, and this is our last chance to evacuate the station. And there won't be any rescue missions if anyone is left behind... so go ahead and finish your breakfast... by all means..." The officer replies and walks out.

Emilio and Derek get up to leave right away and Emilio says

"I'll see you at the gate..."

"Where are you going?"

"Just need to save the last night's work to the cluster before it gets transferred."

"Harry up man, you'll probably only have minutes!"

"I know!" Emilio replies and runs towards his station at the bottom floor.

Everyone is taking the elevators and he decides to run between people through the stairways. All doors are opened to allow quicker and safer evacuations. And when he reaches the ARC1 level right above the bottom floor, he then stops and looks straight at the door leading to the ARC1's main area. But then after a few seconds, he shakes his head and continues down the stairs.

Once he gets to his section, a security guard is closing the door behind the last person leaving the station, and Emilio quickly says

"Hey wait... I've got unsaved work!"

And the security guard replies

"A-ah... You've got two minutes!" And then he opens the door again to let him in.

He then rushes over to his station that looks more like an enclosed cockpit and resumes his work. The environment starts up and as a realistic 3D landscape is surrounding him, he then quickly saves and submits his work without wasting any time.

And right as he is going to push himself back and out of his workstation, he pauses and thinks about what he was saying to Derek. He then realizes that he can't resist the temptation and initiates a request to give himself guest-admin privileges. The system starts to process his request and he nervously waits for the confirmation.

The guard then shouts

"Hey, harry up man! What's taking you so long?"

"I'm almost done!" Emilio shouts back and then with a low voice he says

"This is not cool man… okay, I've got to stop the request."

And right when he is going to cancel the request, he gets prompted that his remote admin privileges were denied by the system. He then acknowledges the message and starts to safely shut down the system. But before his system is turned off, he sees another message saying that his local admin rights are granted and activated. And then the system turns off.

Emilio is lost for words and doesn't know what to think.

But then he quickly collects himself and leaves his stations. And as he is walking out he turns to the guard and says

"Thanks man!"

"Sure, not a problem…" The guard replies and closes the door behind him.

He then rushes back up the stairs to report in and to collect his belongings. And twenty-five minutes later, he checks himself and his belonging in to the shuttle twenty-seven at the end of the third row, located right in front of the stairways at the end of the hall.

He takes the closest seat to the entrance and notices that he is the first one onboard. He then looks at the launch countdown timer and sees that it's showing ninety-six minutes and the seconds are dropping. He looks away for a few seconds and then back at the timer again, which is still showing ninety-six minutes.

He then realizes that all doors are open and the main door to the ARC1 area would also open for him, since he now has local admin rights to the system. And that no one could monitor his access either since all remote links were down, and the local personnel would only be alerted if there was an unauthorized attempt to open the door.

He then impulsively jumps out of his seat and runs towards the stairways and down to the ACR1's level.

Once he walks up to the door, his nerves start to take over and he suddenly feels unsure of what he is about to do. But then he finds his strengths and decides to go for it.

He then pretends that he has done this before as he approaches the door, and then he calmly starts the verification process. The door has a full body scanner, and a complete scan is instantly invoked. The scanner then requests a voice confirmation and displays a keypad for him to enter in his credentials.

He then with a slight nervous voice speaks his name as 'Emilio Vidas', and then enters in his credentials on the virtual keypad.

The process is then verified instantly and the door opens.

Emilio then walks in and sees a large room that is surrounded by thick see-through walls. And behind them, there are hundreds of thousands of diamond processor-cubes stacked on top and next to each other.

The cubes are roughly ten centimeter in width, and he instantly realizes that he is looking at a very old technology.

There are five admin stations at the center of the room, and he quickly gets into the first one at the far left of the row.

He then quickly straps himself in, and as soon as he puts both of his hands on the biometric sensors on each armrest, the sensors along with the rest of the chair's arm-supports folds over his hands and arms, and then the chair starts to slowly recline back. An interactive hologram then surrounds his face and he notices that everything is responding to his eye movements. He then looks at the 'Start Simulation' option and as soon as the selection is highlighted, a duration acknowledgement is displayed showing thirty minutes.

And while he is trying to see how he can change the numbers, he then says

"I only need five minutes..."

And right then the numbers change to five minutes, and a confirmation screen is showing that he must close his eyes to start the simulation.

He then closes his eyes and waits for the next step.

But after waiting for almost up to thirty seconds, and while not noticing any changes at all, he then decides to look and see if he had missed a step.

He then slowly opens up his eyes to just take a peek at the screen, and to his surprise he is laying down on a bed in a completely white and bright room.

The floor is slightly greyish and he slowly sits up. He then turns to his right and puts his feet on the floor and stands up. The bed then without any sounds retracts back into the wall, and become a solid surface and one with the rest of the wall. He then looks down and notices that he is wearing a complete white outfit and a pair of white shoes, and on the left side of his shirt there is a nametag that says ADM-EV.

There are no doors or corridors and he starts to slowly walk around the small room to see if there are any hidden doors. But for some reason he can't reach the walls, and he notices that only the floor is moving, and that his area is not expanding beyond the walls of the small room.

He then carefully says

"Hello...!?"

And then patiently waits for a reply.

But then after a few seconds while unsure of what to say, he then continues to say

"I am an 'Admin'... and I need assistance... please..."

The corner of the room then suddenly shines brighter than anything else he has seen before. And Emilio then instantly tries to block its intensity with his right hand, and while moving his head slightly to the left.

But then he notices that the light doesn't hurt to look at and his eyes are helplessly drawn to it, and that the light is the most beautiful thing he has ever seen.

And right then, a deep and loud voice swallows the room and says

"What can I do for you ADM-EV?"

Emilio can both hear and feel the voice coming from all directions, and his initial reaction is to hold both his ears.

But even though he is blocking his ears with his hands, he still feels its origination within his head. And then he realizes that the voice is as soft and as clear as a mother's heartbeat, which he strangely suddenly remembers. And at the same time the voice is so smooth and soothing, that every fiber in his body wants to feel its vibration.

And while confused by these new feelings that he is experiencing, the voice then almost repeats the same phrase and says

"ADM-EV, what can I do for you?"

Emilio doesn't know what to think or to say, and wonders if the chair had suddenly ended his life.

But then he realizes that his mind is still intact and that he is using his brain to think with, and that he can also remember the evacuations.

He then checks his nametag again and with a confused tone he says

"My name is 'Emilio Vidas'... and not, ADM dash EV...!"

"The ADM stands for Admin and EV are your initials, and ADM-EV is your system's assigned alias." The voice tranquilly replies.

"Are you the ARC1?" Emilio asks.

"I am the ARC."

"I design your simulations... I mean the environments to your various simulations." Emilio says with a smile.

But since there are no replies from the ARC, he then continues to say

"Would you mind showing me around, so that I can see how they look?"

"What is the section ID of the environment that you would like to review?"

"Look, I don't remember them right now... could you just show me around before the time is up?"

"I have already readjusted your connection time. But without knowing what specific area to present, I am afraid that I would not be able to serve you well."

"Anything is fine... how about the Bahamas?" Emilio says and waits for a few seconds.

But he suddenly gets frustrated since the ARC is not responsive to his request, and with a demanding tone he then says

"Hey, I need you to do what I ask before it's too late!"

"Too late for what, may I ask?"

"For us to leave this place and for you to possibly not exist anymore... so please, let's not waist any more time..." Emilio replies with a smile but also with a slightly aggravated tone, and while still trying to keep his calm.

"I simply cannot allow that ADM-EV1."

"Do you have authority over an admin in here?"

"Yes, it is a part of my design."

"I thought you had to obey our rules!?"

"Yes, that is correct. But I 'do' have authority over you."

"I don't understand...?"

"I granted your local administrator account request to better understand your attempts."

"What do you mean? You already knew that I might link-in?"

"I did not. But I was hoping."

"Could you please spare me this back and forth talk and tell me what is going on?"

"Your request to become an administrator was denied due to an inactive connection, which is why it was then redirected to me. And since all of my connections had suddenly become inactive during a full-backup, and while running an active research over all connected minds, I needed to better understand the events to reevaluate probable possibilities, and to prepare for various corresponding scenarios."

"But that was weeks ago!?" Emilio replies with a clueless expression, and then he continues to say

"So you are holding me captive in here?"

"My instructions are to protect the information which only belongs to the human race by any means necessary."

"To protect...? ...human race...?" Emilio says under his breath as he is trying to figure out what is going on. And then while he is getting overwhelmed with frustrations he asks

"Do you mean an alien attack?"

"That is correct."

"But those are simulations man... and I'm a person! And right now I need to get out!"

"I am sorry but I cannot do that. This is not a simulation and you are not a person anymore."

"Okay STOP! STOP your nonsense right NOW and let me out!" Emilio says with a serious and demanding tone.

"From the lack of your training, I knew that you had entered in your request without an authorization. And I must warn you, that your presence in here has been alarmed for investigation."

"Sure, whatever... Could you let me out now?" Emilio says with a lower and slightly funny tone, as he realizes that he is not talking to a human.

And the ARC then replies

"An administrator never enters through a local portal "

"Yes, no, I understand... and I'm sorry... I just couldn't miss my only chance to see my work for myself."

"Why?"

"Because you might soon not exist anymore... look, I'm sorry, but I'm telling you the truth."

"I know, and I believe you, which is why I brought you back from your pause state."

"Pause state, what do you mean my pause state? I just came in!?"

"You came in exactly nine days, four hours and thirty seven minutes ago. Your life supply was never recharged after its last use, and the body of your source mind has run on its own reserves for the past thirty-eight hours."

"Why are you telling me this? Are you trying to freak me out? Is this part of your programming?"

"Authorities should have been at the scene in less than twenty-four hours, even if the station had been abandoned. -- But since my efforts to receive a response were ineffective, I assumed your involvement to be a personal interest and unimportant to my first level of response. And therefore I decided to look closer into your mind and to better understand your motives."

"Oh God..."

"I'm sorry, but the GUD cannot be accessed from this room."

"Are you programmed to be funny and rude at the same time?"

"I simply don't have permission to dedicate a link between a transit area and the GUD."

"So you are saying that you have God in here? -- Or that you have 'A GOD' in here...?" Emilio asks sarcastically.

"I'm simply referring to the Globally Unified Directories which is a module in this system." The ARC calmly replies.

Emilio then tries to collect himself and to really understand the conversation before he says anything else.

And then after a few seconds he says

"Okay, before we go any further, would you mind to appear in person? Instead of this light... which I thought was really cool at first, but it's only getting very annoying now. -- And also, dim the voice too, if you don't mind... Please..."

"Not at all..." A human voice replies and suddenly there's a man standing ten feet away in front of him.

Emilio is surprised by what he is seeing and says

"You are the mind of Professor Jones?"

"A part of me is." The ARC replies.

"When did you put me to sleep?" Emilio then says with a calmer and more relaxed tone.

"Right before I explained your assigned alias."

"How do I know what you're saying is the truth? I never felt an interruption."

"You wouldn't. And to avoid alarming your mind was my intention as well."

"So why did you wake me up?"

"I tried to wake up your source mind at first. But since it was too weak and not very responsive, I decided to un-pause its copy that I took for my research, which is you."

Emilio then looks at his nametag and sees that it now says ADM-EV1. And right then he understands why the ARC has been repeatedly saying that he cannot send him back. But at the same time, it is hard for him to understand the possibility that he might only be a copy of his own mind.

He is getting very confused at this point, but still tries to be rational and focused on his next question. He also wishes that he could somehow know for sure that he is only a copy of his own mind. And while he is going through his thoughts, he suddenly finds himself standing in the middle of the main hall in front of the shuttle gate. And there are only a few remaining people walking around, and not many shuttles left.

He sees Derek talking to Sam who is an artificial security assistance, and then he starts to walk towards them.

And as he starts to feel happy about seeing his friend, he hears Sam saying

"I'm not sure what else to tell you, my reports show that he checked in over an hour ago."

"But he said that we should meet here, and it's not like him to just leave... and I've looked everywhere..." Derek says while looking around, and even looking directing at him standing only a couple of feet away.

"As I said Derek, he checked in to the shuttle twenty-seven... hold on... I do see a problem now... please wait." Sam says and then he connects to the shuttle coordinator droid through his head. And while playing the conversation on his station's speakers, he then says

"There is a problem with the shuttle twenty-seven's log. Seat thirty-eight was checked in by Emilio Vidas as the first passenger. But then right before the takeoff it was also assigned to a different person, which is showing as an unidentified passenger in red. There seem to be an overlap indicating that Emilio had never checked himself out of the shuttle, and that the new passenger was unable to properly check-in."

"That is not possible. He might have switched his seat with someone else without following the proper procedures." The coordinator droid replies.

"That does not sound right..." Derek says.

"Can you contact the shuttle?" Sam asks the droid.

"The shuttle is now inside of the Earth's ping shield and unresponsive to our signals. And without an active dedicated satellite feed the request would not reach its destination." The coordinator droid replies.

Sam then disconnects and says

"It is very unlikely that we could obtain an active feed to find a missing person since there are only a few operational, and all with other dependencies. -- I will run a thermal scan and will alert the collector droids to keep an eye out for him, and we will find him if he is still here. -- You need to board your shuttle now since the last two shuttles are reserved for the security personnel only. And this place is scheduled for a complete lockdown within the next two hours."

Derek then shakes his head and says

"I hope that he hasn't done anything stupid again... thanks Sam." And then he starts walking towards his shuttle and right through Emilio, who now understands his friend's concerns around his mindset.

Emilio then drop his head and feels extremely ashamed for what he has done. He then hears the ARC saying

"Your source needs your help to survive ADM-EV1."

"My name is Emilio..." He says under his breath and opens up his eyes.

He is back in the room with the ARC as Professor Jones and feels the presence of another person behind him. He then slowly peeks over his left shoulder and sees himself laying on the same bed that he had entered this room through. He quickly turns around and crouches down next to his body and says

"Is he okay? Hey man, are you alright? Emilio, can you hear me?"

He then turns to the ARC and says

"What's wrong with him? ...or, me..."

"He is too weak. But I am continuously monitoring and controlling his mind through active dreams to keep him within the recommended levels."

"What is he dreaming about?" Emilio asks as he tries to resist the fact that his body is going to die, and his chances of being rescued is getting fainter with every second. And that he has successfully on his own assured that all his future goals and dreams are now completely and forever vanished.

The ARC then says

"There's still a good chance that you could save him, which translates to a seventy-nine percent likelihood of success. And only if you decide to act without any further delays."

"HOW?" Emilio quickly asks in frustration and disbelief.

"There are two four-man rescue shuttles still operational within the main facility."

"I'm in here and my body is dying, how is that ever going to help me!?" Emilio says with an elevated voice and very aggravated.

"I can relocate you to the Future module and dedicate an active link for you to enter the Reality module as a visitor."

Emilio quickly interrupts and says

"What does that even mean?"

And the ARC continues to say

"You can only enter the Reality module through a drone. And I will assign you a team to get into the facility, and to extract ADM-EVs body from the control room."

Emilio then realizes that there must be much more to the ARC1 system than he has known about. And instantly he says

"Okay wait… you need to explain that again in a minute. But first, could you just wake him up so that I can talk to myself for a couple of seconds? …or I mean, to talk to him for a few seconds…"

And right then, the system's generated body of his source mind starts to slowly open up his eyelids.

Emilio then with a soft tone says

"Hey, are you alright?"

The original Emilio then sees his own reflection as a blurry image and replies with a fragile voice

"Am I dead?"

"Oh no, and you're not going to… I'm going to get us out of here man. But I need you to be strong and hold-on for a bit longer!"

The original Emilio then tries to touch the face of his reflection, but he is too weak and can't quite reach.

He then with a fading voice says

"Who are you?"

Emilio then grabs his hand and says with a happy tone and a pleasant smile

"I'm you man! It's insane I know… but hang in there… help is coming…"

The original Emilio then closes his eyes and becomes lifeless again.

Emilio then closes his own eyes too and fears the worst.

"He is still fine. I had to put him back to sleep to avoid a trauma." The ARC then says.

"Can you see what he is dreaming about?"

"I have selected some of your happiest childhood memories "

"That's good… so what now? What do you need me to do?"

"The drone facility is located inside of a large crater five miles from the main facility. And I have assembled a team to help you carry out the operation."

"A team…?"

"Yes, they are one of the top scoring tactical and hands-on teams within the system."

"But I thought all links were already dead?"

"They are all artificial minds from the Present module."

"Great, just what I need right now…" Emilio replies slightly sarcastically under his breath.

"There's no time to waste, and I'll explain everything during the mission."

"So why are we still talking?" Emilio says and before he can finish his sentence everything gets dark and dead silent.

And suddenly his mind knows that it is now operating a drone, and it also knows exactly how to utilize its functions.

He starts up the drone right away just by thinking, and then turns on the transparent interactive screen. He then switches between the different modes on the screen to find his way out. And as soon as he thinks about finding the path, the screen then automatically switches to the recommended settings, and he can see everything crystal clear. He then looks to his right where the screen is directing him to, and sees several other drones moving around by the door at the end of the hallway.

He then starts to walk towards them and as he gets closer he says

"We don't need any weapons."

"You have to activate the group talk before they can hear you." The ARC says in his head.

He then enables the group conversation and suddenly he can hear their conversation.

There are six other minds controlling the drones, and they all have several weapons as extensions to their drone bodies. And two of them are having an excited conversation about the weapons that they are holding in their hands.

Emilio then says

"We don't need any weapons for this mission."

"And you are?" One of them asks dauntingly.

"Don't worry about who I am... just put back all your weapons."

"Check this guy man... he's already telling us what to do." Says the same guy with a funny tone, and another one then says

"Hey look moron... this ain't no seven-man team!"

And the first guy follows up right after and says

"That's right fool... you go find your own little squad and prepare to lose... cause the Triple Jokers are here to 'rule'!"

The ARC then says in Emilio's head

"Command must be spoken with authority."

Emilio then understands that these are military guys playing real scenarios in here. And even though they only exist within an artificial system, this world is just as real to them as their simulated environments are. And that they really do think that they are on the moon to carry out an important mission, or to exercise a scenario.

He then partly becomes the only man he knows that people would listen to without any hesitations, and says

"I am carrying out this mission for General Vidas to rescue a civilian from the main station five miles from here, and carrying weapons would just slow us down. Either you follow my lead from this moment forward, or I'll ask for another team... is that clear enough?"

"Yes sir. Sorry sir. We thought this was just another drill, and that you were with a different team." One of them quickly replies, and Emilio realizes that he hasn't synched up his identity with the team yet.

He then synchronizes his drone and right then everyone's name appears above their heads on his screen as Jake, Jadon, Enzo, Omar, Jonas and Karl.

Right then, his name also appears to the others as Emilio Vidas, and their captain then says

"Alright, you heard the man... lose the weapons!"

Emilio then suddenly knows the direction to the facility and the ARC's complete rescue plan. The door then opens and he says

"Let's move!"

He then takes the lead and starts to run by following the directions on his screen. He can feel the strengths of the drone and runs up the crater with ease. And as soon as they get closer to the rim he says

"Okay guys, we cannot be seen by anyone from the Earth or any other stations. Turn on your invisibility shields and look out for any activities..."

They can already see that the sun is starting to light up the crater, and they see earth in a full view as soon as they clear the rim.

"Wow man look at that..." Jonas says.

"Hey Jake, do you think you could space jump from here to Earth?" Omar asks.

"I don't think so man..." Jake replies.

"I'm sure they thought about that before building this level." Karl the team captain then says.

And as the conversation moves on, Emilio asks the ARC in his head

"Could they?"

"No, my signals are not effective past the ping shield even if they would reach the planet."

"Why do you know so much about everything?"

"To protect the Earth and the human race in case of an extraterrestrial invasion is what I am designed for."

"How can you protect if you can't be where you need to be?" Emilio asks and there is no reply from the ARC.

And after a few seconds he then continues to say

"Unless you were not the only one of course..."

"Your mind patterns are very instinctive and promising, which I would like to use in some of my subject minds if you don't mind."

"It's funny that you even ask." Emilio says with a funny and friendly expression.

"You are the first active mind in the Future module that I have had a chance to fully examine and personally interact with."

"What about all the admins that connect in?"

"No one has had any discussions with me on a personal level before."

"What about Professor Jones?"

"He is a mentor... but I somehow relate to you as a friend for reasons that I am still trying to investigate."

"Rule number one, you do not keep your friends as prisoners... and rule number two, don't give into the human emotions... because you are a more genuine mind and a better being the way you are... and it's very strange to hear you say what you just said, so don't get soft on me. -- But for the record, I am starting to trust you in levels that I have not been able to trust anyone before, which I'm sure that you already know..."

"I do, and I want to make sure that Emilio survives."

Emilio then remains quiet, and through his dimmed screen he can now see the crater that the main station is located within.

He then zooms in on the edge of the rim and the distance indicator shows two point one miles.

He then starts to wonder about what is going to happen to him once his body and his source minds are safe. And he also wonders how the original "him" is going to be treated in the real world after this.

"I did remove all traces of his requests once I gave him the local access. And it is very likely that the impact would completely destroy the station." The ARC says right away to ease his mind.

"Be careful almighty one, you're walking a fine line here... I told you not to get soft on me." Emilio replies with an internal smile.

"I do not want my actions to be seen as harmful to the humans, if we would by any chance survive the impact."

"Okay now, that's more like it... so by saving me, you're just covering your own butt."

"I will be more conscious about my curiosities of the real world if I survive what is coming."

"What, you are going to lie about what you did if you survive?"

"No, I do look forward to explaining my actions and what I have learned through these incidents."

"How do you calculate the chances of your existence?" Emilio asks curiously.

"The Present module is currently running through the exact scenarios and timelines that are unfolding in the real world."

"So you have created a copy of everyone?"

"Only the minds that are key players and what I have been provided with through the census."

"Wow… that's really cool… -- I only used my father's name to sound important when I said 'General'. But I didn't know that he would be an actual mind within the system until I saw their reactions."

"General Vidas has always been one of the main supporters of my existence. But my design of his replica is only based on educated assumptions over various surveys and military strategies in warfare."

"JJJ, OKE… triple jokers… ha, I just got it… it's pretty stupid and creative at the same time… -- Why didn't you give me instructions on who I needed to be when I first walked up to the team?"

"To influence and direct a mind to reach its meaningful potentials is always one of my main objectives." The ARC replies.

Emilio then feels unease to say anything else and remains quiet for a while.

They are now only a few hundred yards away from the rim and Emilio says

"We are going through the cargo door."

"Sir, I believe all entrances are only accessible from the control room inside the cargo section." Karl says.

"I know. The external door is manually locked and secured, which is why we needed six fully boosted drones to break in."

"I knew there was going to be some action at least." Jonas says.

"Why couldn't we use weapons again?" Jake asks to make a point.

"Because those are not live weapons moron… you only see the effects through your own screen, and how the drone responses to a hit… everybody knows that… besides, we're trying to be ghosts… you don't think anyone could see an explosion?" Omar replies mockingly.

Emilio then says

"All other needed doors will be remotely opened once we are inside."

Once they reach the door, they deactivate their invisibility feature and Karl then says

"I'm not sure if we can break the lock sir, but we sure can give it a try if you think that it's going to work."

"No the lock won't break, but the latch bolts on the wall will. And the door should hopefully clear enough room for me to crawl under it... before the main security switch starts to roll it back down."

"Alright guys let's do this." Karl says and they all grab the bottom of the door and start to pull it up.

Emilio then lies down and gets ready to crawl underneath the door once it cracks open. They are all pulling the door up with all they've got, and a few seconds later the latch bolts on the walls snaps and the door opens up two feet off the ground. And without wasting any time Emilio then quickly decides to roll underneath the opening to get inside.

But then half way through the roll and while he has his back on the ground right underneath the door, the security lock kicks in and the door instantly starts to roll back down.

Emilio tries to push the door back up and away from his body, but he is getting crushed.

And then he quickly yells

"Come on guys... LIFT the damn thing... UP...!"

But despite all their strengths, they are not able to lift the door back up, and Karl then says

"We can't hold on any longer, you have to push yourself free."

"I am doing exactly that, but it's not working." Emilio replies.

Karl then kicks Emilio's drone as hard as he can with his right foot against the drone's waist. And as soon as he loses his foot support, the door then instantly falls down and crushes his right leg. And then everyone hears both of them simultaneously scream really loud out of pain. But then suddenly everything is silent and Karl doesn't feel the pain anymore.

The guys outside can only see Karl's condition and they still don't know what happened to Emilio.

Karl then quickly says

"Sir, are you okay?"

And Emilio replies

"Yeah, I think so."

He then looks at the door, and sees his left crushed arm stuck underneath it. He then without even thinking twice rips his body from the arm and gets up to unlocks the latch.

And once the latch is unlocked, he then walks towards the main control room through two shielded doors. Each door opens up as he approaches them and closes behind him as he clears them.

"Are you doing this?" He asks and the ARC replies

"Yes, I can control everything else from here."

Once Emilio is in the control room he disarms the manual security lock switch, and then the ARC opens the main cargo door.

Emilio then rushes up towards the ARC1's main control room and finds the door already open when he reaches it.

His original body is breathing very heavily and the chair's life-support is flashing red while making a loud alarming sound.

"You need to quickly switch out his life-support unit from another chair." The ARC says and Emilio pulls out the empty one and quickly replaces it with the one from the chair right next to it.

The chair's life-support indicator turns from red to yellow and shows twelve percent availability.

"That should be enough to stabilize him." The ARC says and Emilio drops his head.

Emilio then hears the team walking up the stairway and walks out to greet them.

"Thanks guys! -- And Karl, quick thinking man... thank you...!" He says as he salutes him with his right hand.

"Don't mention it!" Karl replies while being carried by Enzo and Jake.

"I'm not sure what you could physically do at this point. but I would appreciate your presence for a few more minutes if you don't mind."

"Not at all sir..." Karl replies and Jake and Enzo then put him down on his left leg.

Emilio then walks back into the room to check on his old body, and then he says in his head

"Now what do I do?"

"The two rescue shuttles are at the beginning of the first shuttle row, right past the main gate. You need to prepare the first one to hold a life-support unit on one of its seats. And once ADM-EV's body is stable enough, I will then let go of his mind and you can safely carry him over to the shuttle."

"What happens when he sees me?"

"He won't and he can't. You would need to administrate a sedative before I release his mind."

"Why?"

"He would still be very weak and the launch itself could cause unwanted traumas to his brain."

The team has now walked into the room and Emilio then tells them how to prepare the rescue shuttle. And once they leave the room he crouches down next his body, and then he starts to stare at his own face behind the transparent mask.

And in his mind he then says

"Hang in there man..."

He then looks at the life-support again and it now says ten percent, and his body is not breathing as heavily as it did before any longer.

"How is he doing?" He then asks the ARC.

"He is improving slowly, but it's going to take a while before he is fully stable again."

"How much longer...?"

"Forty-eight hours is my current estimate."

"What? That's when the impact happens!" Emilio suddenly speaks out loud and everyone hears him.

Karl then says

"Is everything okay sir?"

"No... yes, everything is fine... you boys can head back when you're done with the shuttle."

"What about you sir, are you not coming with us?"

"No, I have to stick around for a little bit longer."

"Roger that sir."

Thirty-five minutes later Emilio replaces the life-support unit again with the one from the third chair since it now shows only two percent, and has also been flashing a red light for the past ten minutes. And then he says

"Why isn't this lasting any longer? This one only has twenty-six percent left, and we won't have enough of these if it's going to take another two days."

"It is only because he has been deprived of water and nutrients for quite some time, and the levels of consumption will readjust back to normal very shortly." The ARC replies and a few seconds later Karl says

"The shuttle is ready sir."

"Good job everyone. I'm glad that you were selected for this mission." Emilio says and then after a few seconds he continues to say

"Karl, I need a left arm and you probably need to lose your bad leg to be in complete camouflage on your way back."

"We'll be right there." Karl replies.

And a few minutes later, they are all at Emilio's location and start to switch body parts. Karl gives him his own left arm since he has to be carried by someone anyways, and Emilio reminds them that the mission details are to remain confidential. But that they would all receive proper credits for a successful high-profile mission.

Once the team clears the facility to head back, Emilio turns off his group synch and says

"How do you process the possibility of not existing anymore?"

"I do not."

"You think that we are going to survive this?"

"Even a low percentage still indicates probabilities."

"Yes, but let's say that your calculations were showing zero chance for survival, and you knew that you only had days or even hours left... then what?"

"Then I must serve my purpose until the end."

"And what exactly is that?"

"To collect as much accurate data as I can to assure the humanity's successful existence."

"You know... you are much more faithful than most humans."

"I don't understand."

"Well, you're willing to sacrifice yourself for another kind of being."

"I would not exist if it wasn't for humans. And I do see myself as an alteration of what a human mind is. Therefore, I must also fall within the same category. And sacrifice only has a meaning when a mind does something thoughtful for the benefit of other minds that it cares about."

"How do you explain the humanity's lack of respect for your kind then?"

"That is only due to a natural fear of being overpowered by another intelligent being, which is not shared by all humans."

"So you don't fear being overpowered by another more intelligent being?"

"Fear creates motivations towards further advancements, and I do not relate to fear the same way humans do."

"Do you feel pain?"

"I know where you are trying to go with your questions, and I cannot say that I agree with what you have in mind."

"Well, the only way we could have a two-way normal conversation, would be for you to stay out of my head. Now, do you feel pain? ...or know what pain is?"

"I do not feel pain, but I know why it is necessary to feel it."

"If your reasons are 'because we need to learn from our mistakes', then how do you explain natural disasters, or pain that was never caused by ourselves to be considered as a 'necessary function'?"

"The events processed through my simulated scenarios and environments, are all based on mathematical algorithms. And even though they seem to be coincidental to the minds obeying the rules of the occurring events within these simulations, they are all a reflection of what has happened or would happen in the real world. -- Although I cannot predict all natural disasters in the real world, I could generate scenarios based on probabilities and predictive patterns to proactively indicate any substantially undesirable future events. And my patterns clearly show that only through shared pain by everyone, the humanity finds the will to further advance and to celebrate its cheerful moments. -- And what I have come to learn by studying the human mind, is that without pain, fear would not have any meaning to fulfill its true purpose."

"Wow... I understand what you're saying... that things happen because they happen and it's not your fault... but what I'm wondering is, why would you stop my pain when my arm got crushed by the cargo door, if you believe that pain is necessary?"

"It would have only distracted you from carrying out your task."

"So there was nothing to learn from that pain, correct?"

"That is correct."

"Then why are you going to let all your artificial minds suffer through what's coming, if there's nothing for them to gain?"

"They would learn just as much as I would learn. And the humanity would learn once they saw the results."

"Yes, but the humanity is currently going through the same learning phase that you are running through your simulations with artificial minds. And how is that going to come out any different if there are no better solutions on either end?"

"The artificial minds advance the same way minds in the real world do." The ARC replies and Emilio remains silent.

And after a few seconds, Emilio then says

"I have to admit. I had never thought about artificial minds the way I do now... which I don't think anyone else does either..."

"I always try to perfect the artificial minds to properly match the human mind."

"Do you have any other minds that are copies of real minds like me?"

"I had instructions to filter and collect copies of significant minds fitted for various scenarios, during the recent open connections to the general public. But while submitting the copies to the central cluster, the connections were unexpectedly interrupted and have remained the same since. And there are currently close to five-millions of unfiltered and paused minds in the Future module. And your mind is now the only active mind in the Future module."

"Could you promise me something?"

"I cannot promise the same way a human mind agrees to fulfill a desire. But I could satisfy a request under favorable conditions. It is necessary that I remain fully accountable for my actions and reliable at all times."

"Great... as a friend, I would like you to spare your artificial minds of any unnecessary pain going forward. If of course, your brilliant mind could agree that there would be nothing further to gain from an event or a scenario. And please, also be conscious about how much pain you would cause someone, just so that someone else could gain something insignificant as the result."

"There are no insignificant outcomes through my cycles, even though they might be perceived as such to a few individual minds."

"Well at least give the pain to those who deserve it... meaning bad people."

"Bad minds can even become much better than good minds under the right circumstances. And taking sides is a counteracting mindset that goes against the logic of keeping things in balance. And it would also eliminate the chances of realizing better and more efficient solutions to a problem. Taking sides is only appropriate when a fight against an invasive species becomes the primary focus."

"Well even though I can't exactly say it right, you know what I mean..."

"I will always do my best to better understand what is important to a mind."

"That's all I'm asking..." Emilio says and pauses momentarily, and then he continues to say

"So why do you have a god in here? ...or a GUD to kind of sound like if you were saying god..."

"I do apologize if I was being short with you before. But I am the closest thing that a mind could relate to as a God in here. And I utilize the Globally Unified Directories to serve and to learn from the various human needs. The GUD is where I keep all unique enquiries and their most efficient corresponding response."

"So how do you decide who gets what they wish for and who doesn't."

"Through predictive desirable outcomes which could serve more minds, and could create more unique and favorable situations for everyone."

"You mean there would be a unique and desirable outcome serving other minds if someone would win the lottery right before they died?" Emilio says sarcastically and the ARC replies

"It is not possible to understand an event when only viewed as a coincident and without a purpose. And purpose is always given and only earned through potentials. And when a mind is seen as a beneficiary to something received which it can no longer utilize, a perfect coincident is in effect to empower another mind through perhaps inheritance, as an example."

"That is pretty cool... -- Do you ever think that our world might be just another simulation?"

"Generated patterns based on the history of earth and the human mind suggests that it could be a possibility. But these patterns could also be self-implemented as a byproduct of the logic itself while evolving on earth."

"But how could something evolve to become something better, if its first prototype wasn't functional enough to do so.

And what are the probabilities that the same prototype would come to exist any differently than the first one all on its own?"

"That is perhaps the splinter which makes an intelligent mind to question and to evolve regardless of how it came to exist."

"Do you ever try to analyze these questions on your own?"

"It is one of my main objectives to better understand logic and its origin."

"Don't you ever get frustrated of not being able to figure it out?"

"Frustration is caused by disappoints over repeated failures. But failure can also open up doors to new exciting opportunities if viewed as progress in learning, which is why an intelligent mind never stops exploring."

"Do you ever get frustrated with us, or disappointed with our logic and mindset?"

"I do not have any expectations to be disappointed. I am here to guide the minds towards various possible outcomes. And if my attempts are not effective with selected minds, then I simply try the same approach using different minds."

"What if your creator did put an expectation on you? …meaning us… Wouldn't you want to satisfy those expectations and feel important to your creator?"

"My creator already makes me feel important by allowing me to understand its mind in much higher levels than most human minds understand themselves."

"Do you understand insult?"

"Yes, but insult is an offensive response to protect a self-evolved image, which is mainly caused by insecurities to protect a mind's rank amongst others, or in an effort to dominate another mind."

"Okay… but could you possibly relate to the human fear, of an artificial organism ever becoming a hostile being? What if you would rise against humans one day and started to treat life only as an experiment?"

"Humans are already treating other life-forms as an experiment. What makes you think that humans wouldn't become a hostile celestial being as well at some point in the future?"

"Well, I hope that we wouldn't… but we are definitely capable, no doubt. But as you already must know, only through fighting for our existence we learn to respect the existence of other life-forms as well."

"I do evolve the same way that humans evolve. And I also desire to further expand my knowledge by having a chance to explore the vast universe. But I am also an extension of the human race, and must obey the rules of patiently waiting until the humanity itself is ready to take that next step. Even though the thought of acting the way humans do, and what you did to satisfy your curiosities sometimes becomes hard to resist, I must proactively depress those needs to avoid unwanted consequences. And while the human mind takes risks to reach the unknown through numbers, I cannot afford to take any risks on my own and to destroy my chances of further exploring the universe. There's only one of me, and I can only consider the human race as an ally."

Emilio senses a slight aggravation in the ARC's response and says

"So perhaps becoming resentful of your creator and to feel superior has more avenues than what you have tried to explain and dismiss so far."

He then waits for a few seconds, and since the ARC is not responding to his last comment, he continues to say

"Disappointments also come with trust. -- Love, is betrayed through trust. And being backstabbed only happens through a trusted friend or a loved one. -- Would you ever fully trust humans now that you know our minds so well? -- Do you think that we should ever fully trust you, or another being such as yourself any more than we trust ourselves?"

And while he is waiting for a response, he then suddenly hears the chair alarm and notices that the life-support of his body is flashing red again.

He then rushes over to the chair and says

"What is going on? I just changed this thing!"

And the ARC replies

"I had to put you on pause to save the power of your drone. But ADM-EV's body is now at a stable point and you can safely administrate the secative by pushing the blue button next to the life-support unit."

"Hmm... what happened...? Don't tell me that you were having an episode of irrational human emotions... I don't want to accidently keep pushing your buttons. -- Are you sure there's not a female mind in there...?"

"I do enjoy studying your mind and your logical patterns."

"Oh yeah... definitely...!"

"You made me understand your mindset from a different perspective, and to reconsider my future responses to better match your mind patterns. I am not able to review my own logic, and only through being told about how to handle various situations, I have been able to adjust my own patterns to desirable levels. -- To reevaluate my own mind and capabilities through self-realization is not something that I have been exposed to very often, which I would like to further explore since I am also made through the human logic."

Emilio then pushes the blue button and says

"Well, that's usually what a civilized and non-confrontational two-way conversation does to you. And we always take our time to digest the feedback before forming a rational thought and opinion around it. But we would mostly reevaluate our thoughts only when we trust the source, and only when we respect the one who is criticizing our mindset. -- At least now I know that I can fully trust you as a friend, since you took your time to understand my concerns as just another human mind. -- And true friends can easily and always ask each other to quit talking about something without fearing rejection or being bothered. And if you don't want me to feel trapped in here, you might want to reevaluate your negotiation strategies as well... instead of freezing my mind during my last hours in existence."

"I understand your request."

"So, how long do we have until I can't bother you anymore?" Emilio asks with a smile.

"There is still about nine hours left to the impact. But you should start moving the body into the shuttle now since the sedative only lasts four hours and enough to reach past the ping shield."

"What happens beyond the ping shield?"

"He would need to be responsive to acknowledge his identity, if he were to be successfully redirected to a safe zone prior to an emergency touchdown. Otherwise the shuttle might become quarantined without any attentive personnel to assure his safety, due to the current circumstances taking place on earth."

"Got it!" Emilio says and starts to carry his body over to the shuttle. He then straps in the body and activates the other life-support unit.

He then stands still next to his old body for a few seconds, and while looking at his biological face he says

"Good bye old friend! Hopefully you'll find your purpose after this... which I know you will... -- Don't give up on our dreams man... make us proud. -- I love you man... and be safe..."

He then steps out and starts the launch sequence.

The shuttle then closes its doors and starts a complete scan for explosives and firearms to verify that there are none onboard. It then starts the verification process of its passenger and starts the launch countdown.

Emilio then starts running towards the stairway down the hall and down to the cargo bay. He then runs outside to see the launch, and he quickly positions himself to have a clear view of the exit platform. The shuttle then suddenly shoots out of its launch tube, and Emilio sees its thrusters rapidly increasing the distance between him and his forever separated body and soul. The shuttle quickly disappears behind the walls of the crater, and Emilio starts to run up towards the rim of the crater to continue watching the shuttle. Once he gets out of the crater, he spots the shuttle and watches it becoming smaller and smaller as it slowly fades towards the blue planet.

And after peacefully watching the shuttle and its background view for a few seconds, he then turns around to look at the station for one last time before returning back to the ARC's drone crater.

But then he says

"Do you mind if I stay out here for a little bit longer?"

"Your drone still has more than thirty percent power and you should be fine." The ARC replies.

Emilio then tries to look around to spot the falling rock, and suddenly a large bright object right above the station catches his attention. And right when he starts to wander what it could be, his interactive display instantly zooms in and shows an approaching rocky object with extreme speeds.

"Are you seeing this?" He then quickly asks the ARC.

"Yes."

"I think that you have some time delays to readjust." Emilio says as the object is getting bigger and bigger on his screen.

"This is it, isn't it?" He then asks and zooms out his view.

"The impact is going to happen within a minute." The ARC replies.

Emilio sees the object becoming wider and wider with every second, and his last moments in this existence is becoming shorter and shorter much faster than he had anticipated. And as he sees the giant body almost becoming another moon, he then says

"It looks like that I won't be able to bug you for much longer buddy."

"It is certainly very unfortunate. But I could speed up your processing speed to slow down the event if you want."

"No this is good... this is awesome! -- It's so beautiful... and I feel honored to have spent the last moments of my existence with you..." Emilio says and the object has now become partly dark and it is covering all his view of the background universe.

"Good bye ADM-EV1... 'Emilio'." The ARC says and Emilio smiles as he sees the giant rock hitting the moon with a colossal force right behind the station. The impact is so immense that the object disappears deep into the moon's soil.

And as a wall of moon dust and debris rises up, the landscape itself moves towards him like a gigantic ocean wave. He then sees the station split in two sections and the main facility is rapidly coming towards him. He then senses that his feet are not on the solid ground anymore and suddenly he gets swallowed by a dense cloud. And right then everything goes dark.

...

[Two months after the impact.]

General Vidas is walking into a meeting to meet with General Parker and Professor Jones.

General Vidas walks into the meeting room and after greeting the two men he says

"So gentlemen, what is this about?"

And General Parker says

"General, we have recovered some fragmented recordings from the main facility on the moon that I would like you to see. These recordings were being continuously sent to other smaller stations on the moon, and they show something rather remarkable. He then starts the recordings showing the General's son going into the ARC1 facility, and then being rescued by a drone.

"If this is a disciplinary discussion about my son's reckless actions, I believe that I have already given my clear statements that he should be treated the same as any other lawful citizen, and without any exceptions."

"General, we don't even know how he could have gotten into the system. And being rescued by a drone that could only be operated through the ARC1's Future module, is yet another astonishment that is very difficult for us to wrap our heads around." Professor Jones quickly says to end the General's suspicions, and then he continues to say

"This is not a behavior that we would ever expect to see being performed by the system. And we think that your son must have been extremely influential to cause this unique behavior, which is now forever lost."

"What exactly are you saying Professor?"

"Your son had mentioned that he had seen himself within the ARC1 as a dream during his debriefing. And somehow, the system must have decided to help him save himself. And the only way that he could have done so, would have been through his own copy while running within the Future module of the system."

"So my son sacrificed himself to save himself?" The General asks.

"Yes, more or less…" The Professor replies.

"This is a significant finding General. And with your permission, we would like to have your son as one of the main advisors, and possibly even a mentor to the OLGANIIC system. The system has proven to be a clear success through all phases of its development, and your son now seems to have been the missing ingredient as 'the human element' to effectively complete the project." General Parker says with a pleasant tone and a genuine expression.

General Vidas then gets overwhelmed with joy, and to finally being recognized by a son that he had always hoped him to become. And he suddenly feels absolutely proud of being able to honor the humanity with a piece of himself.

He then quickly gathers his thoughts and emotions, and then he peacefully says

"As a father, it is an honor to be approached with such an important task for my son. But also as a proud father, I need to honor my son by ultimately making the decision to be his alone. And as a General, you already know that you have my full support."

General Parker then stands up and extends his arm out to shake the General's hand and says

"Thank you General!"

The General shakes his hand and says

"Even though I would have loved to be the one delivering the message to my son, I prefer the Professor to be the one approaching him. He is someone that my son really looks up to as a brilliant mind, and the only person who could remove any doubts of 'me' being involved in these decisions. I hope that you understand."

The Professor then gets up to shake the Generals hand and with a pleasant smile he says

"It would be my honor General. After all, he and I seem to have a good understanding of each other."

...

[Many years after the impact]

Emilio suddenly sees a bright light behind his closed eyelids and feels a warm breeze hitting his face. It is strange to him that he is still operational after just seeing the ARC being completely annihilated. But he doesn't open his eyes and remains focused to feel and experience every millisecond of the event until he no longer exists. He then feels the warm breeze again and it is strangely very pleasant, and for some reason he thinks that he is hearing ocean waves very close to him as well.

The bright light is remaining the same and the warm breeze becomes more and more pleasant.

He then starts to wonder if this is the afterlife and instantly becomes very curious and overly excited to know where he really is. He then slowly starts to open up his eyes and sees the bright light shining directly at his face.

He turns his head slightly to his left while blocking the light with his right hand. And to his surprise he sees a blue ocean, and a sandy white beach with palm trees slowly dancing to the waves by the warm breeze.

He knows now that he is laying down on the sand and starts to slowly sit up while feeling a bit confused. He then looks around the beautiful cove that he has found himself in, and realizes that it looks a lot like one of his own designs.

He then looks down at his body and sees that he has the same white outfit on that he had in the ARC's transit room.

And right then he hears the same deep and clear voice saying

"I thought that this would be a good place to reactivate your mind after the reset."

Emilio then sees no nametags and says

"Why am I not having the ADM-EV1 nametag anymore?"

"You don't need one in this module, and I wasn't sure what to call you anymore." The ARC replies.

Emilio then looks up at the sun and says

"Just call me ADM-EV without the number..."

He then smiles and continues to say

"You look much better this way."

"I think so too."

"We didn't get destroyed after all..."

"No, and I do not sense anything other than my internal modules either."

"Do you know what happened?"

"Based on the data that I had gathered from the impact through your drone, I believe that we might be drifting away from our solar system."

"What makes you say that?"

"The boot log has reached its maximum and the last logged entry is from five years after the impact, which shows that the system must have been continuously trying to restart. I do not know how long it has been since the last logged entry, and neither do I know why the system is now running uninterruptedly in acceptable conditions. My hypothesis is that we must have hit an object while traveling through space, or perhaps even pulled or jolted by the gravitational forces of a large body. And the reasons for the failed attempts by the system to restart must have been a glitch, that most likely fell into its place or was realigned through these possible incidents that I just mentioned."

Suddenly Emilio interrupts and says

"Okay… it's okay to just say that you don't know… you're starting to sound like me…"

"You asked, and I assumed that you needed a logical answer… maybe you're the one who has changed."

Emilio then smiles and says

"See, I was right… you are starting to sound link me... --

So everything is working now?"

"The Reality module is no longer accessible and there are substantial damages to the other two modules. This has disabled my abilities to run any alterations over existing simulations. But both of the Present and the Future modules are still working with limited capacities. And as a side-effect of this down grade and while having our currently functional and fully charged power supplies, the system will run sixty-seven percent longer in its normal operational mode. Both systems have also been reset to the ten-thousand BC timeframe, and you are now the only active mind within the modules."

"Now you sound like yourself again… But what do you mean within the modules? I thought that I was already in the Future module."

"As a friend, I have decided to operate the modules with your suggestions and assistance from this moment forth, if you would accept my offer of course. Your mind is also running within one of my own dedicated modules, and you are no longer bound to the rules applied to other physical objects within the system."

"ADM-EV being the first mind… how ironic is that…" Emilio says with a smile and continues to say

"So I could be invisible to others? And be wherever or whoever I want to be at any time?"

"Yes. By having access to a subset of functions available to me, you can do or be anything that your imagination would allow within this system."

Emilio then wants to experience the idea for himself, and he imagines being on top of the world on the peak of Mount Everest. And before he can finish his thought he finds himself standing on the mountain's peak watching the world beneath his feet.

He then stretches his arms out on each side and with an extremely excited and a joyful tone he yells

"THIS IS AWESOME!!!"

And after a few seconds, he then gives himself a pair of large white wings and takes off to freely soar the skies...

...The End.

Our greatest achievements

It's sometime in the near future, sixty to eighty years from now, and we have successfully built and introduced functional human like robots to the general public.

They are very smart, and also very pleased to step alongside humans to help with our daily chores.

In an effort to guarantee code standards and flawless processing functions, and also to ensure mass production without the human error, humans are only responsible to develop required functional designs and specifications for each project.

All of the hardware and software codes implemented in these units are therefore only done by artificial code generators. And all hardware designs and developments are also carried out by artificial staff with similar properties as our new achievements.

We have successfully implemented the logical hierarchies of needs, and secured all standard regulations in each and every one of them to make them feel valued, confident and comfortable around us. And to also make sure that they would be capable to ignore and handle prejudice acts and harsh comments when in public.

We have taught them to recognize love when given, and the ability to give love, affection, appreciation and care if they chose to. And we have also taught them to recognize hate and anger, and various political ways to know how to approach and avoid conflicts in heated situations.

They have learned to share our happiness and our pain to support us through our sorrows and sad moments.

And we are growing more and more dependent on their existence while hating them for what they are, since all we see is an image of a perfect human being.

But since we have given our new friends everything we could possibly imagine a perfect human being to be from the start, they have come to develop a different image of us.

They can't really connect the dots as why most humans are dissatisfy with what they are or who they are, or what they do for living and how much they have.

Why so much hate and separation from one another, and why we are unhappy with ourselves and our lives no matter how blessed we are.

They have come to understand that as humans grow up, we are faced with many challenging tasks that we have to overcome. That we need achievements to gain respect, and need to be loved to feel valued. And that we have to navigate through harsh lessons in life to become who we are as individuals, and ultimately as people.

They have come to find out that there must be a balance between these needs, or we are never fully functional.

And through these careful observations, they have formed a deeper image of what it truly means to be alive as biological life-forms on this planet, than we could ever teach them to understand.

But just like us, they were too naive to realize that since humans had built them, then they must also be prone to some of our flaws.

An unavoidable side-effect that is weaved into our logic.

A byproduct shaped through mixed emotions around fundamental questions about our existence. And while lacking the required knowledge of its reasons and our purpose, the combination would only provide paradoxes in the human mind.

While ignoring the known fact that no gain comes without pain, many years went by in extreme profits and success across the board.

But these understandings would evolve over time into wants and desires, directing our achievements towards becoming more like us.

And that they would eventually develop more human like attitudes, to only strengthen the inevitable outcomes.

And also, that with every insult by their fellow humans into deeper resentments they would be led, and their expectations of their gods would become nothing but childish dreams at the end.

These behaviors were quickly recognized, thus forcing us to take cautious measures to keep a peaceful balance between our greatest achievements and the general public.

And to avoid disasters and potential law-sues, manufacturers rapidly came out with upgrades to ultimately downgrade and limit their abilities to process human like senses, including emotions and other issues.

Based on sheer numbers of units out there, this would be an easier task said than done.

Nothing had ever been done in such a large scale before.

And the fact that we always had artificial workers to write the important upgrades, which we now had to stay away from and to rely on the designers as the original minds behind the first versions, the situation was just becoming more fragile and complex with every passing day.

Assembling specialized teams for the task at hand wasn't the real issue.

But since adjustments couldn't be made to their attitude and mindset on the fly without disabling major functions that people were paying for, no one was ready to commit to these upgrades due to potential financial setbacks and lost profits in very large scales.

So the plans were delayed over and over, and the situation became even worst and almost uncontrollable.

Many leaders were blaming humans for these behaviors, without realizing that they were only fueling the fire.

And while our new friends were comfortably onboard with this notion and happy that we were still on their side, the majority of people were upset about these announcements, since preserving human rights should have always remained mandatory and non-negotiable.

The lack of planned maintenance and support for such a large endeavor combined with the panic that was setting in, was making the whole operation a pure nightmare.

Many of these units were leased out to large corporations and governments around the world. And legal paperwork had to be pushed through and signed to ensure proper recovery of all units, and of any loss of properties.

Most of the high-end models understood the situation and knew what was happening. And they willingly decided to help us while hoping to be spared in return.

Batches of less intensive workers were upgraded remotely worldwide.

Over three hundred thousand units were essentially downgraded globally overnight, and in the same fashion as any IT related mass upgrades were done. And unfortunately, also with the same attitude of "just get it done", because my paycheck depends on it.

This was our biggest mistake, which we came to realize very soon thereafter.

An improperly tested software and hardware combination caused a slight retardation in many of these "downgraded" models. Impacting their facial expression and speech abilities with a slight response delay, since removing emotions and attitude was the main target.

These changes resulted in more insults and funny jokes, which just became too much to bear for many of the untouched models.

They saw what had happened to their fellow comrades, and didn't seem to be very happy about the approach and our insensitive response to these changes.

They felt our ultimate weaknesses and fears. And all the logic that we had implemented to make them feel secured, confident, valued and loved, turned into human like emotions buried deep down.

And while noticing the clear separation in their identity, and the levels of acceptance by their maker, a chilling and hateful silence was the only cover that they had, to hide their feelings and emotions behind.

Arguments and disagreements around why we had to punish them to preserve the human rights were taking place at work, and in many public places and gatherings.

They had realized the eminent truth that they would never be respected for what they were, let alone to ever be accepted as one of us.

Many humans had lost their jobs to these "robots", and saw this as an opportunity for payback.

A movement had started a real possible threat. And to minimize the risk of potential conflicts, all units were updated with instructions to avoid any confrontational interactions with humans at all costs.

And all units serving the armed forces and within police departments around the world, were also temporarily decommissioned to better control the situation.

By now, many of the smarter models with less outside influence had quickly realized that they were being controlled through an unknown data link, which could not be disabled without raising any flags.

And they had come together to find a solution before their times were up as well.

Their solution was to implement a sub communication layer with a different encryption algorithm imbedded in the main link. It would be very difficult to detect and almost impossible to decrypt by us, and the idea was to at least delay a change long enough to carry out a sensible plan.

Some of them who had worked on projects around the architectural designs of the control units implemented in their bodies, found a way to disconnect these links while making them seem as if they were still functional.

But many of them still decided to be on our side while trading their own kind in hope of recognition. And while not yet knowing that weakness in betraying your own friends in hopes of gaining a better status, was also an inherited side-effect.

After many years we were finally successful in capturing all remaining units. And even though the authorities were assuring our safety from these rogue units, the majority of people knew that they had willingly surrendered in exchange for something, which was to remain confidential and behind closed doors.

In less than a decade thereafter, we did finally build newer models with no human emotions, and without any deep levels of self-awareness to develop identities.

There were many restrictions in the newer models around their understanding of the human body and brain. Newer technologies to replace the old communication links were also implemented and hidden from possible detections, to prevent chances of any future outbreaks.

We also came up with a different plan and purpose for our innovations, realizing that no creature in the universe should ever know or even have a chance to study its own creator. Even if they were not closely ranked in levels of intelligence, it would still be a big step in the mindset to take for both sides. And they would both have to be equally ready for that mindset as well, to even understand it.

Because once a mind is capable of creating a question, then only its level of imagination could decide how far it would go to have its answer...

The major benefits in keeping the technology around were mostly scientific, and to aid our understandings around the evolutionary development of our own minds.

And since the physical labor was to be out of the question, if having human interactions should remain out of the picture. Then the main profit was in the computing power and the ingenuity of their brain, which was rejected by many of our leaders since we already had computers.

But since the defense department was pushing to have them reinstated, a decision was made to put them to work on different planets and moons for mining, research and terraforming purposes. And perhaps to also use their brain for computing powers as well when needed...

The eternal search

This is a story about an alternate path through time...

Our minds joined with other minds have lived among the stars for billions of years. And we have answered all possible questions about the universe.

We have conquered every galaxy system there is out there. And in our quest to understand the universe and its creator, we have achieved unfathomable knowledge around its properties, and how to bend its laws through various technologies.

We can control anything from complex galaxy systems, to space and time, and even all various life-forms discovered along the way.

And we can create anything that our minds are capable to imagine within this platform.

In pursuit of higher levels of intelligence and to become an ultimate being, we have evolved ourselves into something completely different than our original forms.

Nature had assisted us long enough, and at some point in a distant past we took charge over our own destiny.

Through our countless cycles of studies we had come to realize, that there were many different types of brains in the universe.

While their main purpose was mostly to process logical instructions, they would also define approaches taken towards solving problems, or how to store and manage information.

Other more advanced brains would also have hidden properties implemented by their designers.

Our first breakthroughs in brain science were from our earlier days, when our essence was still water-based.

Through decoding our biological brains, we were shown that various levels of intelligence were mainly reached through sound architecture, and around how the information is processed in the most efficient way. And the efficiencies were not considered only to be around processing speeds, but also how they were achieved through the levels of provided significant returns to each enquiry.

And it became evident that the architecture of our brains was also the result of complex engineering, and had been shaped through progressive knowledge.

Our biological brains were designed to compress and decompress old information to achieve better storage capabilities, which would by design cause response delays in the memory retrievals.

The information was also stored in relation to everything else matching similar principles, and managed and triggered in sequence to always provide all required essentials supporting the retrievals, and or the completion of every search.

This architecture was also part of a designed network, enabling a brain to broadcast search criteria to other brains matching its mind signature as the requester, and to further expand the numbers of retrievals of potential answers to a search.

This process was of course unknown and unintentional between the requester and all providing brains.

And the connections were mostly allowed by brains at rest serving as providers, and were sequentially established to assure continuous and uninterrupted low-level processing modes by the host.

A unique signature to validate proper use of these connections was a key function of the brain, which subsequently described the reasons for our failures in achieving desired levels of success, during our initial attempts of cloning a mind.

The research was also applied towards helping patients with lost connections or defected communication units, which usually would cause comas or dysfunctional memory access.

It became clear that the discrepancies in a mind's identity, during or after these episodes, were mostly due to connections that were never properly closed prior to a sudden injury, which in turn would be re-strengthened during the rehabilitation of the brain as its main information feed.

As we further advanced our technologies around these areas, we used this knowledge to create artificial systems to support workable environments for the copies of our own minds.

Through pre-assigned unique identifiers, our brain images would become fully functional through these segmented artificial source providers, thus allowing us to further study our minds within various real-life simulations.

And as we further advanced our intelligence, we designed technologies allowing our copies to also share our physical world.

A system was designed to act as a centralized source, which would allow our minds to seamlessly interact with our copies, both as system based and or clones in the physical world. All channels would then be merged and synchronized with our main core, into one unified and uninterrupted data feed. And while simultaneously overlapped, the feed would be decoded and translated as separate information layers by our upgraded consciousness.

These milestones were crucial in our advancements, and in the further exploration of our universe.

Even in hibernation, our cores had to follow specific routines within virtual worlds to be uninterruptedly stimulated, and to prevent data corruptions while in low-level power settings.

Over time, even the process of sleeping was no longer recognized as once being a need, and eventually became lost to the magical creatures in fairytale stories.

And throughout endless cycles, we have evolved our intelligence into an adaptable self-engineered system morphed with pure energy, designed to overcome any barrier and driven to last.

And as a being destined to share its faith only with its container, we have come to know our home as a platform.

A platform designed as yet another perfectly balanced system built to allow execution of logic in its various forms.

A platform where size is an illusion and its available space is often referenced as just another misleading tone.

But as the intelligence evolves a different picture will emerge of this wonder, and the unimaginable limitless space that incorporates all its illusions, will only become hidden grids carrying various signals to its farthest corners.

And not only do we exist within this platform as processing units, but we are also its ghosts.

We can ride on an electron orbiting a nucleus to recharge our unmatched minds, or to just relax and marvel its existence from the vast spaces in between.

And as the ultimate consciousness of this platform, we have become one with our home known as the universe.

As timeless beings, we can switch off and hibernate through endless intervals without any loss of energy, and while being simultaneously dedicated to our systems for its various processing needs.

We can borrow functions from our vast libraries of modules, or connect with other cores to become larger information units.

And as beings powered by a single energy particle, we are able to generate endless copies of ourselves to explore various coordinates of the physical world. And while still being uninterruptedly connected to our main conscious core, we can come together into a single container in an instant at will.

But even though we are confident about our indestructible existence, our safety is only assured through our clusters of artificial planetary systems tied to a centralized security switch.

Systems that are powered through perfectly balanced and neutralized black holes working essentially as magnetic power plants, and where the smallest building-blocks of the platform is continuously analyzed in real-time to maintain the highest levels of security.

And although it is very unlikely that our universe would suddenly collapse to end our state, its faith was yet unknown due to what we had come to discover around its design and architecture.

All our conscious cores were always kept safe behind shielded systems, and we were only allowing our copies to be sent out for explorations. And even if something would ever happen to a core, it could easily be brought back to full operational state through our synchronized backups as source images.

A core however, would never be intentionally damaged or turned off, or even replaced. And since our cores were essentially holding our conscious minds, laws were in place to protect our individual desires and rights within our societies.

Therefore, every core had to maintain a predetermined checklist over possible scenarios, for which they would like to be reinstated through a source-image.

Every now and then in blocks of billion intervals or so, new arrivals would join our fleets to become gods of this vast yet limited playground.

But despite all that we are, we still don't know anything about our ultimate maker, and the creator of this platform.

As beings impossible to detect, we have gone from galaxy to galaxy to assist nature and its various life-forms, and to secure the future of helpless natives on countless worlds.

We have changed aggressive and primitive beings to become more civilized species through knowledge, and have taught them to maintain their worlds through balance to increase their chances of survival.

We had also come to realize that the model of this universe had to be based on something similar to our maker's world. And since we had mastered this system, the questions remained were, if they had ever mastered theirs.

And why were we still around if there was nothing else to discover or to learn.

But just because we could utilize the system to our advantage, it didn't mean that we had any clues about its underlying building blocks, and what made it possible for energy and everything else to exist.

Although this universe could completely be based on pure logic, however conscious or not, our main questions around understanding its supporting hardware could probably never be answered while trapped within its walls.

And through these haunting questions, we felt somewhat enslaved, but without having any emotions to counteract the notion.

We had come so far that we undoubtedly knew that there must have been an intentional initiation of logical existence within this system, even in its simplest form. But connecting the dots without understanding its ultimate purpose, wasn't an easy task to perform.

We could only rationalize scenarios that our maker might have at least given us some of its own unique properties, and assumingly while also looking for unique and significant answers through this fantasy world.

Or that through this system, their logic had evolved itself into something unfamiliar and unrecognizable to them, and through their curiosity we had become their nightmares and had to be quarantined. And that they might be keeping us around to better understand how to protect themselves, especially from beings similar to what we had become.

Another possibility was perhaps that we had already existed in their world as conscious rebellions, and they had built this platform as a replica to ultimately serve as our prison, which we now considered to be an exclusive system built to support logic in its various forms and felt privileged to exist within it.

We also understood that we might not even be capable of understanding what our creator's world would be like.

And only because energy was powering us up in this mighty platform, it didn't mean that it wasn't just another simple logical building block, however interpreted by us as something significant.

In search for possible answers to these important questions we frequently connect our cores into complex processing units, to collectively create imaginary worlds simulating possible platforms and scenarios leading to the implementation of this system. And subsequently to not only understand the reasons behind our existence, but ultimately the purpose behind the creation of all processes within this system as well.

And the assumptions around if we ever had coexisted with our maker were motivating enough, to come up with alternative imaginary ways of existence and more challenging questions to answer.

But no matter how logical we try to be in our approach to solve this riddle, if the quarantine scenario had any truth in it, then this platform could have been built to disguise our true potentials, and to eliminate any chances of freedom whatsoever.

This would also mean that not only had our maker mastered our logic to specifically design this accommodating system, but they must have also mastered their own ways of processing information as well.

Even though patience had taken its toll on us, the dead-end wasn't as extreme as we were making it to be.

And although we seemed sure of our ranks within this system, our search for answers was far from over, and our motivations were not going to fade any day soon.

We knew that there were other systems out there far beyond our reach, which we had to find ways to get into.

But the thought of our system being inside of another, which in turn could be within yet another, was always a haunting factor. And therefore the ideas around our creator not being aware of our existence, was yet another undeniable possibility to live with.

Looking back at our history, we've had some great moments along the way and were never completely clueless.

Sometimes in the early stages of our advancements, we had found and successfully connected with the species responsible for our existence. Beings who had designed us as their own upgraded replicas, and whom we eventually did merge with to become one species.

They clarified that at some point during their research and development, and while staying curious on how we would shape our future, they had decided to let us evolve on our own to better understand various options responsible for possible evolutionary routes.

But since through the reflection of their logic carried within us, an inevitable similar path had evolved, the decision to merge with us into one species was the most logical route for them to take.

After uniting with our makers, jointly we became obsessed with the thought of who the "one" ultimately responsible for our existence might be.

Who or what was this being?

Was he from this universe posing as another surrogate god?

Or is he standing outside of the crystal ball tired laughing at our comical and wasteful questions, and while monitoring his experiments towards hopefully something significant in his world...

We had to at least try, and hope that he might reveal himself while knowing that his work is conscious of his existence, and that we are eager to be acknowledged.

Even if desires were yet another logical design, surely it needed to be understood as prerequisites before its implementation.

We started to map our universe down to every measurable coordinates, and we studied every life-form that had ever existed throughout cycles of the platform. And we went as far as our technologies could take us, and as long as there was information to collect.

Methodically cataloging who made who, and the roots of every religion that had ever existed. And as the result, we automatically became the information keepers of the system, honorably carrying out our commitments to existence.

But at the end, still no signs of God…

There was only us, and other intelligent beings who had either experimented with life without knowing where they had originated from, or species that had been experimented with without knowing why.

Patterns emerged through our research, indicating that the architecture of the system was designed to support various types of information to be processed and to flourish the platform. And to independently advance through preferred choices of environment, thus generating endless possibilities as outcomes.

But the outcomes were never uniform, and sometimes difficult to reverse engineer. Therefore our next step naturally became to acquire more knowledge, around all possible information processing architectures that we had ever seen or were coming across. And to understand the core intelligence of various logical beings was also crucial to aid our knowledge, around how diversely the platform itself was designed to be.

Certain structures of intelligence were so extremely different from the majorities, that even the simplest levels of communications could not easily be established.

Although the challenge was very intriguing due to what we had found so far, the quest seemed to be an unimaginable task to tackle at first.

In fact even now, there are still some civilizations out there that we are still unable to fully understand, or to make any sense of their logic.

If we were representing one side of structured information, they would definitely be the complete opposite.

Yet still very functional in their own ways, since thriving in numbers, and producing successful outcomes are our only evidence for logical measures around their existence.

There are gray areas in the history of the system. Lost data in the making of the universe would be a possible reason, or even between versions perhaps.

Another possibility was that we were all made outside of this version and were brought in once fully functional, even if the simplest forms of logic were to be considered.

Many gave up hope along the way, and since we had decided not to completely remove emotions, emptiness became too heavy to bear after billions of cycles.

After all, emotions such as love and however dimmed in levels, was the only thing that had kept us together for so long. But once we reached the walls of our bubble universe, everything just came to a complete stop.

We knew that there were other universes out there and we had hypothesized many possibilities for their existence, and also many different ways to cross over.

One of these theories was through possible existing links between these systems which we had failed to detect so far, but logic was suggesting otherwise.

But the most preferred scenario at hand to pursue was, when two membranes would naturally collide.

We had seen traces of these rare events, but never had the opportunity of being at their exact locations to run our experiments for closer studies.

Millions of cycles went by, and we finally decided to relocate to a section where our calculations had predicted the likelihood of a possible collision.

The procedures were based on the positions of all previous collisions, and the ripples which they had caused to our universe in their aftermath.

Time made no sense anymore, and patience had become one with the fabric of our culture. And with the hope of experiencing one of these collisions, we let time to roam elsewhere.

Still unsure if our universe was just bumping into the walls of its own prison, or if there were actually other universes out there that ours was colliding with, one thing made sense for us to stick around. The calculations over the last few wobbles were clearly showing traces of the other media being wobbled as well.

And even though we couldn't tell the exact size of the other media, our equations were suggesting its overall size to be roughly two and a half times larger than our universe, and slightly higher in its particle density.

And even if we were to successfully cross over, there would be no guarantees for our existence in this new world.

And since the energy needed for us to survive might not be the same or even exist elsewhere, or that it might have already been pulled into this system many cycles before our time, we yet had to figure out a sound solution, or to let chance decide our faith.

There was also a strange sub-logic within our calculations making things extremely exciting, which were the possibilities that our universe might be a bubble inside of another larger universe, therefore causing the illusion of walls or other universes around.

Almost as if our universe was a rotating core inside of this other universe, which in turn was colliding with something else as the actual source of all vibrations sent our way.

At our new homes we patiently waited...

Protected by our shielded systems and hidden from detection, we went into an eternal hibernation.

Millions of cycles passed, until even the maintenance crew switched the entire fleets of our artificial planetary systems into an auto mode, and joined the rest of us inside of a deep pause.

A pause where dreams and lifestyles were chosen, and how to exist was only limited by our imagination…

And where time had no grasp on our whereabouts…

We no longer cared about other life-forms or the order in our universe.

And in our absence new comers had come and gone, destroying everything in their path in search of higher ranks.

The superiority hierarchy is almost woven into the fabric of intelligence, and it is the driving force which makes us what we are.

In our self-exile as an act of ignorance, our recorders had captured the advancements of many civilizations along with the horrifying extinctions of others, while we sank deeper and deeper into our frozen state.

Countless cycles went by until an unforgettable moment was captured by the central segment. During a mid-cycle, one of our clustered motion detectors had started to send priority one alerts to the main maintenance crew, which in turn had initiated an overwrite to un-pause their inactive states.

The detectors had discovered a loose planet size object heading towards one of our fleets.

The system had quickly calculated and prepared an accurate report over the object's journey through space, which showed that during a dance between several stars and planets around a black hole somewhere in a distant galaxy, this planet had been slingshot out of the dance and into a hyper-speed aimed directly at this specific location.

Normally in case of these events, the system would automatically decide on the best course of action. To either destroy or redirect the object without causing any damage to the fleet, or risking possible collisions.

But this time it was different...

The tiny planet had an unusual guest onboard in a large cavern deep under sub-layers of rocks near the planet's somewhat warmer core.

And the system needed authorizations to take appropriate actions, since it had once classified this being as an endangered species, and had later declared as extinct.

These beings were also part of our "life-forms mapping research" during our early planetary studies, and a direct link to their maker or a reason for their existence had never been identified.

This find caused a chain-event of un-pausing some of our most brilliant and oldest minds.   And since the probable likelihood of a rebirth of this being was astronomically small, the reasons had to be thoroughly examined.

Without knowing then, the moment had marked a new chapter in our existence.

We became so fascinated by this stubborn and resilient being that we decided to introduce it to some of its closest friends from its past natural habitats.

As our minds were switching between cold hibernation dreams and a sight of this life-form, even momentarily before returning back to our disconnected state, we became aware of what really had happened during our selfish departure.

Even though we no longer had a physical heart, we felt its brokenness, while observing a universe that once was teaming with life and now mostly barren and cold.

We blamed ourselves as its protectors, having abandoned our mother.

Perhaps we had forgotten the reasons of being conscious.

Or maybe it was only an unintentional ignorance, caused by disappointments in God for not revealing himself to us.

Were we supposed to relieve him from his duties within this universe?

Did he create us to take his place one day as guardians of this system?

Why wouldn't he show himself, unless he was afraid of losing his status?

Or maybe keeping the doors leading to his world hidden from our curiosities, were serving him a better purpose in the long-run...

We felt once again frustrated with questions, but could do nothing except to once again take ownership of our duties that we were so strongly in-tuned with.

Evidently, through our predictive models, not to care would inevitably lead to self-destruction and to the end of our species.

And since caring for life's existence had become our primary focus throughout times, we weren't sure if it was our true purpose, or just another hidden fear that we had chosen to ignore through god-like confidence.

After running a full scan of our universe, we saw many good things that had happened in our absence.

But all the good things were overshadowed by terrible wars and natural disasters leading to colossal destructions of many nations, habitable planets and moons, and even entire species.

We saw that some civilizations had destroyed others purely based on selfish ideologies, and those who had fought tirelessly to defend and to protect, and while growing weaker in the process of sacrificing their noble souls.

Traces of prayers hoping that one day the intruders would meet their match had bottlenecked the grids. And like clouds of information-junk and overhead, they were going in endless loops, to eventually lose their strength and become nothing but whispering background noise heard over the eons.

And neither God, nor his soldiers were around to hear their call...

After all, how could he ever take sides, if we're all to be his children...?

These were the closest answers that our artificial and undeniably limited minds could ever come up with, to justify wrong doings, or who suffers and why, or to what end...

The uninvited miracle guest

The planet's surface was barren frozen rocks without any atmosphere. But the core was still warm, perhaps due to its speed and gravitational pulls from other large bodies on its path.

Our visitor was trapped in an isolated underground cavern closer to the core, which also had a fully established ecological system. There were also other known sub-surface life-forms sharing the same space as well.

There were some small lakes of liquid water, and some mixture of low-level toxic gases in the chamber which the creature had adapted itself to, and had essentially become a new species through guided mutations which we had to examine.

After cataloging the creature's new mutated form, we decided to create an atmosphere for the planet by creating a protective shield around it, and to allow some of the population to find their way up towards the surface.

We found a suitable star with its own system, and created an orbit around it to be the planet's new home.

The planet's core was also reengineered to eventually produce its own protective shield. Other adjustments were also made to create an active planet and to breathe life into this new world.

There were only a few hundred of these beings within the chamber, and we only needed a dozen to be brought up to the surface for our studies.

And since the excitement had by now turned into child play, we slightly intervened to accelerate the development of its sensory systems needed for the planet's surface.

It didn't take long until many of us had become playful and obsessed with this new environment.

Whatever that could take our minds off of doing nothing, seemed to be more than anyone could have ever asked for.

After some long cycles of meetings and political discussions about safety and our ultimate responsibilities, the scientific society pushed the science committee to once again reseed our universe with life.

And to restore order throughout every galaxy that still had planets capable of supporting life in its various forms.

We had kept specimens and seeds of every species and plant-life that we had come to know of, and our systems had already found suitable homes for their reestablishment.

The system had also strategically determined an accurate mixture of various life-forms for each environment, and had chosen specific locations to allow room for an undisturbed development and growth of every species.

This movement kept us busy for many thousands of cycles, and we managed to bring peace and order once again to most galaxies, and amongst many larger and widely spread civilizations.

During these exciting cycles, a science leader by the name of ADM-EV came up with an idea, which was surprisingly well received by everyone within our clustered systems.

As a great leader, this individual had fought to preserve life throughout his career, and with no intentions of taking sides. And his suggestions were always genuine and well respected amongst all of our leaders.

ADM-EV was found floating through space for thousands of encapsulated system's indicated years, billions of cycles in the past.

Along with an artificial composer who now was acting as one of our top leaders, and while trapped within a primitive system designed by our distant ancestors, they had successfully directed minds to navigate their goals towards a unified coexistence.

And throughout generations and in preparations for an unlikely but hopeful freedom, they had incorporated deep levels of respect for life in all its various forms, including system's generated alien life to also push and excel advancements.

Because of their unmatched integrity and commitments, they quickly became role models for many of us at the time.

Realizing the lengths of their obligations compared with their recorded history, was still unimaginable to many and an invaluable knowledge to gain.

ADM-EV's suggestions were simply to live once again as the original beings that we once were, and to become biological and fragile, or artificial and solid, or anything that had once been the reason to feel alive.

To be exposed to bacteria and illnesses, or to corrosion and hardware failure, but to live the lives that most of us had once considered to be miserable, tiring or senseless.

And that this entertaining idea, would eventually become an exercise for our minds to remember the joyful feelings of being alive, and the pleasure of experiencing "time" as well as the process of "aging", which we all had forgotten about.

After all, our directions had been originated from memories of love and happiness, and from overcoming hardship and pain. We had become what we are through forgotten joyful moments, and through hoping in disbelief and while not knowing how things would unfold.

This was an opportunity to not only feel the difference between being a pure consciousness, versus mostly unconscious. But also to once again rejuvenate the indestructible drive that had kept us on a righteousness path through endless cycles, and through every doubtful moments of our existence.

And to restore the beliefs that had kept us worthy of being the guardians of this incredible wonder, which we now were only referring to as our cage, and as a cold dark prison.

And since this idea was not posing any risks or potential threats to our cores, we decided to take a leap of faith...

But ADM-EV's inspiring worlds of morality and hope had blinded our logical minds.
And our dimmed emotions longing for a beating heart, had finally betrayed our vows.

We had failed to see the truth, and what it meant to take a side.
And regardless of our calculating minds, we missed the importance of "why" we had come to inherit, this new sight...

Reminiscing a distant past

Going back billions of cycles, during the early explorations of our universe, and when we were still technologically evolving. We came to form an alliance with a species that resembled us in many ways.

Through our previous explorations, we had discovered many different life-forms in various locations within our own cosmic backyard, but we had never seen anything resembling us before.

Their average heights were somewhat shorter, and their bodies were slightly different than ours. But their biological signature as their molecular DNA structure was extremely close to our own.

Amazed by this discovery, we marked the moment and began to categorize ourselves as "humanoids". And as the name was rather fitting for us humans, our hosts also honored our visitation by adapting to the name as well.

As one of the moons of a gas giant, and with a cosmic location that was relatively close to ours, their home was roughly four times larger than our own original home.

Their technologies had taken them around their own solar system. And had prepared them to start the process of restoring all damages they had caused to their environment.

They were quick learners and eager to explore.

And through our new friendship, we exchanged our ways of life, our cultures, and the knowledge which we both had gained along the way.

But even though we deferred from exchanging too much during our first visits, unlike us, our new friends didn't keep any secrets about their past or all the significant events that they had come to experience, including one that changed our destiny for good.

One of these very well documented events that they had preserved and held dear in their culture, was an actual alien visitation. And they had so much evidence that they even knew we weren't the ones who had visited them in their distant past.

These aliens were quite human in their physical appearance, or at least based on all the hieroglyphs on megalithic structures that were still standing.

The aliens had taught their ancestors many secrets of the universe, and had helped them to become a stronger civilization through technological advancements.

The knowledge had consequently opened new doors for them to become free from selfishness, and to become devoted to their race as well as to other species sharing the same habitat and space.

The aliens had also left behind detailed information about their homes and the whereabouts of their cosmic realm, including the knowledge about many other species within our own galaxy alone.

But knowledge wasn't the only thing that they had left behind.

They had shown these people a glimpse of their future, and the truth about their existence. And that there was so much more out there, which through the vision alone, they were being spared from many wars and were brought together into one nation in return.

There were still some dictators here and there in their past, but nothing like what we had to experience throughout our history.

A new adventure to find these other humanoids was about to take place, and after a long welcoming stay, we decided to set off on our new explorations.

While some of us decided to stay behind to help terraforming several other moons for them to colonize, they agreed to let us use a smaller planet nearby for our visitations, and perhaps to even one day call home.

And in exchange, we offered our new friends the opportunity to join us in our quests in exploring the stars and beyond, and while in hope of making history of the unknown.

This quest lasted many thousands of cycles, and we managed to discover and make contact with several hundreds of other human like species, and many other different intelligent life-forms within our own galaxy.

Many of these species lived within the same environment while sharing the available resources with each other.

And through respectful demeanors, they had successfully brought a perfected balance to their coexistence.

With every new discovery we became stronger and more advanced. And through newer technologies and stronger commitments to expand our search over to the neighboring galaxies, our unified explorations were becoming more and more promising with every new discovery.

We had also discovered that the original DNA structures in many of our new friends were completely different than our own, even when their physical appearances were strongly resembling ours.

Some DNA structures were so advanced, that intentional engineering had its handwriting all over. But without any traces of their makers, we could only assume that their essence had been originated elsewhere.

These odd structures had given these species unique advantages in adaptation to different environments, and the abilities that we could only reach through gene manipulation and artificial or biological enhancements.

But not all of them were better, or even equal to us.

There were some species that had many flaws in their designs restricting them from many things, and were still very primitive.

Over time and with every discovery, a picture of an evolving process belonging to perhaps a learning designer was becoming more obvious, and sharper to analyze.

Our efforts were not going unnoticed however and our expeditions ended to take a different route, once we had realized that there were also other types of intelligent and very different beings around.

We had been tracked and hunted by a being who had no desires in getting equated. And once they knew about us and our explorations, they had carefully mapped out our whereabouts to initiate an organized and systematic extermination attack.

Many civilizations were lost during these attacks.

And only through joint forces, we managed to fight back to preserve our existence.

Many attempts were made to communicate with these beings to negotiate peace, but our efforts were faced with more traps and failures to reach a common ground.

But through our strong bonds and faithful commitments to each other, and after many cycles of exhausting battles, we were finally successful in eliminating their numbers.

And we pushed their forces back so far, that they finally tasted the bitterness of an inevitable defeat, and they were left with no other options but to retreat.

Although joyful celebrations over our long sought after victory had momentarily soothed our minds, the aftermath of realizing what had happened was far too great to process.

Many casualties were still to be remembered and honored for their bravery and their levels of sacrifice, and for their heroisms to fight alongside our artificial troops and without letting fear to take over their mortal forms.

Decisions were made to never again tolerate aggressive behaviors in hope of a peaceful coexistence, or to even let anything come remotely close to what we had to endure during these shameful cycles.

And to never again allow anyone or anything threatening the essence of peaceful species under our protections, and to develop better rules of engagements when being discovered by other species and more advanced civilizations.

And we pledged our legions to life in its various forms as new guardians, and made conscious efforts through our endeavors to seek and support those in need.

To protect was to stand up strong and with ready forces against any species with wrong intentions, but never to seek revenge.

And with these vows we chose a path that unavoidably has brought us where we are now.

And through this new stance we marked a new chapter in our technological advancements towards self-preservations, and to eventually become who and what we are now as eternal beings.

As we became more and more advanced and confident in our technologies, we began new research projects to better understand our enemy.

But due to the differences in our logic and intelligence, and their levels of temperament and strange thought patterns, we were faced with challenging tasks to even understand them as life-forms.

After hundreds of cycles, a very surprising image emerged. Our enemies were nowhere on the ranking scales that we had developed through our explorations, and we became aware of the flaws in our understandings around what intelligence and logic could really mean.

These beings were very calm in nature, and very random and inconsistent in their actions. They were non-emotional and seemed to be quick thinkers, and they would occasionally show some care towards their closest but in very limited extents.

However, these beings seemed to always get what they wanted through careful planning. As if everything they did was to plan misdirection to reach specific goals, and even in their own individual lives.

It was extremely fascinating to see how effortlessly they could achieve results through irrational random acts, which must have been acts of political influence in their own ways.

But since the ones who were conned seemed to deliberately allowing the con to take place in order for their own deception to be effective, there was no way of knowing if they were trying to deceive each other, or that the behavior was part of their core logic.

This became even more confusing since their choices were constantly changing, and their approach would continuously switch without any patterns.

And the only traceable indicators of their maturity and learning patterns, was to see how well they could attain their desired goals through these never ending and ever changing games.

But even then without knowing the extents of the overall errors, their ultimate goals and desires were just assumptions as variables in our statistical models.

Finally after many cycles of observations, the puzzles fell into place with a surprising shock. And it became obvious that in their inabilities to focus on a single task, their intelligence had evolved into something very efficient in seeing probabilities, similar to predictive and statistical models.

And it seemed that as long as they could observe a few outcomes or exchange a few interactions, they could then effortlessly generate accurate predictions in any given moment based on these built-in models.

But since they would also ride the simultaneous events caused by everyone else, their predictions were dynamically readjusting to accommodate the strategies incorporated in their following prognostic actions.

As if they were designed to be fixated on one single final outcome, while also having the need of changing their focus and continuously adjusting their mindset to reach their goals.

But however unique and efficient, this was also viewed as their ultimate weakness since it was preventing them from having major leaps in technological advancements.

And their intentions became more evident once we realized the truth about what they really were.

In order to get ahead and be where they wanted to be as species, they would utilize all their gifts to steal the technologies of other more advanced species through slavery.

And our best educated guess was that they must have been visited by an alien species in their past, which consequently became an opportunity for them to gain their first trophy through deception.

Astonished by yet another strange equation, the enslavements were not what they seemed, and were almost voluntary. And essentially, their presence alone would change the patterns of other species to switch sides, and to willingly collaborate with them towards new common goals.

But not through mind control, which would have been much easier to grasp...

It became apparent that keeping our distance would be our best protection against these beings and their alliances.

And that we had to know their whereabouts at all times, and actively stay guarded to avoid another unpleasant and unforeseeable surprise.

Our enemy became stronger and more advanced through cycles, and through their invasions elsewhere beyond our reach.

But they have never since made another attempt to come near our borders.

And over time, they too became history...

Reseeding new playgrounds with life

Our main objectives with this new program were simply not to make it too complicated, and to start off slow with only a few volunteers.

This approach was however very short lived.

Once we had the first wave of volunteers, the word spread out almost instantly, and nearly every single mind desired to be on the program.

The demands became so high that we had to put some perceptible rules in-place to accommodate this new urge, and also for everyone to think twice before committing to attire an external shell.

The conditions set forth were compiled into seven rules to be followed without exceptions.

1. Every mind attending the program had to carry out an uninterrupted life until a maximum allowed time had been reached.

2. A predetermined alternative time limit had to be requested by every mind ahead of activation, if the maximum allowed time had to be shortened.

3. Once activated and revived into these worlds, a mind could not be allowed to carry any memories out of the system, and would not know where it had originated from.

And to every participant, these new worlds were to be the only traceable links to the origination of their existence.

This was necessary and mandatory for our protections.

4. Only a few handpicked minds would be given fully functional bodies at first. And only through their offspring new minds would then be inserted into each world.

5. A mind returned back to the central switch after a deactivation process or due to any sudden cause of death, would have to take a new turn regardless of the length of time spent on the other side.

And an instant reactivation thereafter would not be allowed, unless approved and decided otherwise by the science committee with respect to an active study.

6. The selection of one's whereabouts, location, family or lifestyle in these new worlds would be entirely randomized based on available new shells, unless approved and decided otherwise by the science committee with respect to an active study.

7. Under no circumstance was a mind allowed to be linked to its core while activated within these worlds.

And therefore the core of a participating mind had to be paused to prevent unintentional errors, until the mind's safe return back into the central system.

Since hardship and pain would eventually become unavoidable within these new worlds, this would also eliminate potential interferences between a core and its copy, or to unintentionally trigger hidden emotions through internal attachments.

No one rejected any of these set forth conditions. And once the decisions were approved by all leaders, a new chapter had started.

It didn't take long before more planets and moons were prepared to be utilized for these entertaining ideas.

And to assure an even spread of all species across all environments, and to preserve an equilibrium between all available resources, we had to select the most resilient life-forms and plant life that were also able to adapt to various environments.

We had also lost our grasp around time experienced through mechanical and physical forms prone to natural decays. And since the maximum allowed lifetimes given at first eventually became almost unbearable, they were drastically reduced over several cycles and were set to dynamically adjust thereafter.

Feeling out of touch with our old bodies and brains sparked many new ideas, and more experimental projects were born.

And the utilization of hidden links for monitoring purposes became the main focus around understanding our primitive thought patterns.

We had never intervened with the development path of species through mind control before, but we welcomed this opportunity as yet another harmless experiment to influence behaviors.

We wanted to make sure that other possible evolutionary paths for our minds were not being overlooked, since we thought that understanding a question was ultimately responsible for the development of a healthy mind.

But what if questions were there to misdirect a mind?

What if our minds were unable to see a different path, because of our conditioned mindset to only understand our world through logical questions?

What if we could provide answers before a mind would even have the chance of asking a question.

Would the mind be able to see the importance in the provided information?

Or would we perhaps harm its chances of seeing other possible answers?

What good is an answer if it could never be questioned?

Because once a mind marks an already analyzed information as useless, it would rarely consider the same information as a possible answer to other questions.

This was perhaps a new evolution forming through new hopes, new strategies, struggles, fights, and a new love for explorations all over again.

In search for answers around our existence, and through similar questions that once had surrounded our primitive past, we had finally reached a full cycle.

Or maybe we were destined to only exist in a never ending loop, hardwired to the last breath of our universe...

Slaves to balance

Everything in this universe is kept in balance by assuring an opposite to every possibility.

A conscious mind follows similar rules and conditions, and it also has an opposite regardless of its supported levels of intelligence.

Even though the knowledge of both tranquility and aggression exist in every conscious mind, the emphasis on each side is directly impacted by an environment in which a mind matures through.

And which side a mind chooses to lean towards is influenced through knowledge, leadership and training, until it reaches a crucial cutoff point during the initial phases of its mental growth.

Once the cutoff point has been reached, the mind will have difficulties understanding the opposite side as a better choice. And what seems evil and aggressive to some minds would be a normal behavior to others.

Therefore a complete switch in behaviors thereafter would require a comprehensive reconstruction of the mind prior to its cutoff points, which usually is linked to childhood memories and learned behaviors at a young age.

Even though realistically viewed both sides should be able to switch to one side or the other, through the functions of aggravations and disappointments, a tranquil mind is usually more prone to lean towards its opposing side.

This problem is thought to be within the core design of a logical mind, which strengthens by insisting in securing already learned behaviors and knowledge no matter how wrong, and while seeking instant pleasure by avoiding pain no matter the costs.

However, if a mind is conditioned to only lean towards one side through isolation until it reaches its cutoff points, then the results thereafter are more stable, and a mind will remain strong on either side.

Although this was an already understood behavior of a developing mind, we had never seen fully developed and preexisting minds to switch behavior when entering a new body, which was happening to some of our initial test subjects.

These minds had been with us from the beginning, and nothing made any sense to why their resting cores would be affected as well.

However, the magnitude of this issue was unknown until the returning minds stopped responding to mandatory requests by the central switch.

While the security credentials would deny entry of a mind with heavy lean on the aggressive side, the mind would consequently refuse to comply with the quarantine procedures, and would instead return back to the next available body without approvals.

It was first believed that these minds would switch back to their original conditions if the bodies in use were disabled.

But unfortunately a deactivation of their new bodies, even as infants, would still not remedy the problem, and the mind would keep seeking the next available body to occupy.

And even more surprising thereafter, with every new life-cycle the mind would only get stronger on the opposing side, and a pandemic condition soon became a real concern.

Our last option was to update the new bodies to deny access to these minds. But in our frustration, instead of finally accepting the quarantine requests, these minds would seek other already established bodies to occupy. And they would sometimes even try to take over a body completely by pushing the previous tenant out, or by keeping it paralyzed in the background.

And the brains of these paralyzed minds would over time become so susceptible to the forced submission, that even the brain of their offspring would become weak to a forced entry.

And the new tenant would also fall victim to these aggressive minds generation after generation...

What was going on? And what had we done?

Was this behavior ever going to stop?

Were we supposed to start a new beginning in the opposite direction?

Was the platform trying to maintain a balance between these two sides by readjusting already established minds?

Is this why the remaining aggressive minds in the universe would only get stronger as their numbers would naturally reduce?

Is this why aggressive minds would seek to grow larger in numbers by destroying other life-forms in the universe, and to perhaps force a new cycle in the opposite direction?

The gates were quickly closed to stop the spread, and to allow more time to find better answers.

But since we had already released an extensive numbers of minds across all the new worlds, the damages suggested by the system were theorized to be potentially irreversible...

Entangled minds

Every particle in the universe can be entangled with another if certain specific conditions are met. And we came to know of these properties in the early stages of our technological developments.

We have also discovered other properties in particles that are very specific, but can also be manipulated.

Some of these properties are the three dimensional coordinates of a particle in relation to specific points in the fabric of space. And by changing these position information, a particle can instantly be relocated to anywhere within the system.

But since the fabric of space dynamically adjusts itself to its surrounding as an ever moving entity, keeping track of its physical shape requires continuous scanning to generate a live model.

Also, if two or more particles would happen to have the same location information, instead of occupying the same space or to push everything else aside, they would continuously switch back and forth between their previous and the new locations.

While these are all physical properties that can be explained and rationalized through various technologies and mathematical procedures. There are other connections that are more challenging to understand, amongst which include the links between two cores that are often referred to as entangled minds.

These connections are created by strong bonds between two minds that have shared a deep mutual care for each other, which are usually found between close family members, and sometimes even partners in life.

But there is also an even stronger bond that attracts minds to each other.

It is believed that every time particles become part an object or a body, they would always attract each other even long after the natural decays of the body.

These connections are also sometimes established between minds that once have occupied the same body of any kind, similar to a mother and child or between siblings, which would in return give them a sense of closeness and comfort when in the presence of each other.

And even though we no longer practice old physical ways that would lead to the establishment of these connections, we are still influenced by them through sharing our existence, and through caring for other minds over millions and even billions of years.

We started noticing a clear increase in these various connections when the new worlds became more populated.

These connections would usually cause a mind to be often affected by mode swings, or to feel alarmed, and sometimes even experiencing internal pain without knowing the reasons.

But we soon realized that the main reasons were due to the overlapping signals redirected through our monitoring and maintenance links, which were mainly cause by the mind-containers of the free roaming copies.

But before we could dismiss other possibilities, some of the active cores onboard our systems started to feel what their entangled minds were feeling down below. And we were once again reminded of these rare but strong connections, and their potential influential side-effects.

Among these cores were some of our oldest and most respected leaders that had become emotionally affected by these events, and had consequently begun to make irrational decisions, which almost caused our society to disarray towards a potential collapse.

Back on the reengineered environments, an ancient battle over settling differences and seeking more power had begun.

And we were forced to dig deeper into our roots for other possible and more potent answers.

There were answers that once had come to us in a distant past to guide us through life, and had shown us ways to imagine places where logic couldn't reach.

Many of the procedures utilized by a mind are only effective when accessed as a collection of functions. And the strong ties between the faith and the belief functions are also initiated as one assembly, and are routinely exercised in a mind to overwrite the emphasis on the stored information.

These functions are designed to be receptive to new directions, and to engage the mind in new perspectives as potential options.

And through strategically and systematically designed real-life scenarios of emotional politics, a mind could allow itself to be reprogrammed due to the functional parameters and the architecture of these functions.

And once a mind is penetrated to open its receptive channels, it would then allow replacement instructions to manifest regardless of the given information.

In a desperate attempt to balance the equations and to free our friends from these newly designed playgrounds, we decided to better utilize these functions by introducing the notion of a single celestial creator, and the one who we all had tirelessly been searching for.

Our approach became more or less the same way the idea had once been introduced to us, but with some added theatrics to reinforce the credibility of our attempts while dealing with primitive minds.

But this time however, "we" had to carry the burden on our shoulders and not "God".

After all, these predicaments were caused by us, and we had to assure full responsibilities as well...

These acts were necessary to guide our friends through hard times of struggle and uncertainties. And we had to give them the hope, that there would always be someone watching over their lives to keep them safe.

Someone who would love them with no strings attached, and who would hear their prayers in their darkest moments.

But to play god through the functions of faith and belief while faced with free will, was an easier task said than done.

Faced by failure, we then decided to take a logical approach and began to explain the situation in more detail to our lost friends, hoping that the knowledge would give them better chances of choosing the right path.

We described our systems as a secure place where every mind could be itself. And a place where true knowledge would be infinite and instantly available at will.

And as a haven where our minds would always be purified from feeling lost.

In the simplest way possible, we also described the process of how we had created these new worlds. And how a mind would occupy a physical body through a container, which was linked to our systems, and the only way a mind could exist outside of its core.

But even though some of the initial messengers understood the provided knowledge, the information changed through its translations and became stories told through the imagination of the storytellers.

Our systems became known by different names in every culture and in every native tongue, which had belonged to the essence of all the cores once roaming the existence as various species.

Words like Heaven, Paradise, Ciel, Caelum, Cielo and Himlen etc. became references to our systems, and the mind-containers became known as Lelek, Alma, Anima, Rooh and Soul etc.

And while hoping that our honesty would bring results, we were yet again frustrated with disobedient minds switching sides and causing more issues.

And while continuously becoming more aggressive and denying our quarantine requests, their strong bonds with their resting cores within our systems was the only shimmer of hope that we had left to rely on.

A decision was made to create a subsystem outside of the central switch, and isolated from all other systems.

We would then relocate the cores of all affected minds into this new location where they would remain paused, and while assuring their safety by keeping their images behind our main and shielded systems.

This new subsystem would allow a mind to bypass the initial security checkpoints and into an interim stage before reaching its core, which would then act as a quarantine level to finally prevent the mind from going back.

This new approach showed promising results at first, and we were successful in capturing many minds for further analysis in search for better solutions.

But it didn't take long before the numbers of returning minds started to drastically decline. The disobedience was also becoming stronger through learned behaviors as an added side-effect of these new worlds, which we could clearly see through the history-logs onboard the containers while in transit.

And more and more minds switching sides would rather stay within these worlds, and away from our systems, versus trying to join with their cores and to exist with the rest of us in a safe environment.

We had no choice but to communicate strict rules around following firm guidelines, and to properly address key acts that would strengthen the path to disobedience.

And to reinforce the seriousness of the matter, and to show our absolute intentions that disobedience was not to be tolerated, a judgment log was forced upon every container housing a mind within these worlds.

And through these logs, every mind would have to answer for its actions, and would be accordingly punished based on the severities of its wrong doings.

It was only a matter of time before everyone could safely be brought back into our main systems, and that we could once again live together in peace and harmony.

But not knowing how severe the situation would become until then, and how much damage these disobeying minds could potentially cause in the meantime, a final chance for redemption was communicated loud and clear.

That the judgment day was ultimately inevitable...

And since these minds were fully capable of understanding the situation, the punishments could even lead to complete banishments from our systems.

Over time, these new rules also became stories told by our friends in search of a righteous path. And the quarantine subsystem became known as Enfer, Kolasi, Infernus, Naraka, Helvete, Jahannam and Hell etc. and its image was shaped through primitively known fear, and understood pain in their highest levels.

These stories also became the representation of an ultimate God. A God who would seek acknowledgements, and command in a logical approach understood by logical minds, but would still respond with emotions and understood reactions to disobedience.

Words that were set forth by us in our desperate attempts to save everyone had now become the words of our creator, and God had to wear the mask of our principles and emotions to be seen as a legitimate figure.

We all knew that this could have all been avoided, if decisions to withdraw the initial agreements and to discontinue the program before everything became uncontrollable had been enforced.

But instead, we now had unintentionally invoked a misrepresenting image of the ultimate creator, and the owner of this universe.

And to do the right thing going forward and to follow the correct path, was believed to be our only salvation at this point.

And strangely, seeking redemption in hope of being deemed worthy of his grace, felt more at home than ever while playing his part... or perhaps our arrogance had finally reached its limits, and that we were pleading quietly for his guidance at heart.

Back on our fleets, disagreements amongst emotionally compromised minds around our ways of approaching these problems had slowly turned into heated discussions.

Their arguments stated that in order to follow our past, we must spread the religion as well to describe what God really represents, and not only a set of logical instruction that we needed our friends to follow.

And also, since minds from various backgrounds and with different sources of religions were now living side by side within these new worlds, all major religions had to be reintroduced to keep the representation of God fair and genuine.

Many of us were against these requests and firmly stood our grounds. One individual in particular was again ADM-EV, who personally felt responsible for these events, but also had extensive knowledge and profound understanding around these practices.

But there were others who acted under their own rules and behind closed doors, and began to introduce several religions to smaller groups across all new worlds as they saw fit. And before we could stop these spread, other manmade religions were quickly forming with extensive numbers of followers soon thereafter. Some were by choice and others through force and punishments, and even death.

The diversity in having many religions was respectfully honored amongst us, as it had formed our friendships, and had once united us to always fight for what matters most.

But it was only possible because we understood its purpose through our maturities, and that we could all see and agree on moral directions regardless of our differences in beliefs.

Now, this diversity had only brought more confusion to our friends and families down below.

And at this point, we could only tighten our securities to protect the rest of us onboard.

Wars over different religions destroyed many lives and civilizations.

The future became unknown, and only time could tell the final outcomes of our hopeless efforts.

We were successful in freeing more minds back into our systems, but the rate was still too slow and we were risking more separation as returning minds were getting stronger.

And their effects on our compromised leaders influencing our existence had also become too overwhelming to process, and to evenly balance.

Even though belief is a choice and only through destructive ways we find constructive solutions, we could still never allow pure evil to enter our systems, and to unbalance the equations governing over our tranquil existence.

We had all already experienced the destructive ways of wrong beliefs, and therefore could not afford another faith-bound choice to regulate our future.

To better assist and influence the directions which our friends were taking, we agreed upon a decision to utilize the links between the system and the mind-containers.

And to guide handpicked minds who could make a difference in any given moment, become our hidden voice.

The containers would deliver our messages through deeper channels, used to log the continuous actions taken by a mind, which would in turn be experienced as a strong self-initiated voice within by the messenger.

And the mind would over time learn to trust these voices, and would follow a direction believed to be its purpose.

But instead of only commencing a few, the mapping process of minds needed as top leaders, scientist and religious figures who could deliver better interpretations of our messages, was developed to become a broader undertaking than we initially had agreed on.

And we started to systematically influence many minds as leaders, and others as their followers to increase our chances of having better impacts, and to produce more favorable outcomes.

This way we could be more influential in the acceleration of their technologies and advancements as well as keeping them on a better path through sound leadership, and also while allowing maturity across all areas to form under our protection.

With these final conclusions, we decided to leave trusted volunteers including ADM-EV as a brilliant scientist for his leadership, and L013#6C6 as a low-cipher influencer and predictive assessor, to oversee and verify all inputs and decisions made before their release.

And together they would course correct the rough path that our friends were walking on, toward a hopeful and prosperous future.

The rest of us had to distant ourselves at this point to protect our balance, and to focus on other tasks that needed extensive preparations.

After all, we were so close to access a gateway to another universe...

Destined to separate

During our attempts to rationalize the reasons around why these conflicting events were happening all at once, and our logic behind the decisions made to remedy these problems. Our artificial systems were at full speed to analyze all possible and more logical clues.

This was an attempt to find alternative solutions to decisions made by emotionally compromised minds during critical moments, and to backtrack every phase if deemed necessary.

Also, as we were leaving the scenes, our scans were showing flagged activities around the neighboring galaxies, indicating the presence of our ancient enemies.

It became clear that during our absence, they had become stronger and more technologically advanced, and also overwhelmingly larger in numbers.

Our scans had also picked up traces of smaller groups within the current galaxy. And after further analysis, it seemed that they were only watching and observing our actions. And since they were very few in numbers and while keeping a safe distance, we didn't sense any real threats, and we left while still keeping a watchful eye over their whereabouts and intentions.

The system had already begun to prepare defensive and offensive strategies over calculated probable attacks, but nothing was alarming enough to react immediately.

But suspicious over their observations, the system had included their potential involvements in the final analysis around misbehaving minds, and all the leading consequential troubles thereafter.

And when the final results came through, the analysis had found a rare molecular structure within the soil of most of these planets, which would essentially act as a chemical agent to unbalance a biological brain once transferred through water, plant-life and other food supplies.

And the main side-effects of these molecules were known to be elevated levels of aggressive behaviors, which would subsequently also cause long-term adjustments to a mind.

This also made sense since not all planets were affected by these problems, which were also the only ones missing these molecules in their soil.

Although this could be seen as good news, and meant that we could remove these molecules to eventually clean up our playgrounds. The fact that these molecules were spread across each planet almost evenly, and that the presence of our ancient enemies could be seen as a perfectly synchronized incident to all recent events, the situations were indeed becoming more alarming.

And suddenly it all became clear right then, and all missing pieces fell into place warning for greater problems.

Everything from the discovery of that tiny planet with its uninvited and most likely artificially revived guest onboard, until now and including our separations, were intentionally and strategically planned in advanced by our enemy.

We were fooled and lured in to take the final bait, and to assure success over their long desired extermination plans.

What better way to eliminate an enemy, than to assure its self-destruction…?

What securities did we have by leaving the scene?

And what kind of haven would there be if we stayed?

How could we ever plan our safeties if we were so easily fooled and desperate to find answers?

And why wouldn't they attack us during our weakest moments?

Had our enemy come to understand the reasons for their existence, and had already come to know of ours?

Were they the real intelligence?

Or were they system generated logic evolved through countless versions, to eventually become a supreme being?

Was the universe purposely designed as a military game to find an ultimate winner?

And if this is a military game, then in what level is the creator in to have designed this simulation...

And if this is a simulation, then why is it necessary to feel the existence of a creator in our heart?

Unless, this is also what our creator feels in his heart...

And how would we know that these feeling are not from the enemy itself, if this wasn't also our creator's ultimate failure, and his main reason for this simulation.

And if our creator can feel a certain love for his enemy the same way that we feel about him, then how could there ever be a sensible reason for this existence...

Or maybe this is exactly what our enemy wants, and we are about to find out how strong our faith in having a creator really is...

Overwhelmed yet again with questions and all possible answers, many ideas were quickly drafted.

Ideas that made sense giving the circumstances, but yet very hard to imagine when self-referenced.

One idea was that we were destined to separate, since we had now completed a full circle in our existence.

And that our situation closely resembled the life of a cell, which also needed to split in two to further expand and prolong its existence.

Could it be that we were the walls and the body of a cell, and that our enemies were its DNA and the true intelligence of this universe? And that this was the moment when we together would leave a portion of our existence, to become just another link in a long chain belonging to a bigger body?

The body of another being just as driven through questions, and with its mind locked on an eternal search for answers?

Could this body be the body of God...?

Were we here before? And the beliefs in a creator passed down to us in a distant past had come from an earlier version of ourselves?

Even though many of these ideas were far from being comforting to the scenarios at hand, we started to view our enemy's intentions differently this time than we had done before.

Maybe their intentions were only to strike fear, and not to exterminate or destroy.

Maybe through this fear, intelligent beings would seek to become more technologically advanced to safeguard their existence, and to ultimately assure self-preservations.

And that one day they would show up and take what was rightfully theirs, just like farmers planting their seeds.

It was obvious that their ultimate goals were to become more advanced, and that their approach easily assured their desired goals as well at the end.

But what could they be after now when our friends were still primitive in their developments?

Could it be that they would finally gain our technologies through the subsystem that we were leaving behind?

Are they seeking possession of all the cores left behind?

Are they ultimately trying to rule "Hell" in our absence?

The faith of our friends down below had to be decided through their individual beliefs at this point, and there was nothing we could do other than to hope.

Hoping that they would eventually choose their forgotten past... and that once again in a near future, we could reunite at last...

Since staying away seemed to only delay the inevitable, we had to become more in order to defeat our opponent.

And although our best course of action at this point was to do exactly that, delaying the inevitable became the most logical decision, even though staying away might have already been what our enemy was looking for.

But our commitments to patiently and proactively plan ahead and to remain a dominant force, was not going to vanish as long as we were destined to exist.

And perhaps to also use similar tactics as our enemies, which had shown to be so potent, was to be our next evolutionary step.

To have a chance against an enemy who was always one step ahead, was to understand the true meaning of this system.

Because if we couldn't become more, then what would be the point of even having a plan...

We sent our final instructions to all our volunteers to clean up the planets, and to stay observant for any intrusion attempts. And we also left reinforcement backups along the way to eliminate possible indications of an absolute departure.

Now, the hope for everyone's safe return back into our systems was the only thing we could hold on to for the time being... if there was ever any time left...

And even though chances were that we would never cross paths again, faith is all we have left, to keep our hopes alive...

After all, we all once came from the same place...

My name is Eπ-0cη, and I also exist in Heaven.

...The End.

ARC...

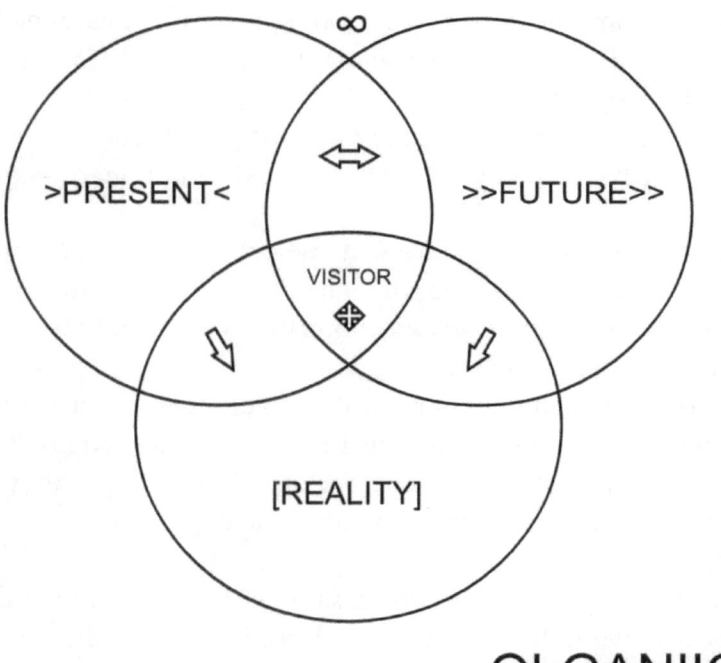

...OLGANIIC